RENEGADE KISSES

Small Town Enemies to Lovers Romance

LARISSA LYNX

Literary
Madness!

Contents

RENEGADE KISSES

Renegade Kisses Copyright © 2020 by Larissa Lynx
Published by Literary Madness - First published March 2021

ISBN 978-1-949426-07-6 (Paperback - Rev 10.21)
ISBN 978-1-949426-02-1 (E-book)

Cover by Literary Madness

Chapter Header Images: © Victoria Novak, © Torky, © Lindwa, © Evgenii Naumov via Dreamstime

At Literary Madness, we strive to create a book free of typos. If you notice anything amiss, we're happy to fix it. litmadness@yahoo.com

RENEGADE KISSES

TEXAS BAD BOYS, BOOK #1

Something old and something new, something borrowed and something blue, and a lucky sixpence in her shoe.

—Emily Post, *Purple and Fine Linen*

ONE

Something Old - Three years ago

BUCCANEER PRIVATE CAMPGROUND - EAST TEXAS

"GOD SAVE US. Here comes another coddled coed who'll gripe for an hour the moment she snags a nail." The normally upbeat Brett gave a disgusted sigh. "When will they stop already?"

Nico finished pounding in the last tent stake before he stood and stretched, glancing the thirty yards or so across the clearing to scope out the newest, unwanted arrival. "Huh. I thought they'd give up after the first four failures. Shows what I know."

Nico marveled that his reply sounded so coherent given how the latest piece of rich, spoiled fluff they'd been saddled with captured his full attention.

She'd arrived in a boxy bunker of a car that might as well have been a limousine, it was so big. What was up with that? She didn't wait for a chauffeur to jog around and open her door, no...the female herself exited from the driver's seat, bold as she pleased.

Easy on the eyes or not, her kind had absolutely no business crashing their weekend campouts with their goody-two-shoes ways and richer-than-thou attitudes. "Give her one night in a hot, humid tent minus a shower and her maid, and—"

"And bet she calls Daddy for a ride home," his fellow weekend counselor concluded.

Not if she drove herself.

What a surprise.

Nico and his camping compadre, Brett, had met a dozen years ago in juvie when they were fourteen. Not long after, they'd been a couple of the "underprivileged, disadvantaged adolescents afforded a chance" on various field trips and camping expeditions—always under strict supervision, of course.

It was one of those weekends that had helped turn Nico's life around, meeting Coondog, the mechanic who'd shown Nico he had as much talent fixing engines and suspension systems as he did pinching the cars they were housed in.

Coondog, the old coot he still worked for Monday through Friday, had taught him more about being a man than Nico's deadbeat, currently incarcerated father ever had.

While Nico remained stateside, his buddy Brett— who had a softer record—did a four-year stint in the Marines. Came back all grown up with loads of muscles and motivation to match.

Now they both *voluntarily* volunteered as informal camp counselors for the same kind of "loser" kids they'd once been labeled as. Kids who were due to arrive in just under an hour.

Problem was, some hotshot in the big city had decided these troubled teens needed multicultural—

read "cultured"—exposure too. So now, in addition to the paid supervisory adults and unpaid volunteers such as Nico and Brett, they kept getting burdened with these highbrow, snooty types. Girls—excuse him, *women*—usually college seniors or grad students working on some useless liberal arts degree who thought it'd look good on their résumé if they "roughed it" a couple days a month with the rough kids from the wrong side of the tracks.

The last ten months, they'd seen no less than eight different females traipse through, wiping their dainty fingers with moist towelettes, their sweating brows with starched handkerchiefs, and their shiny white, highfaluting asses with their heated leather seats when they hopped in their eighty-thousand-dollar SUV and escaped, usually before their backsides ever made it *inside* a tent.

"A twenty says she's on her phone by midnight," Brett said, pure derision in his tone, "begging Big Daddy's chauffeur to come rescue her."

Not if Nico could help it.

"It's a bet." Nico flipped the mallet he'd used to hammer in the last stake and then caught the handle. "You okay finishing up here?"

At his friend's nod, Nico tossed him the mallet and headed over to meet the newest Society Chick, curious about this one. And bothered by the realization.

Why her?

Just because she had thick hair, dark and rich as black coffee—strong, how he liked it—and not bleached blonde like all the others?

Or was it because she was the first one to arrive

early, *before* the kids, as though she might actually give a damn about something other than her manicure?

Nah, man, be honest. It's how she fills out those jeans. All curves and booty.

Okay, that.

But also how she unloaded her own suitcase—no, make that a *duffel* (his brows rose at that) and backpack —from the trunk, didn't wait for or expect someone else to do it for her. What *was* she doing driving that monster vehicle?

Or maybe it was because after dropping both duffel and backpack straight on the ground without a second's hesitation, she reached back into the trunk and started hauling out gallon jugs of water. More prepared than any Boy Scout.

Get real. It's how she reminds you of Lila Delgado.

Nico snapped his fingers. That was it.

Pretty Lila Delgado. Nico's very own first crush. And first babysitter.

It didn't matter that she'd been his cousin or ten years older than him. No, what mattered was how she'd made his young, innocent heart race. How she'd made him happy—the six bucks an hour his mom scraped together to pay Lila had translated into as many video game car chases or shootout competitions he wanted to play. Ice cream for supper and crank calls to any number he wanted to dial.

What mattered, when his aunt Rosa—Lila's strict Catholic mom—kicked out her only daughter when she became pregnant at fifteen, was that his vague, romantic yearnings had been shattered.

A more broken-hearted five-year-old he couldn't imagine.

But with *this* female?

The one who'd just swung around, upon hearing his approach. The one now struggling to lift a *five*-gallon container out of the trunk...

"Here," Nico said, reaching in past her, half expecting her to slam the trunk lid down on his fingers. "Let me get that for you."

He hefted the water up and out, then did the same with the last one remaining in the spacious interior. Placing it next to her bags by the others, he straightened. "Ready for Armageddon," he observed. "Welcome to the front lines."

Up close, she was even prettier than Lila, with a voluptuous figure that put young Lila's to shame. With full lips and a generous mouth, parted and nearly smiling, with startled jade eyes blinking at him in surprise, strong, sculpted cheekbones—

Hell, why'd he care what she looked like? What she packed? He wanted her gone before she insulted the kids. Kids who had enough difficulties in their lives without adding Miss Fancy-pants Number Umpteen to the mix.

To give himself some space while hopefully squashing his insane interest, Nico leaned back in over the trunk. As though he couldn't tell they'd already cleared everything out, he lifted the thin carpeting then laid it back flat, smoothing it all the way to the edge as he completed his introduction without glancing at her. "I'm Nico. Thanks for arriving early. The kids will be here in an hour, give or take."

He knew better than to extend his hand. For one thing, society labeled "his" kind beneath her notice, much less her touch. For another, it was stained.

No matter how clean it was, how hard he scrubbed —whether with soap, vinegar, bleach, GOJO, etc.—a man couldn't work under the hood all day and not show it. Grease still found a way to embed itself in the lines of his palm, the crevices of his nails.

Using the action of closing the trunk to move to the side of the vehicle, he waited, ready to let reality squelch any silly comparisons to childish infatuations. The first time she prissied out her name—a Heather or Ashlynn, he'd bet; no last name, *ever*—in that pinched, nasally voice he'd heard so many times the last ten months, his unfathomable attraction would say *adios*.

"Hi there, Nico. I'm Alexis Templeton. Pleased to meet you and *so* excited to be here."

Ah, damn. A last name.

One that kept repeating in his brain as though she'd said Alexis *Temptation*.

He'd better nix this fascination and fast.

Before he could politely direct her to the largest tent that had been set up for administrative details and get the heck out of Temptation's Way, she started up again.

"Where, ah, should I put my stuff? I know I brought a lot, but I wanted to make sure I didn't forget anything." She lifted the backpack by one of its straps. "I've got all sorts of snacks and energy bars. Are the kids allowed to share? What'll we do when they get here? Take them hiking or what? Do we grill dinner? Or have to catch it first? What about..."

As she continued to exuberantly ask her questions,

to bathe his ears in the husky, made-for-sin voice she blessed him with, Nico knew two things for certain:

He was a goner.

And he *had* to win that bet, couldn't let her call for evacuation by midnight. Or drive herself.

As she kept going, asking questions in a cheerful, ninety-to-nothing way, he realized better make that *three* things:

1) His interest wasn't going anywhere.

2) Neither was she; he'd steal her keys if he had to.

3) And he was definitely, totally in lust with someone more out of his reach than Lila Delgado ever was.

TWO

Something New - Present Day

SAINT ANTHONY'S CATHEDRAL - HOUSTON, TEXAS

THE SCENT of orchids wafted from the bouquet she clutched and flowered through Alexis with every breath she took. Longing, love, and loneliness combining into a cocktail of Reluctant Bride-To-Be.

No, I'm not! I'm not lonely. I'm not reluctant. I'm marrying Bradley tomorrow and I couldn't be more delighted. We're perfect together.

Want to lie to yourself a little more?

Alexis ignored the annoying taunts and stiffened her spine. She'd get through this rehearsal if it killed her.

She was marrying Bradley tomorrow. Nothing would stop her. Bradley, former high school sweetheart and current fantastic fiancé.

You really think you're right for each other?

Of course!

You really think you're truly over Nico?

Ah. Shit.

That question had been popping into her head with

frustrating frequency as the big event drew near. Today, it had been a near constant.

Doesn't matter, does it? Nico dumped me.

The reminder only left her sighing. Breathing in again. Choking on the stupid scent of her favorite flower and remembering all the times Nico, not Bradley, had given them to—

Ugh. Why couldn't she stop thinking of Nico?

This was the day before her wedding. Her darn nose needed to stay out of it.

But oh, how her body craved Nico, wouldn't stop reliving his every touch, every word...

It'd been like this since she'd entered the church building and her mother had surprised her with the fancy "practice" bouquet.

Stupid flowers!

Stop blaming the flowers and your nose. Blame Jenny!

Now that was a good idea.

Alexis never should have allowed her best friend to talk her into using the Ben Wa balls. Jenny might've meant well, but Alexis didn't think the sex toys shoved up her hoo-ha were doing their intended job.

They were supposed to be strengthening her inner pelvic muscles for her wedding night, while gently arousing her, so that by tomorrow, she'd be ready to jump Bradley like a horny hooker. And maybe enjoy sex with him again.

Instead, all she could think of was Nico.

Nico, Nico, Nico. Thoughts of her ex-boyfriend were driving her insane.

"Alexis? Did you hear me?"

Smoothing the skirt of her long summery dress,

Alexis turned toward Deacon Joe, who was standing in tonight for the pastor. She wanted to whimper as she squeezed the muscles of her vagina, clasping the balls tight. "I'm sorry? What?"

Gently arousing? Ha! With all the forbidden thoughts of Nico, her inner thighs were slick clear to her knees.

The elderly man nodded, the lines of his face wrinkling in subtle humor. "Getting anxious again?"

Crap. Had she done anything weird? Anything to counter the confident act she'd put on the last few months, convincing everyone—herself included—that this was exactly what she wanted?

Deacon Joe had conducted their premarital counseling, and when he'd questioned her previously, she'd blamed it on nerves. Pre-wedding jitters.

"Of course not." She shifted her stance and sensation radiated through her loins. She *had* to stand still. "I'm ready. Can't wait."

To get laid.

She heard a snicker and glanced at Jenny, whose brown curls bounced as she vainly tried not to bust a gut laughing. Alexis could strangle her. Jenny mouthed *Are they working?*

When Alexis scowled, her friend had the audacity to wink, to nudge Calli who was standing next to her, the petite blonde giving Alexis a thumbs-up.

Great. Her former college roommate was in on it too?

Alexis crossed her legs at the ankles and prayed.

Earlier, when she'd been cruising from one spot to the other in the vast sanctuary, practicing her Here-Comes-the-Bride walk, goofing off with the younger wedding-party participants, she hadn't much noticed the balls at all. Why now?

Because you're still. For once, in body and mind. Finally allowing yourself to contemplate the giant mistake you're about to make.

Shut up! Alexis shook her head so vigorously, her neck popped.

"It's natural to worry, my dear." Deacon Joe's voice was soothing, but doing nothing to help her current affliction. "Never fear, we'll all be here to support you, to make sure things go perfectly tomorrow."

"Thank you." She just wanted everything to be over with. The bouquet in the trash, the balls following right behind. She strove to speak evenly, to not give a hint of the inner turmoil tormenting her since two of her youngest friends had left a few minutes ago, taking their vibrant, and distracting, chatter with them. "That's what I'm counting on."

"Now, we're all finished here with the rehearsal," he continued. "Unless you have any questions?"

Is it wrong to marry one man while pining for another?

"No. I believe I'm good." Alexis choked the bound stems and constricted those naughty inner muscles for good measure. "Um, I'm good."

Except for the part where I'm losing my mind.

And about to orgasm in a church.

"Then I'll see you all tomorrow, along with Father William." Beaming at her, the deacon clasped her wrists then released them and turned to make his farewells to her mother and Bradley's grandmother as Alexis and the wedding participants relaxed and moved off.

"*Thank God* that's over." Her fiancé sounded as though she'd been putting him through labor.

Bradley Langston came from old money—even older than Alexis's mom's—and was considered a prime catch by everyone's standards.

Tall, fit, and blond, with refined yet chiseled features that belonged on a black-and-white men's cologne ad, he wore Armani suits as though he'd been born in one. And he *could* be great company.

In high school, dating him had been a blast. They had fun together, whether going out one-on-one or with a group of friends. He was considerate, solicitous, and could handle her mother like a champ, better than anyone not counting her dad.

Best of all? Bradley had been enamored with Alexis, complimentary about her talents, scholastic achievements, and appearance, even when she didn't always feel like she deserved it. He'd refused to put up with her mother's criticisms about her weight or anything else, able to casually deflect the conversations away from Alexis often before a harsh word could be uttered. Or, if not, he'd graciously contradict whatever her mom said, somehow able to shut the critical woman down without ticking off Mother in the process.

For that, he'd earned her undying gratitude.

Lately though, everything he did annoyed her. Either he tried too hard or not hard enough. His kisses were too brief—or too deep.

It hadn't helped things when she'd decided they needed to stop having sex a couple months ago, to wait for their wedding night. So it'd seem more special.

She hoped.

Impatience rising, he checked his watch with a groan. "What time's our dinner reservation? I'm starving. Come on, sweetheart, let's roll."

Bradley headed for the church's immense doors without even waiting for her, his best friend in tow—a crude jerk she couldn't stand. Most of the wedding party followed quickly behind them, murmuring among themselves, making her feel like a huge inconvenience. Was everyone so hungry? Should she have chosen an earlier rehearsal time?

It had been the rare instance when she held her ground against Mother's wishes, scheduling a time when the two girls Alexis mentored through the Big Sisters program could attend. Drea and Kisha might be too old to be flower girls—or so they both insisted—but Kisha happily assigned herself as junior bridesmaid and her younger sister as the Official Guestbook Guardian. Alexis made sure both girls had appropriate versions of the bridesmaid dresses, and they'd been delighted. Even happier still to be invited to the rehearsal.

Their mom, Dawnese, who'd hoped to join them after work, had picked up her daughters fifteen minutes ago when she'd been called in to her second job unexpectedly.

Alexis gave a deep sigh. She'd been looking forward to getting to know Dawnese better, having seen the single mother work hard to turn her life around during the time Lexi had befriended and mentored Drea and Kisha.

It didn't escape Alexis that some of the spark had gone out of the day the moment her two LSFs (Little

Sisters Forever) decamped. Between the two of them and three distant relatives under the age of ten that Mother had dug up from somewhere to act as flower girls and ring bearer, there'd been more than one interruption as they practiced the processional. Could Alexis help it if she found more joy joining the kids in locating the best spots in the cavernous cathedral to test the echo of various whispers, whistles, and fart imitations?

Maybe if she'd been more focused on the rehearsal they'd be eating already.

It was all her fault. She was screwing everything up. But this was her wedding. She'd only get one and she wanted it to be absolutely perfect.

Yet it felt far from. Everything was in order but something felt wrong. Dreadful, in fact.

It had to be the Ben Wa balls.

That...or Nico.

She really had to stop that—thinking about him was off-limits. From here on out, *Nico* no longer existed in her vocabulary. Or her thoughts.

With a sigh, Alexis glanced at the elevated platform at the front of the sanctuary. By tomorrow the high-ceilinged room would be overflowing with guests, happiness and fresh orchids lining every pew. Which was exactly what she wanted. Wasn't it?

"Excited?" Jenny came up beside her.

Not like I should be. "Not like you mean," Alexis told her darkly. After the long rough patch, it was nice seeing her friend so gleeful, but Alexis wasn't ready to forgive her for suggesting the damn balls.

"I was talking about the *wedding.*" Jenny laughed. Too bad her enthusiasm wasn't contagious.

"Yeah. So was I."

Jenny grabbed her arm and tugged her closer. "As soon as we can escape after dinner," she whispered, "I'm throwing you one heck of a bachelorette party and then, in just a few short hours, you'll be getting married—to Brad! You lucky dog!"

Now why can't I be that eager?

I am!

Alexis had long suspected Jenny had a tiny crush on Bradley, but her friend had never spoken so much as a syllable about it, so Alexis wouldn't either. "Bachelorette party? I thought my mother said not to waste—"

"*Pfft!* What your mom doesn't know won't hurt her. Are you ready? The sooner we eat, the sooner *va-va-voom*." Jenny shimmied and held her mouth open, as though she was watching a male stripper.

Alexis laughed, squeezing her newly toned PC muscles for all they were worth. Her crotch had a date with the bathroom. "I'll catch up with you guys at the restaurant."

Calli approached, smiling widely and holding up one finger as she finished a phone call. "Great news, y'all," she said, tucking her phone in the back pocket of her cargo pants. Alexis was lucky she'd agreed to wear a dress tomorrow. "Jaz was able to wrap up things at work, so she can meet us for dinner."

Entertaining and opinionated, Jazmin had been noticeably absent tonight. "Terrific," Alexis exclaimed with relief, ready for anything to provide a distraction. "I was hoping she could make it."

"And after?" Jenny asked. "She can join us then too?"

Calli's eyes went wide and sliced toward Alexis. "You

told her? Dang it, Jenny, I thought we were keeping that a surprise."

"It's okay." *I needed something to look forward to.* "I'm glad you planned something. Can't wait to see what."

"You sure you don't want to ride with us?" Both her friends were practically dancing on their toes. Just what had they planned?

Alexis nodded. "I'm sure. I've got my car. Plus, I just need a few quiet minutes."

"Planning to catch a quickie with Brad?" Jenny gave her a high-five.

Not even close. Alexis flashed what she hoped was a sultry smile. "You know I'm not one to kiss and tell."

Nudging each other knowingly, both girls gave her a quick hug and then joined the other bridesmaids who were already jostling and flirting with the groomsmen as they all exited the building.

She suddenly wanted to cry. Or hit someone.

Or have an orgasm.

"Alexis, dear? Aren't you coming with everyone?" her mother called once she'd left the sanctuary and was headed down the hallway toward the ladies' room.

Alexis stopped and turned. Waiting by the main exit, Mother gave her a look that could only be described as *politely harassed.* "We're late for our reservation, dear."

"I need a moment, all right?"

Her mother continued to stand there, waiting, brows pinched in a familiar frown.

How that woman dared convey displeasure when Alexis was doing exactly what she wanted—marrying a groom Mother practically chose and dished up on a silver platter—only made Alexis steam. And want to cry even more. "Alone. *Please?*"

Her mother's eyes narrowed and a ladylike huff emerged. "Fine. But don't be long. I'll tell Bradley to wait for you, shall I?"

"Thanks." *No! You need more time.* "Uh, Mother—no. I'll drive. Just tell everyone I'll be there soon. Go ahead and order—"

"A salad? For you, dear? Nothing too heavy the night before you need to squeeze into your bridal ensemble. You *know* you want to look your best."

Alexis wanted to tell her where she could shove her stinking salad. What she could do with her too-tight wedding dress. The one Mother insisted be purchased in a size too small. *To encourage you, sweetheart,* her—naturally slender—mother had murmured in a low enough voice that no one else overheard. *Think how lovely you'll look for Bradley when your special day arrives and you've maintained proper portion control throughout.*

Proper portion control her plump ass.

Some people weren't instinctively skinny. Alexis had tried. God, how she'd tried, especially throughout late elementary and junior high.

Tried to eat just like her mother, tried to change a body type that insisted on being husky or chunky or chubby or fat or whatever other word came to mind when her society-conscious mother told her what she could or could not eat. Told her how much, then told her to go for a run or do some aerobics to work it off.

After years of misery, Alexis finally garnered the gumption to talk to her dad. Who, with his long hours at work and frequent out-of-town business trips, hadn't been aware of how controlling his wife had become, especially in reference to their daughter's eating regime.

His wonderful foot had come down fast and hard, putting an end to the blatant efforts employed by Alexis's mom. Which had done a world of good, but hadn't stopped the occasional remark or the looming disappointment Alexis constantly felt emanating from her maternal parent until coming into her own shortly after she entered the private prep school her parents had selected for her high school education.

Everything changed during her wonderful freshman year. She discovered drama class and having fun on stage. She found her absolute best bestie, Jennifer "Jenny" Beckman, who might be thin but who had a hard time disguising and learning to live with the pair of size Ds that had sprouted on her chest practically overnight. That was also when she met Bradley Langston, two years older than her, athletic, smart, and instantly interested.

Their parents moved in the same circles; Alexis learned later it was the Langstons who'd recommended the school when her parents started asking around. She and Bradley really didn't start dating until the following year, when she was in tenth grade and Bradley a senior, but all throughout freshman year and beyond, whether via school activities, things their parents were all involved in, or just as part of a group, his friendship and then romantic interest really boosted Alexis's confidence and self-worth.

For that, if nothing else, she'd love him until the day she died.

But you're certainly not in love with him any longer, now are you?

Ugh.

"Alexis!" her mother said sharply, regaining attention that would rather wander. "You know the restaurant won't serve until the guest of honor is seated, not with such a large group..." She trailed off, expecting Alexis to jump.

Well, that wasn't going to happen. Not tonight. Her nerves felt too raw, her spirit too downtrodden.

And you question if you should be getting married tomorrow?

"Do you know if Dad will be there? Is his friend out of surgery yet?" The only reason her dad hadn't been present this evening, ready to run interference with Mother, was that one of his closest friends had a stroke or seizure and was currently in surgery. Dad had gone to the hospital, with Alexis's absolute support, to sit with his friend's wife. To provide comfort where he could. "Have you heard from him?"

If not, she'd know once she retrieved her purse and phone, where she'd left them in the Bride's Room, and could check whether he'd texted her with any updates. Jenny had already sent him a few posed and candid pictures, so he wouldn't feel like he was missing out on *everything.*

Instead of answering, her mother only huffed again. "*Hmpft.* I suppose you don't care if you inconvenience everyone."

When Alexis only stared back, trying to display her own calm annoyance, her mother gave a little sniff, followed by, "Just don't be late, Alexis."

"I won't!"

Before Alexis could feel remorse for snapping back, the giant wooden doors closed behind her disapproving parent, the loud click echoing in the sudden stillness. She was alone. Finally.

Clutching her crotch muscles for all she was worth, Alexis didn't beeline for the ladies'. Instead, she walked back into the sanctuary. She stepped forward to run her fingertips over the carved side of one wooden pew. Tomorrow each aisle would be adorned with beautiful orchids and satin bows—*then the scent will really knock you on your ass!*

Alexis circled the room, her fingers fisting against the bound stems she carried. Why wasn't she happy?

Bradley was perfect husband material. Well-muscled, handsome as a Greek god, with a solid reputation throughout Houston, a respectable upbringing that matched hers, and his own thriving import-export business. Not to mention, he was heir to the Langston family shipping dynasty, something that really impressed her yacht-loving dad.

What more could she want? Her parents loved him. Her friends loved him. He loved her.

You love Nico.

Alexis gritted her teeth. She had to get these damn Ben Wa balls out of her vagina and *him* out of her mind. Tomorrow she started a new life. Time to leave the old one behind.

Resolved, she spun on her summery sandals, aiming for the bathroom. As she passed a side door, the sound of deep laughter made her pause. A sound she didn't hear nearly as often these days.

Men talking, laughing.

Memories welled up. How she'd loved seeing her dad and Bradley together back when she'd been in high school. Both of them, along with Phil whenever he was home on leave, had been avid sailors, always ready to take out the Langston family's boat. Always ready for a day on the water.

She hadn't joined them, not then, having zero interest in fishing or what came after—the cleaning. Yech.

And that memory only brought more, this time stupid ones of her and Nico, cleaning fish and laughing. Having fun and falling in lo—

No more!

If only her dad was there now! She could talk to him, maybe admit the doubts plaguing her, growing stronger. Perhaps seek his advice on—

"My balls can't get any bluer," she heard Bradley complain loudly through the slight crack in the side door. "The way Alexis has been holding out on me, I've been *dying*. Well, except for that hot little—"

Tom chuckled. "Bet you can't wait until tomorrow night. Until the whole damn honeymoon."

"Are you kidding? It's past time I shifted gears and drilled into her sweet little ass."

Alexis's eyes widened. Her stomach churned. The oaf! She shoved the door with all her might, knocking into one of them. The ugly scent of tobacco greeted her nose. Disgusting.

Her fiancé stumbled down two steps, almost dropping his cigarette in the process. "Shit, Alexis! What are you trying to do, break my leg?"

A rumble of thunder growled in the distance as she stepped outside. Above the nearby skyscrapers of downtown, heavy, dark clouds loomed. A warning...from God perhaps? Or a portent of things to come if Alexis proceeded in going through with this sham of a wedding?

She shook off the unwanted thoughts.

"Oops," she said brightly, secretly wishing she'd knocked him on his butt. *Perfect husband material?* He couldn't wait to *drill* into her? "Smoking, Bradley? You told me you'd quit."

Why aren't you asking about the "hot little—" whatever he just mentioned?

Alexis tamped down the suspicion. Lying to her about smoking was bad enough; the last thing she needed right now was to deal with possible cheating.

Don't you mean probable cheating?

"I had, truly." He actually had the grace to look guilty. "Just one. I'm celebrating." He straightened, painted on a charming smile that could make any woman melt. Even her. He was handsome, he was rich, and he came from good stock. Mother always said breeding counted for everything.

Tom glanced between them, puffing away after raising his cigarette like a toast.

"Celebrating? What?" Drilling into her?

Or maybe his hot little—

Bradley stepped closer. Her nose wrinkled from the stench.

"Tomorrow I'm marrying the prettiest woman in Texas. My beloved Alexis." His fingers brushed her hair and she warmed inside. His beloved? That was sweet.

Maybe she hadn't enjoyed sex with Bradley this time around but she *would*. It was just...different...from how things had been with Nico, from how she'd remembered the innocent abandon of having sex with Bradley her senior year.

That he saw her as his beloved had to be a good thing, right?

Sounds old-fashioned for Bradley, doesn't it?

She tried to drown out the worrisome niggle. It only got louder.

Sounds like insincere bunk to me.

But we're perfect together.

Yeah, perfectly boring if you're honest—

The dress!

Ah, yes.

The dress Bradley had surprised her with. The dress that now canceled out the annoying little voice in her head. The wedding dress he'd somehow learned about and purchased *in the correct size*. The one he'd delivered personally to her, when no one else was around, with a polite kiss and comforting hug, along with the message: "This is between me and you. Something for my future wife, to hopefully help make her wedding day extra special. And no, I promise I didn't peek."

Somehow, her prince of a fiancé—who cared if he smoked and drilled?—had learned about Mother's devious Diet Plan and had purchased a duplicate of the dress that Alexis loved and adored.

It had hung in Jenny's closet ever since, Mother having no idea that the switch would take place in the morning. Jenny having no idea she didn't have the original dress they'd all picked out that day.

Alexis forced a big smile. Of course Bradley was perfect. Any man needed grooming, right? As soon as they were married, she'd talk to him about respecting her in front of his friends and not smok—

A sliding sensation in her vagina grabbed her attention. *The balls!* "Oh, crap!"

Both men stared at her.

One of the Ben Wa balls had slipped free and was now rolling around in the crotch of her panties. Alexis fought back a moan then couldn't help but laugh. Thank goodness she hadn't worn a thong.

She clenched her inner muscles to hold the second ball in place and squeezed her thighs together. "Bradley, I don't want my car to smell like smoke. Why don't you ride with Tom and I'll meet you there?"

"Sure thing, whatever you—"

She thrust the malodorous bouquet toward his chest. "And take this too."

While he fumbled with the flowers and his stupid cigarette, Alexis ducked back into the building.

THREE

Something Determined - Present Day

SAINT ANTHONY'S CATHEDRAL

OVER HIS DEAD BODY.

Tucked away on a side parking lot, concealed behind a couple of trees and overgrown bushes, Nico tightened his white-knuckled grip on the steering wheel of his '57 Chevy convertible and weighed his options. He'd been staking out the ornate church long enough to consider several.

Then why are you still here? Watching? Waiting?

It took all his restraint not to jump from the car, chase Brad Langston down and pound the pretty boy's interest in Lexi away.

Nico watched his girl—his *ex*-girl—dash back inside the fancy building while Langston and his butt buddy headed to a pathetic excuse for a sports car. Nothing but a tin bucket—just like Langston and his crowd. Flimsy outside, empty inside.

What was the man doing, anyway? Leaving her? It was their rehearsal, for Christ's sake. Even Nico had better manners than that.

Better manners? Is that why you tracked her down and have been lurking in the parking lot the last hour, working up the guts to crash her rehearsal?

The gumption to pick her up, sling her over your shoulder, and bang on your chest like Tarzan while yelling that you finally claimed your woman?

Nico frowned, clenched the narrow steering wheel so tight his fingers hurt. Hadn't that been part of his problem? The lack of courage to claim her in front of her set? To stand up and announce she was his in front of others more educated, more refined, more wealthy than he'd ever aspire to be?

Refusing to let the weight of that thought settle on his shoulders, he shrugged it off, closing his eyes against the temptation to send her fiancé to the emergency room—*that* he could do blindfolded and with one hand tied behind his back.

Closing his eyes against the temptation that was Lexi. Reality trumped his memories in spades.

Just that quick glance, watching her interact with the two men, was a sucker punch to his gut. Bringing back everything—every memory, every laugh, every kiss.

Every longing, to have her in his life.

You said goodbye for a reason. Put the key back in the ignition. Go home. Leave her alone.

He just couldn't.

Then grow a pair and go after her.

She'd looked so beautiful, even surrounded by the two jackwipes. She wore a long white dress—the irony of the color not lost on him—with straps that crisscrossed in the back and came up over her shoulders to support the top part modestly covering her breasts.

But it wasn't just her full-figured body that boiled his blood. It was everything. The way she smiled, frowned, gestured. No matter what she was doing, his Lexi oozed sensuality, from her silky, cocoa hair to her heavily lashed, huge eyes and full, pouting lips.

Never mind that he couldn't currently see either her eyes or lips, he *had* to stop Lexi from marrying Langston. She was making the biggest mistake of her life. Langston could never make her happy. Not that Nico was positive he could, but Langston damn sure couldn't. Sweet Lex was too extraordinary to suffer a pig like that.

He'd never sleep again if he didn't stop her. His conscience was keeping him up at night, every night, hence his presence here, at the eleventh hour. Despite thinking that he'd talked himself out of doing anything stupid or spontaneous, he was here now, with a little prodding from his friends.

Not four hours ago, Nico had wandered into the office at the auto shop and over to the booze fridge, so named because it mostly housed Coon's latest home brew, to grab a Dr Pepper in between jobs.

Only instead of enjoying cool, carbonated refreshment, Nico found himself under attack when Coon and Brett had come at him, barrels blazing.

"You know it's tomorrow, right? *Lexi's wedding.*" As if he needed a reminder. Brett leaned forward, causing the old chair to squeak, irritation lacing his voice. "Tonight's your *last* ethical chance to set things right between you two."

Hell yeah, he knew what tomorrow was—the end of his dreams. But, glutton for punishment, he played dumb. "What're you talking about?"

"Boy, I taught you better 'n that." Coondog spat a stream of tobacco spit into a paper cup. Then he reached for his bag of chew where he kept it stashed behind an old framed photo. "Don't lie to us—or yourself. You really gonna let her go? Without a fight?"

The walls started closing in on him. Regret from the past weeks and months looming, pressing in like life-threatening razors, ready to shred his resolve.

Holding on by a thread, he put the unopened soda back in the fridge. Slammed the door shut and spun to face his attackers. Legs crossed at the ankles, he braced himself against the counter, folded his arms in front of his chest and glared. "You two busybodies don't have anything better to do than harp on me? On my nonexistent love life?"

"Nonexistent because it's what *you* chose," Brett said. "Not her." Easy-going Brett's words were all the more powerful because of the quiet intensity behind them.

"I didn't have a choice!"

"Bullshit," said Coondog, the tats climbing up his neck flexing as he spoke. "Your daddy being in prison? No choice." As he talked, he hauled the trash can over with his booted foot, spit out the chewed-to-death tobacco and started prepping a refresher. "Your mama tryin' to do it all and dying too damn young? No choice there either. But now, abandonin' Lexi? Standing back with your thumb up your ass while she marries someone else?"

Like the two were dancing a tango, Brett picked right up, ticking off Nico's mistakes on his fingers. "Choice. Choice. The texts you didn't respond to? Choice. The times you ignored…"

Brett kept going, guilt kept growing.

All the calls from Lexi he'd declined.

All the times he'd driven by her house first, then her apartment complex when she'd moved out on her own.

All the minutes wasted. The *seconds*! The—

"Choices, dammit." Brett's voice turned hard. "Bad ones. Don't ignore your last opportunity to—"

"What opportunity?" Regret crawled through him like a mound of angry ants, stinging his stupid pride. "Get real. Like either of you really think I'd ever fit in with her crowd? For the long haul? Lacrosse?" Hell if he even knew what it was. "Golf? Sailing?"

"Golf's not so bad." Coon grinned as he folded up his bag of chew. Then he speared Nico with a look. "You might want to try it sometime."

Yeah. Like never.

"You might try minding your own fucking business," Nico spouted off. Then immediately said, "Hell. I'm sorry."

He scrubbed the heel of his palms into his sore eye sockets; the recent sleepless nights were getting to him. He lowered his arms and looked at his boss and mentor, the closest thing to family he had these days. "I apologize. My life *is* your business. I wouldn't have much of one if it wasn't for you."

Coon saluted him with the bag of Red Man before tucking it behind the old picture from his Army days he kept on his desk: *all forgiven*. Why couldn't the rest of his life be so easy?

"Who cares if you don't like sailing? Golf or Lacrap?" Brett asked. "Lexi never belittled you, did she? Gave you a hard time?"

Or ever once tried to change him or make him "fit in". Not once.

"No. Never." She'd ask or suggest but was always willing for him to hang back or skip an event if he wasn't interested. He was the one who'd left her. Not the other way around.

The one who'd made the biggest mistake of his misbegotten life. "What can I do now? It's too late."

"It's never too late, son." Coondog looked ridiculous, dispensing advice with a chew the size of a baseball pooching out his cheek. "Not till one of you's in the ground."

"Since when did you start rooting for me and Lexi?" Come to think on it, though Coon had warned him off a time or two in the beginning, that was before he'd met her. Once she showed up at the garage that first time, never mind that it wasn't at her best, Coondog had changed his tune.

"Boy, anyone with eyes in their head can tell the two of you belong together."

"Hell, Nic, I'd give my left nut to have what you and Lexi did," Brett said solemnly. "What you could get back if you'd only make an effort."

Coon nodded, as if it were the easiest thing in the world. He spread his tattooed arms wide, reminding Nico of every time the hardened geezer had given him valued advice over the years. "I have it on good authority the rehearsal is tonight. At—"

"What do you mean 'good authority'?" Nico could feel himself starting to unravel. The date and location hadn't been on the engagement announcement, he knew. Because he'd looked it up two nights ago, curious. Desperate. "How do you know that?"

"Does it matter?" Brett said, pure exasperation in his tone as he leaned back in the vinyl chair to another round of creaks. Stupid thing had to be two decades old. Right now, Nico just wanted to kick it out from under his interfering friend. "If you're not man enough to fight for her, maybe you don't deserve her."

"Damn straight, I do!" Nico fired back, the truth of his words roaring through his blood. "Okay." He glared at them both, fighting mad and ready to do something about it. "Okay, I admit it. I've been a fool. How do I convince her? What kind of grand gesture can I make to prove it?"

Prove that I need her. Will never let her go.

Coondog spat again. "Now that's up to you, Nic. We can't do everythin' for ya." He wiped the side of one wrist across his lips. "But from what I know of Lexi, she's not 'xactly a grand gesture kind of gal."

"More of a *sincere* gesture kind of gal," Brett added.

"Since when did you two become Tweedledee and Tweedledum, finishing each other's thoughts?"

"When you became Humpty Douche," Coondog said with a snort. "Too afraid to hop on the wall because you might—*might*, mind ya—fall."

"That's just"—Nico couldn't stop the strangled chuckle from emerging—"plumb awful."

"Here." Brett tossed him the keys to his newly restored '57 Bel Air. "I know you want to show off this beauty."

He sure did. Had been envisioning Lexi riding with him, wind in her hair, smile on her face since the first moment he'd bought the in-need-of-TLC clunker over two years ago. Now restored to its original glory, the silver classic drew attention like a magnet. Since that wasn't why he'd gotten it, Nico tended to keep it housed at the garage more often than not. But today? For Lexi? He was pulling out all the stops.

He snatched his jacket from the hook beside the door. His fingers gripped it tight.

As always, touching the supple black leather brought back so many memories of their time together. Especially their first Christmas, when she'd given him a vintage, signed edition of his second favorite book, his favorite being outrageously expensive. How the one she'd ended up gifting him, *King Solomon's Mines*, meant so much more than any amount of secret treasure. How their second Christmas together, she'd given him this jacket, saying even a reformed hoodlum needed to look the part. Year-round, he kept it close—even though she wasn't.

"Hold up." Coondog roused himself enough to dig something mangy out of his pocket. He reached out and pressed the pathetic thing in Nico's palm. "Good luck."

Nico looked at the yech bit of dirty fur. Great. His future happiness depended on the good fortune from the worn, once bright green rabbit's foot Coon won during a trivia contest last St. Patrick's Day? "Gee, thanks." He caught Coon's eye. "So tell me, does your good authority extend to *where* this rehearsal's taking place?"

"It does." The bearded shop owner stopped there, just stared, eyes glittering.

The bastard.

"Do I have to take a crowbar to your head to pry it out of you?"

"Nope." Coondog grinned, enjoying Nico's discomfort. "At that fancy church on Capitol."

Oh, hell no. "You mean Saint Anthony's?"

The church he knew Lexi wanted to get married in. The one she'd dreamed about since first visiting as a kid. Where she'd invited him to attend Christmas Mass and Easter services with her family, but he hadn't gone. Because he'd abandoned her.

Coondog gave half a shrug. "If that's the one downtown, then yep."

The church parking lot where Nico had now taken up residence, just as soon as he could clean the garage off him, grab a couple things, and fight his way through evening traffic to reach.

Only to sit and cower.

No more!

Resolved, he blinked open his eyes. Pure determination thrummed through him. He *had* to talk to her. Convince her to take another chance on him.

Langston's butt buddy revved a sputtering engine that was in dire need of a tune-up and peeled wheels from the parking lot. Showing off...how mature.

He'd seen everyone else leave earlier, bridesmaids and groomsmen, her mother and a few other folks, both young and old. Lexi's respectable Honda Accord being the lone occupier of the main parking lot.

Acting on instinct, he pocketed his keys, leapt from his convertible, and sprinted to the side door he'd seen Lexi disappear behind. Easing it open, he stepped inside the long hallway.

Hallelujah!

There before him, by the grace of God, was Lexi—bent over, with her hands in her panties.

Nico grinned, feeling instantly lighthearted. Better about confronting her. "Now, I don't doubt a pansy like Langston can't satisfy you, Sweet Lex, but is this really the time and place?"

FOUR

Something Old - Three years ago

BUCCANEER PRIVATE CAMPGROUND

"HI. Do you mind telling me where I should put my stuff?" Alexis asked the man who'd come over to welcome her, eager to stash her belongings so she could get the lay of the land. It'd taken over two hours to reach this remote, wooded area about sixty miles northeast of Livingston, Texas.

There were several regular-size tents arranged in a large semicircle, nestled among towering pines, with one large open-air, cabana-type tent dominating the space off to the side. That one seemed to be the gathering place for the half dozen or so adults milling about.

"What about The Tank? Do I need to move him somewhere else? Or is this okay?" She motioned to her father's old Lincoln which she'd only driven because her modest import had made a frightening clanking noise as soon as she started down the driveway. Tankster here had been the closest vehicle at hand with enough fuel to get her all the way to the campsite, and she hadn't wanted to waste any time starting her new adventure.

Fortunately, after swapping vehicles, the drive had gone off without a hitch.

Because she'd packed enough for a small army, she sheepishly indicated her bulging backpack. "I know I brought a lot, but I wanted to be prepared." For once, her mother hadn't censored Alexis's food intake. Instead of telling her what she *should* eat, Mother had panicked about there not being enough *suitable, healthy options in the wilds of beyond* and encouraged the array of snacks she'd brought. "I've got all sorts of granola, jerky, and energy bars. Are the kids allowed to share?"

And when are you going to stop flapping your tongue? Barraging him with questions?

Him...

The man who stood silently while her jaws worked up a breeze. Who evaluated her in a way Alexis couldn't decipher. She was exhilarated to be here. Excited to start the foreign adventure.

And she had to admit his presence only amped the feelings.

From the moment she'd spun on her brand-new hiking boots to find him at her back and taking command of her unloading efforts, Alexis had been angling to get a better look. All she'd glimpsed upon his arrival was tattoos aplenty, facial hair, and a better tan than any salon-paying customer could buy.

It wasn't until he plucked out those giant cases of water Mother insisted Alexis bring ("What if there isn't a shower available? Alexis, you'll thank me. But you really shouldn't be going off on this asinine little jaunt.

Be reasonable—"). Alexis slammed the lid on that line of thinking and focused on the man who faced her.

She wanted to stop babbling, afraid she might be coming across as a dipshit. But she positively could not wait to call her best friend, Jenny, and share that she'd found him, the very incarnation of her teenage "rebellious" crush, a.k.a. Dave Navarro from the *Strays* album when he was with Jane's Addiction: The black hair, the goatee, the tats, and attitude minus the earrings—and eye makeup, she was relieved to note—now stood before her. Jenny would applaud, knowing Alexis usually went for refined, well-groomed men.

Her words should have dried up. This unexpected awareness of the definite bad boy in front of her should have caused an instant retreat into the reserved, circumspect behavior that had been drilled into her since she'd escaped her mother's womb.

Instead, Alexis learned something about herself: A surprisingly stark and instant attraction made her chatter. Who knew?

She'd never done that before, not with the boys, or men, she'd dated.

It's the danger factor. That's all.

Which made sense.

He did look like a Hoodlum's Hunk of the Month, with that mixed Italian-Hispanic-Question-Mark heritage; that long, sin-black hair pulled back in a low ponytail; those jet eyes more intense than any laser beam—and that neatly trimmed goatee.

That had to be it. Her lips tingled the longer she tried not to stare. Not because they were turning blue due to lack of oxygen—hard to breathe when one is yakking up a storm. But because they wanted to slide against his.

She'd never kissed a man with facial hair.

Stubble, sure. Three-day, too-lazy-to-shave beard growth, certainly. But not an honest-to-God lip-lock with a man and his mustache and chin hair.

Shake some sense into yourself, woman!

She'd long since outgrown those silly, girlish fantasies about rock stars. Hadn't she?

But as she continued to blather, she kept having to yank her gaze away from his supple-looking lips, where they were framed by that gorgeous goatee. Why'd she find it so sexy?

Goes with the tats.

It did indeed. She didn't have time to catalog them all, but beneath the sleeveless denim shirt he wore—the sleeves having been ripped out who knew when—his muscled forearms, biceps, and shoulders were all decorated with interesting ink. The faded denim shirt was only partially buttoned, leaving the upper half of his torso exposed to her ravenous gaze.

Her stomach swooped at the thought of being held against that gorgeous chest, of having those dark-skinned, strong arms wrapped securely around her. Was he that tan from hours outside or his natural heritage? Would she ever get a chance to look her fill at the designs adorning his skin?

"What'll we do when the youngsters arrive?" Ack. She sounded totally out of breath. "Take them hiking first or what? What about—"

Stop talking! Give him a chance to answer.

But the uncharacteristic nervous chatter wouldn't

stop. No doubt about it, forbidden attraction aside, Alexis was thrilled to be here. Away from the latest ongoing drama at home.

She hadn't intended to gabble like a stuck goat. *Play it cool,* Drea and Kisha had advised with all the wisdom their eight and eleven years possessed. *And go by Lexi,* Drea had added. *Alexis sounds stuck-up,* she'd said. *Lexi is hip. Dope.*

Nobody is using "dope" anymore, you dope, Kisha had told her younger sister, as she folded Alexis's most casual two outfits and placed them in the canvas duffel bag the girls had brought over for her to borrow. *Gucci ain't cuttin' it, girlfriend. Not this weekend.*

Inside, Alexis smiled at the memory from yesterday. Being a Big Sister to the real sisters the last three years had been a bright spot in an otherwise often blah life.

Privileged and rich didn't necessarily equate to happy or content.

Add in the uncertainty concerning her brother's whereabouts—United States Air Force pilot, currently MIA in enemy territory—and, well, Alexis had needed to feel good about herself, to do something other than worry or pamper her distraught mother.

With only one afternoon a week dedicated to her "little sisters", she'd had way too much time on her hands. So when her former faculty advisor contacted her to ask if she "might possibly" be interested in another volunteer opportunity, one that hadn't panned out to date but an effort he thought worthwhile, Alexis had jumped at the chance.

Anything to feel useful again. To regain some of the

precious independence she'd lost when she'd stopped going to school.

Camping? Whoa, boy. Definitely not what she'd expected. Nothing she had any experience at but was totally willing to learn.

She could do this. She wanted to do this. *Needed* to do something before she either grieved herself sick or strangled her annoying mother. Since matricide wasn't an option, Alexis became one very determined college dropout.

With only a semester and a half left, she'd taken Incompletes when her brother went missing, Dad had a heart attack, and Mother fell apart, all in the span of one short week.

Now, two years later, Dad was doing great. Still no official word on Phil, though, and her mother's nagging attempts to turn Alexis into the Perfect Society Hostess, complete with unwanted marriage and—oh, horrors!— tennis lessons, made Alexis more determined than ever to get out of the house and—

You have got to stop talking!

When she realized her mouth had kept going, ninety to nothing, while her thoughts had spun in circles, she forced herself to wind down. "...really a waterfall off the trail? I'd love to see it."

Ta-da!

Alexis gulped in some much-needed air after that unintentional monologue. What must Mr. Strong, Intense, and Tattooed think of the flighty, wordy female who'd just invaded their midst?

His low, appreciative whistle filled the air. "Wow. Alexis Templeton, huh? Fancy that, you're either a really good actress or hyped-up on something. Because we both know all that crap you just fed me about wanting to be here is just that—bullshit."

While she worked to process the accusation, he spewed out more, in a dark and sexy voice she wanted to hate.

"The last thing you want to do is be here, and if you stay past supper, it'll be a miracle. Already planning your Clorox shower and night out with your frivolous friends, I bet. Can't wait to report back to whoever was stupid enough to send you out here about how grimy and beneath you we all are." He nodded abruptly toward The Tank. "Why don't you just climb back into that irresponsible gas hog? Make like a princess and bow out before the kids get here? Before you go getting anyone's hopes up."

By the time he finished, he was scowling at her, leaning forward, hands on his hips in a fighting stance. Challenging her right to be there but more than that, questioning her integrity.

Alexis just stood there.

Dazed. Hurt. Surprised silent by the unwarranted attack.

Options, girlfriend, she could hear Kisha repeat one of the things Alexis had taught her. *Consider all your options before you react.*

Okay...

1) Slap his sexy face. Hard.

2) Shove his sexy chest. Harder.

3) *Yell back. Defend yourself. This asshole piece of Italian-Mexican trash doesn't know anything about you! And he's ready to be judge and jury?*

4) *Kiss him. You know you want to.*

5) —

Alexis stopped right there. This was getting totally out of hand. One and two were out—she wasn't physical by nature. Three wasn't her style. She might think trash talk, but she'd been raised not to voice it. And four?

Not going to happen. She didn't make out with just any stud who caught her fancy. She had principles. Respect for herself, even if he didn't.

"I am so out of here," Alexis muttered.

In her most refined manner, she knelt to retrieve the duffel and backpack. He could tend to the water himself —she didn't care if she grew body odor enough to fell a crowd with one whiff. Hefting the moderate weight of her casual luggage, she turned to him, steeling herself against his appeal. "I'll be removing myself from your vicinity now. Wouldn't dream of getting your hopes up."

Or anything else, huh?

Down, crazy-insane libido. Down!

He stepped in front of her, grabbed one wrist. "So now you're proving me right? That quickly? Running home to Mommy because I don't buy your act?" His fingers tightened against her skin. "Why am I not surprised?"

His touch was firm, not frightening. His hold around her wrist warm, not unwelcome. Stupid, traitorous body!

Be Lexi, she'll be cool. Those kids'll like Lexi. She could hear the girls as if they were right beside her. *Did you know our half-brother Sticks has gone on those campouts? You might even see him!*

"Not sorry to disappoint you, but 'home' isn't my

destination. I'm simply getting away from your undesirable"—ha—"presence."

His grip had somehow turned caressive, his thumb downright stroking her skin. Felt good, too good. She didn't want to move.

Respect.

"I'd like my arm back, if you please."

Without another word, he unfurled his fingers one by one and moved off, both hands upraised in surrender, eyes narrowed in distrust. "If I misjudged, please accept my apology. These kids have been through a merry-go-round of useless society types and—"

"Nice to know what you think of me." Worst part was, he hadn't misjudged. *Useless* socialite was exactly what she felt like these days. But she wasn't about to admit it. "How about you stuff your sorry, insincere apology up your prejudiced ass?"

Huh. Maybe she could talk trash after all.

FIVE

Something Mortifying - Present Day

SAINT ANTHONY'S CATHEDRAL

"NICO?" Alexis hissed under her breath.

Her fingers grappled in the crotch of her underwear for the elusive ball. Frantic, Alexis crammed her middle finger as high inside as she could, pushing the remaining ball back into place so she wouldn't lose it too.

Where was the other one?

She heard a small thud.

"Why me?" she squeaked.

Is that all you have to squeak—er, say—to the man who haunts your dreams? Still holds your heart?

No, he doesn't have anything to do with my heart. He can't.

You shouldn't lie in church.

I'm engaged!

You don't have to be...

"Looking for this?" Nico swept down and picked up the missing ball where it'd landed on the carpet. Whipping her hands free, Alexis wiped her fingers and faced the bane of her current existence, Nico Tonetti.

"You absolutely cannot be here." Hungry for him, she devoured the vision of sin personified—shoulder-length black hair (for once not pulled back), triangular goatee, captivating jet eyes. Tanned and tattooed. Wicked and wonderful. Irresistible. And he'd been hers. For a time.

He shifted closer and she caught a faint whiff of the garage that always seemed to cling to him, even fresh from the shower. Leather and motor oil, two things synonymous with Nico. Two things guaranteed to turn her on.

Where was his ever-present leather jacket? Summer or not, she could practically smell it on him.

Today he wore snug, well-worn jeans and an even snugger black t-shirt, bulging in all the right places. Her fingers itched to trace his sculpted pecs, to raise the left sleeve of his shirt so she could set her eyes on the detailed cougar blessing his muscular arm.

Her ravenous thoughts scattered when Nico lifted his right hand to hold the gold, glistening ball at eye level. His nostrils flared. "Smells like you. Would it taste like you too, I wonder?"

Alexis shook free of her stupor and reached for it, but he snatched his hand away and she lurched, almost losing balance. The movement jostled the second ball between her legs and she tried to will it back up. She could *not* take any more humiliation right now. "Give that back!"

"Uh-uh. Tell me what it is and I *might* let you have

it." His wicked grin reminded her how much she loved him. Him? *It, it, the sex, anything but him!*

"What are you doing here?" She clenched her thighs in an effort to prevent further embarrassment. Why had she listened to Jenny? Her pelvic muscles were fine, thank you very much. "You can't be here."

"But I am." His piercing eyes took her in, said a lot more than his words. He spread his arms out to the side, looking way more comfortable than he had a right to. "In the flesh."

"I mean it, Nico. Tell me what you're doing here."

Bringing the ball back to eye level, he gave her a speculative look. "Tell me what this is first."

"Nothing."

He looked at the ball, then popped it in his mouth, swirling it around. His cheeks inverted as he sucked. "Delicious."

"Disgusting." Alexis looked away. She had enough to deal with without...*that.*

"I used to lick you all the time. You didn't think that was disgusting."

"Maybe so, but that fell on the *floor!*"

"Now that you mention it," he said, shifting the ball to the other side of his mouth, "I see what you mean. That is kinda gross." Putting his hand to her nape, he pulled her to him. Their noses brushed. "Watcha say we get dirty together, Lexi?" His voice had gone all hoarse. "I've missed you like crazy."

A heartbeat later, he meshed their lips. At the taste of him, Alexis shattered. Forgot where she was, what she was supposed to be doing, even who she was. Instead, she became Nico's sex-starved *Lexi.* His *Rene-*

gade. She sucked on his tongue, loving the thick glide of it against hers as he plundered her mouth.

His hands roamed her back and butt, warming her, heating her crotch to boiling. When he grabbed a handful of ass and kissed her harder, Lexi moaned.

How she'd missed this. Missed him. And not just the way he kissed, either. The way he looked and acted so very bad, but in truth was so very good. Kindhearted, charitable even, always willing to donate the important stuff—more than just money—to those kids he cherished.

How he'd made *her* a better person too.

And, man, could he kiss. It was even better than she remembered.

Bet he's been getting in lots of practice since you guys broke up.

Lexi refused to think about that. To even consider it. How could she, when he kissed her with such raw passion? Such urgency?

Her heart hitched.

Did he want to get back together? Give them another chance? Make things work after all?

Something clanked against her teeth—the ball! Nico was trying to thrust the damn ball into her mouth. Dick-whipped for him or not, she drew the line there.

Lexi broke free, spitting out the hated ball. It fell to the carpet with a plop.

"Stop!" She turned her head to the side, unable to believe what she'd just allowed. Just participated in. *Encouraged.* "A kiss doesn't change anything. I could have just kissed the deacon and I'd still be getting married tomorrow."

The deacon wouldn't have had a Ben Wa ball in his mouth.

Lexi licked her swollen lips. Nico's taste, mingled with hers, brought it all back. All of her dreams, all of the heartache.

His fingers brushed her chin, pulling her gaze back to him. "But you didn't. You kissed me." The look in his eyes went straight to her soul.

At the thought of marrying anyone but him, she wanted to puke. "Why are you doing this?" She wrenched away, looking over his shoulder. What had she done? She was getting married tomorrow—to the perfect guy.

The perfect guy who smoked and drilled? Now she just plain wanted to puke. And paw Nico till he made her purr. "Leave me alone! You had your chance. You threw it away." *Threw me away.*

"Lexi, you can't marry that asshole." His voice was firm. As if it was his place to tell her what to do. "You just can't."

She wanted to smack him. The absolute nerve. Showing up out of nowhere, thinking he had any say in her life. "Move," she told his left earlobe, determined not to get captured again by his gaze. "I need to get to the restaurant."

"Lexi, hear me out. Langston isn't the guy for you."

"Neither are you." She tried to shove past him and met immovable muscle. "Or did you forget that long letter, detailing all the reasons why?"

Now she just sounded whiny. Pitiful. A weak woman who'd held on far too long to a man who no longer wanted her.

"Lexi." He grabbed her again, shook her shoulders as though trying to force her to meet his gaze. "You *can't* marry him."

He's not exactly acting like a man who doesn't want you, now is he?

True.

Needing to see the look in his eyes, to see if he felt anything, she lifted her gaze. Concern, love even, sparkled back. She'd never seen his gaze glow like that, like the hottest part of a flame.

What was he doing to her? Nico had made it clear she was nothing but a fling. He'd had *months* to convince her otherwise.

What they'd shared hadn't ever been just "a fling" to her. Okay, yes. Maybe at the very beginning, but something changed a short while in, when she'd told him about her brother...

From that point on, she'd given Nico her heart, her loyalty, and for nearly two years, they'd been in dating heaven. Lexi hadn't pushed for more, being delighted with exactly what they had—they saw each other every chance they got, and she never had any reason to think he wasn't as happy as she. Then came the Disastrous Dinner. Followed by his Dear Alexis-Jane letter. And mountains of heartache.

Heartache she'd assuaged by becoming dutiful little Alexis all over again. Mother wanted a hostess for afternoon tea? Alexis was her gal. Mother wanted Alexis to start taking tennis lessons again? Fine by her. Mother wanted Alexis to start dating—and it should be someone in their "circle"? Sure. Who better than her former high school boyfriend?

Mother wanted her to say *yes* when Bradley popped the question just a few weeks in? And in front of her parents, no less. Well, why not? It wasn't as though she hadn't enjoyed dating him in high school. Had even, for a short time when she was younger, thought herself in love with him. And because of that—the "high school sweetheart" label—nobody raised an eyebrow when they announced their engagement so soon after getting back together.

Nico shifted. "I know I broke things off abruptly—"

"You think?" Lexi contemplated kicking his shin. Making a run for it.

"But I'm here now. Ready to do anything it takes to keep you from marrying the wrong man."

"Why now? How dare you have the gall to come here uninvited and tell me I can't marry Bradley." Why wouldn't her stupid voice stop quavering? She cleared her throat. "I think I can. I think I *will*. Now go home. I don't want to see you ever again."

"I won't force you to," he said swiftly. "Promise me you won't marry Langston. Do that and I'll vanish. Get out of your life."

"Oh, I see. This isn't about you—or, heaven forbid, *us*—you're just here to save the day?" She couldn't face him another second. He was killing her inside. "To screw up my life? When did I ever do anything to you?"

He started to say something, then clamped his mouth shut.

"Well?"

A muscle ticked in his jaw, and Lexi had the impression he was fighting with himself. About to tell her something meaningful. Insightful. *Real.* "Langston's not for you."

That was it?

Her heart collapsed. Ridiculously disappointed all over again, Lexi glared to keep from crying. "And you call *Bradley* an asshole? Try looking in the mirror."

Nico's hold on her shoulders shifted, became almost soothing.

She jerked out of reach. "Don't touch me!"

Don't talk to me. Don't make me think of you. Don't let my heart flare with hope by showing up, then shatter it to pieces all over again by not fighting for me. Wanting me...

Seeing that he finally got the message—he hadn't taken a step toward her—Lexi fled toward the bathroom, struggling to hold in a sob.

How could he do this to her? Now?

After all this time, she'd finally gotten him out of her system. And he just pops up out of nowhere, determined to ruin all her plans.

Out of your system? What do you call mooning over him all evening? Before he ever showed up?

Squaring her shoulders, Lexi increased her speed. She'd forget all about Nico, retrieve the remaining gold ball from her girly bits, then she'd rush to the restaurant where—

Strong arms wrapped around her and lifted her feet off the floor. Nico swung her around and hauled her against his strong body.

"Stop! Don't. *Please.*" She twisted in his embrace. Up this close, leather, aftershave, and the faintest hint of motor oil invaded her nostrils, throwing her off-guard. She pounded against his granite chest, trying to push him away, when it was the last thing she really wanted. "Nico!"

His hands left her shoulders only to cup her bottom. Without warning, he spread his fingers, firmed his palms, and propelled her right over his shoulder. Her stomach landed against hard muscle. *"Ooomph!"*

"Ahem." From behind her butt, a throat cleared. The deacon! *"Eh-hem!* Is everything all right, Alexis?"

Thanks to Nico's caveman tactics, the long skirt of her dress had gotten bunched under her stomach. Cool air hit her legs. *All* the way up.

The aroused part of her inner workings cinched—with shame or desire, she wasn't sure. The rest of her burned with embarrassment.

Nico swung to face Deacon Joe, leaving her dangling over his shoulder. Then the jerk had the nerve to pat her bottom.

Good Lord, she was practically mooning the poor deacon. Why hadn't she thought to wear leggings? *Or pants!*

"Everything is fine, sir, just fine," Nico told him in a calm voice that belied the effort he made to hold on to her protesting body.

Deacon Joe walked around and bent at the knees, looking up at her from the awkward position. Through her curtain of hair that separated them, his eyes studied her. "Alexis? Is this Neanderthal part of the wedding party? A late arrival perhaps?"

Blood rushed to her face as she tried to slip free of Nico's grasp. He *slap-popped* one of her exposed thighs. With a sigh, she gave up. Nico wasn't letting go.

Maybe she didn't want him to.

"*Men*," she whined.

"Hmm," Deacon Joe murmured, gazing at her with a knowing smile. "This explains much, I'm thinking."

"What does that mean?" Nico wanted to know.

Lexi shook her head frantically.

No way was she going to explain that during premarital counseling, the man of the cloth had questioned her privately more than once. Questioned her commitment to the upcoming marriage, her devotion to Bradley.

She'd worked on her acting skills and must deserve an Oscar because after the third visit, he hadn't quizzed her further.

Until now.

"Shall I call the authorities?" Deacon Joe persisted. "Is this man hurting you?" In ways he couldn't imagine. But not enough for her to plead for his help. "Or shall I let you two possibly work through some things, hmm?"

"I never noticed how very red the carpet is," she mused, staring at the floor. Being in Nico's arms was making her lose her mind. Hanging upside down wasn't helping.

"Miss Templeton," more sternly voiced, "do I need to call the police?"

She smacked Nico on his legs. "That's not necessary. He's putting me down. Now."

Nico jiggled her, stilling her complaint. "What time's the wedding?"

She couldn't believe this was happening.

"Two." Deacon Joe answered firmly, then he moved Lexi's hair back and caught her gaze with no barrier to block her expression. Or the rising concern she saw in his. "Miss Templeton? The police? Yes or no?"

"No." Boy, that was weak. She cleared her throat and tried again. "No. Please don't."

"Your parents? Shall I call them?"

"Heavens, no!"

"Sir, I won't mistreat her. I'll have her back in time tomorrow. Word of honor." Nico grunted as if he were doing them all a favor. "*If* she still wants to be here."

Swinging around, he stormed down the hall then shoved open the massive doors. His strong legs pounded down the stone staircase, the motion jarring her with every step.

Lexi couldn't decide whether to be agitated or elated.

Whether his secure hold promised heaven.

Or guaranteed hell.

SIX

Something Old - Two years and eleven
months ago

BUCCANEER PRIVATE CAMPGROUND

NICO WAS BEYOND IMPRESSED. And feeling crummier by the step. He'd royally misjudged her.

Not only had Miss Temptation returned for the second month—something he couldn't decide whether to be pleased or resentful about—she'd gone on the Sunrise Seven Miler with nary a single complaint.

In truth, the famed hike was closer to nine miles, but he supposed some clever adventurist had given it the nickname. The Sunrise Seven sure sounded better than the Four-in-the-Morning Nine. Throughout the year, no matter when he'd gone, the view of the sun climbing its way from behind the distant horizon remained spectacular, always worth the effort.

Staggering out of their tents about 4:30 a.m., they'd all been on the trail shortly after five. For the kids and paid caregivers, jokingly—for the most part—referred to as jailers, the early morning hike was mandatory; for the volunteers, optional. Nico had been more surprised to see Alexis Templeton emerging from her tent, flashlight in hand, her hair slapped haphazardly into a high ponytail, her jeans, flannel shirt, and light jacket just right, than he'd been to see her show up Friday afternoon—which was saying a lot.

A rare summer cool front had blown in, dropping the early-morning temps and clearing out some of the typical humidity.

After making it to the overlook, where the vista stretched for miles and enjoying the birth of a new day, then resting up for a few, it was time to tackle the remaining six miles of the loop.

They were nearing the homestretch now, just over a mile left before they returned to camp. Though she hadn't voiced a single complaint, Nico had watched the perky, upbeat female fade from the front of the line, cheerful and energetic, to the back. She was no longer vivacious or smiling—unless one of the kids was talking to her. And despite her determination to mask both grimace and limp, he saw them clearly.

He'd bet next week's paycheck that blisters had set up camp inside those spanking-new hiking boots.

Her thick ponytail had wilted, now lay limp and low against her nape. Along with the rest of them, once the sun came up and they worked up a sweat, she'd taken off her jacket, tied it around her waist. But she'd trudged on, keeping up until the last couple hundred yards.

Now that he thought about it, *impressed* didn't begin to describe the emotions the determined beauty roused in him.

Last month, after he'd unfairly laid into her—a stupid self-defense mechanism, aiming to scare her off because he could tell if she got close enough, he'd take everything she might be willing to give—she hadn't spoken another word to him. Hadn't looked his way once.

But the justified animosity he'd felt emanating toward him like a toxic cloud couldn't stop him from watching her. Some sixth sense kept him wholly aware of her location every minute that weekend. Damned if he didn't eavesdrop on her conversations, observe her interactions. Wish he'd been part of them.

Not once did she behave in the spoiled, entitled manner he'd accused her of. She got down and dirty, digging up worms with a couple of the younger boys—when they dared her—and even tried her hand at fishing. She was utterly hopeless at casting her line, certainly couldn't be quiet long enough to lure a fish anywhere near the hook, but she'd laughed. She laughed and made friends of the less reserved, less hardened kids.

She'd laughed, and made Nico feel all kinds of rotten.

The same thing had happened since she'd arrived Friday. Interactions. Participation. The ability to zap him with guilt-inducing poison arrows—without ever glancing his direction.

Knowing he needed to make amends, needed to salvage something between them if they had any hope of working together peacefully, he loped up front to tell Brett he was going to hang back for a while. Try to smooth things over with their latest volunteer.

"Good luck with that," Brett said. "I may not be the most female-savvy guy around, but even I can tell the only way that woman is welcoming you with open arms is if they come bearing chocolate and jewelry."

It'd been that obvious? How much she couldn't stand him? He had to fix this. "If you'll help occupy the troops with food, I thought I'd take her out to the waterfall. See how bad those blisters are."

Brett looked skeptical. "You think she's actually letting you within ten feet of her? Much less close enough to inspect her *feet*? In your dreams."

Nico waved off his friend's negativity. "I'll turn on the charm."

"Charm? You?" Brett nearly guffawed. They both knew if *charm* was a word to ever be applied to either of them, it'd be Brett, hands down. Nico? Never. "Is that pool deep enough for drowning? Judging by the scowls she's sent your way, I wouldn't put it past her."

Really? Nico hadn't caught a single one. He'd only felt them. "Yeah, well, I'll make sure all the stragglers are headed back to camp. You keep everyone there."

"Will do."

That taken care of, Nico returned to the back of the line.

Toward Temptation.

DON'T COMPLAIN. Don't complain. Don't complain.

Alexis's new mantra. She'd finish this horrible hike if it killed her. If her left foot gave up the ghost, she'd crawl.

Stupid blisters! Around mile three, just before they'd reached the viewing spot, one had started on the back of her heel. She'd ignored it. By mile five, one by her pinky toe had joined the fold. Then her big toe. Not to be outdone, in the last mile or so it felt like the blade of a knife carved into the side of her ankle with every agonizing step.

She gritted her teeth and kept going. Tried not to imagine what her foot must look like. Whether the blisters had popped. Were oozing inside her sock.

Tried to ignore the glances of concern Nico-The-Bonehead shot her way the last five minutes. Knowing he was watching stiffened her spine, strengthened her ankle.

If she could muster the energy, she'd start singing "Supercalifragilisticexpialidocious", make sure she sounded absurdly chipper so he knew how merry she felt. How enthusiastically happy and joyful.

Hardly.

Knowing they were nearing camp—and a hearty brunch—several hungry teenagers took off ahead, leaving Alexis behind. Way behind.

She didn't mind. With no one to chat with, she allowed her steps to slow. The pain increased, and her entire world narrowed to the dirt path in front of her.

Step over the broken branch.

Avoid the roots.

Don't walk on the loose rocks!

One foot in front of the other.

Plod. Plod. Plod—*ow!*

Damn rock.

Another step. Another. Another—

"Hey." At the unexpected touch to her shoulder, she wrenched her head up. "You ready to rest?"

Alexis wasn't about to admit defeat in front of

Jerkwad Nico. "I'm fine." She made herself smile and turned her head, looking through the thick foliage on either side of the trail. "Just enjoying the view."

"Liar." The gentle smile in his voice softened the accusation.

"What? You're going to try and make nice now?" *Too little, too late, you accusatory schmuck.*

She forced herself to lift her sore foot in pathetic semblance of a step.

"Wait, Alexis."

She ignored him.

"Please."

Yeah, as if that was going to work.

Fabric *whooshed* past her waist. Alexis looked down, stumbled to a painful halt, then spun to face him. "You took my jacket."

He shrugged. "I stopped you the quickest way I could." He pointed to her stinging foot. "You're hurting. The waterfall's not far from here. I know you want to see it. And I bet soaking your foot in the cool water will feel like heaven."

Torn, because though it sure sounded good, she really didn't want to spend another second with the sexy hoodlum musical-crush look-alike, she indicated the path the kids had disappeared down. "What about camp? Shouldn't we...?"

"Nah. I told Brett we might take off for a few minutes. We can still scrounge lunch when we get back. I know I haven't done anything to earn it, but trust me, okay?"

She debated with herself a full four seconds before giving in. "The waterfall it is." She yanked her jacket from his loose hold. "But keep your hands off and your nasty opinions to yourself, got it?"

Was that a spark of admiration in his inky gaze? "Yes, ma'am."

NICO SLOWED his pace so the stubborn woman wouldn't lose sight of him. The waterfall wasn't far off the main trail, perhaps sixty yards or so, but the path got narrow and muddy, the rocks slick, as they neared the oasis.

Maybe sixteen feet across, the spring-fed pool nestled among both large and small boulders and was surrounded by dense greenery on three sides and the seven-foot drop of water on the fourth.

As always, the private spot waited to welcome him with serenity and solitude.

Nico loved coming here, had since the first moment old Coondog had introduced him to the magical place. He usually preferred being by himself. But today...

Well, he only hoped that the tranquil locale would cast its peaceful spell on Miss Prickly back there.

Since they'd turned off the main trail, it'd been one complaint after another.

No, don't touch me, she'd cried when he offered a hand to help her over a fallen tree trunk that stretched across the narrow path.

I said I can do it myself, she'd snapped the second time he dared catch hold of her when she'd tripped, hopping—more like hobbling—over a particularly damp patch.

Fine. Without a word, he'd hiked ahead, putting a few feet of distance and miles of space between them.

And he'd thought to make amends?

Joke's on you, dickhead, he could practically hear her say—like she'd ever use that sort of language—*if you thought I'd ever want anything to do with you.*

Yeah. Whatever.

Frustrated, and unsure whether more with himself or her, Nico stomped around the last curve and shoved aside a low-hanging branch, his jagged temper instantly soothed by the welcome sight.

The crystal surface of the pool glistened in the dappled sunlight. A startled squirrel chattered an objection before taking off through the underbrush, its fluffy tail giving a wave of protest at the interruption.

Nico nearly laughed. Would have if part of him wasn't still worried about Miss Pain-in-the-Butt back there.

He'd apologize. Make sure she still had both feet securely attached, then he'd beat a hasty retreat back to camp. Why torture himself?

Alexis Templeton might have developed into some kind of odd fascination for him, but he knew his place. And it definitely wasn't flirting—not that he anticipated *that* happening—with the spunky socialite.

Even if she did have more grit than he'd ever imagined.

CHOP it off and feed it to the sharks?

No sharks in this neck of the woods, silly girl.

Fine. Alexis huffed, clenching her fists, her teeth,

and her sore toes against the excruciating pain. *Then I'll whack off the blasted foot and leave it for coyote bait, for the snails!* She didn't care. "Oh God, just make it stop."

"Make what stop?" her nemesis asked from behind a curtain of leaves just before he swished them aside with one arm.

The pain. Good God, the pain. "Your annoying presence."

"Ouch." He laughed and gestured toward a mostly flat rock about three feet across at the water's edge. "Your seat awaits, Your Grumpy Highness."

"I should argue that one," she said without heat as she trudged the short distance to the rock's smooth surface. She fanned out her open jacket and wilted straight down on top of it. "But I don't have the energy."

Alexis just sat there, took a few deep, slow breaths, trying to work up the strength to unlace her boot.

"So I could say something else and you wouldn't argue back?" He sounded overly delighted by the idea.

"Try me." Two syllables. That's all she could muster. It was as though waking up at insane-thirty and hiking for hours on the fuel of two water bottles and a couple of energy bars had totally done her in.

Now that she was stationary, no longer forcing herself to keep going, to put on a brave face, whatever reserves she'd relied on had vanished. Left her zapped.

Drained. Exhausted. Miserable.

That's me. Alexis Templeton, Wimp Extraordinaire.

Immune to the beautiful surroundings, Alexis felt her body wavering. She blinked. Then flopped backward and closed her eyes. The minimal padding of her jacket the only thing between her back and the rock—and a deep, healing sleep.

"Gonna nap on me, princess?"

"Not you," she said. *Perish the thought.* "The rock. Going to...rest on the rock."

"Okay, then." From the sound of it, he sank down next to her. "You do that. I'll keep an eye out for snakes."

"Ha. Ha."

"Think I'm joking, princess?"

As a lifelong Texan, she absolutely knew he wasn't joking. More than one type of poisonous snake slithered through the woods. Especially near water, if they behaved like other wildlife. "I know you're not joking."

She also knew, somehow, that she could relax with him keeping watch.

Alexis still hadn't opened her eyes. Had no intention of doing so. "Just too tired to care. And don't do that."

A few seconds later she felt a tug on her left foot and realized he'd pulled her leg toward him and planned to unlace her boot.

What she found odd wasn't so much what he was doing, which more than surprised her. Who knew the crank had a gallant side? No, what should have freaked her out was that not only was she content to let him, as freakishly tired as her body remained, her mind started perking to life, becoming more alert by the second.

Pliant, her foot wobbled as he rolled her pant leg then tackled the double knot she'd tied. "Don't do what?" he asked in a low growl that did shamefully sinful things to her insides. "Mention snakes?"

Why wasn't she pushing him away? Unlacing her own stupid boot?

Because it feels soooo good to be taken care of for a change.

"Don't call me 'princess'. It makes me sound spoiled."

"And you aren't?" He gave a rougher tug and her breath hissed out when her abused ankle screamed.

Immediately, his warm hand covered the skin above her sock. "I'm sorry. I didn't mean to hurt you."

Yeah, right was on the tip of her tongue. But he sounded sincere.

Didn't matter that her eyes were closed, his vibrant image had imprinted itself on her brain. The picture of his dangerous, so-fine face. Faded jeans, worn to touch-me softness. Snug black t-shirt with unbuttoned flannel over it—his only nod to the cool start to the morning. The deep hues of the Black Watch plaid echoed in his dark gaze.

Ill-mannered or not, he fascinated her, drew her like a junkie needing a fix.

Too weak to resist the lure of his touch, she nudged him with her toes, inviting him to continue.

Two beats later, he did, drawing the long laces through the eyelets backwards, the snug-fitting leather around her ankle and foot slackening with every second, her tongue loosening right along with it. "I was fortunate enough to be born into a wealthy family. Money and spoiled aren't the same."

"Oh no?" Tug. Tug. "So you work full-time? Live on your own? Support yourself?"

She grimaced, but didn't answer. Refused to confirm his accurate assessment that she had no job and still lived with her parents.

"Okay, so no *earned* income," he concluded. Tug-*thwap*, the lace slapped back on the leather. "So let's see...you're still in school? Playing at being grown up while getting that five- or seven-year *Mrs.* degree? Letting Rich Daddy foot the bill?"

It would have been easy to take offense. Appropriate to lay into him for the rude assumptions.

But despite his words, his actions were considerate. Someone was actually going out of their way to do something *for* her. An alien occurrence, given the current state of her life.

Alexis curled her nails into her palms and refused to call him on his narrow-minded assumptions. "If you must know, I had to take a sabbatical from college. A temporary leave of—"

"I know what 'sabbatical' means." He sounded royally ticked at her for presuming he didn't. Gentle pressure started easing the boot off.

"Yeah, well... Some pretty major stuff with my family hit all at once, and I was needed at home." She sighed. Why was she explaining herself to him?

Because he's just slipped your boot off with more consideration than Prince Charming put the glass slipper back on. And, admit it, you're attracted to him. Tattoos, vile assumptions, scruffy exterior and all.

Especially this softer side. Alexis swallowed hard when he started drawing down her sock with careful fingers. She determinedly kept her eyes closed. "That doesn't automatically mean I'm spoiled, you know."

She yelped when he reached her ankle and the sock stuck to raw, abraded skin.

"Let's soak it," he said. "Then I'll try again."

She offered no resistance when he shifted her leg and lowered her foot off the rock and into the cool water below.

And if a tiny, "Eek. That's cold," escaped, she couldn't help it. "That *wasn't* 'spoiled' me complaining, FYI. Just a statement of fact. It *is* cold."

"Okay, not-spoiled you..." Alexis swore she could hear a grin in his voice. "Gimme the other foot."

"Hi-ya!" She made a muted karate-chop noise and swung her opposite leg over until it connected with his firm grip.

She shifted with her leg and now lay partially on her side, one foot soaking in the spring-fed pool, the other leg crossed over her body. Instead of messing with her laces, he simply cradled her booted foot, let the silence around them settle.

Alexis felt her muscles relax. She listened to the musical gurgle where the waterfall splashed into the pool. Listened to the wind singing quietly through the trees. Heard the slight scamper of a lizard or squirrel. Imagined she could hear his breathing, his curiosity.

So even though he hadn't asked, she told him. "I hope to make it back to college. Eventually." Once she decided what she really wanted to major in. "And no, not for a M-R-S degree, if that's what you're thinking." She almost snickered at the thought. She'd spent so much time lately caring for her own family, the thought of adding a husband into the mix nearly made her gag.

"Good for you," he surprised her by stating. "I skipped college, went straight to work after high school. I've done okay, since I'm good with my hands." *How good?* she wanted to ask. "But if there's something you want to study, I'd like to think you could get back to it."

The support staggered her. Warmed her. "I hope so too, thanks." Her eyelids fluttered, as though enticing her to look at him. Alexis squelched the urge. It seemed easier to confess in the dark. "And just so you don't think I quit for some inane reason like a sale at Nordstrom's, my mom's a total mess right now. My brother's MIA overseas. Dad—"

"He's in the service? For real?"

She nodded, wondering at his incredulity.

"I'm impressed. Sincerely." His hands shifted on her leg and he started rolling up her jeans. "Coondog, my boss and mentor, he's ex-Army. Has remained lifelong friends with a couple of the men he served with. I guess I never suspected someone in your income bracket would even think to enlist. Or did he go in as an officer?"

"No. Phil enlisted when he turned eighteen. Said he wanted the experience before college. But between me and you, I think he wanted to get away from Mother. Lucky for him, he liked the Air Force enough that he chose to stay."

As it always did when she thought of her brother, the uncertainty of his fate weighed heavily. When she felt her lips tremble, her breath hitch, and her eyes water, Alexis reminded herself brightly, "He loves it." Present tense. "Says he's found his calling. We talk when we can. At least we did. He even wrote—*writes*—a lot. Emails *and* letters."

Nico's fingers touched her bare leg above her sock,

gave a gentle squeeze. "Phil sounds like a great brother. A true friend."

"He is. Older than me by four years. He's the best." *I miss him like crazy.*

"You're just blasting my preconceptions right and left." Almost with a caress, Nico's fingers left her skin and drifted down her sock to the leather of her boot.

"Go me." If she sounded a bit sarcastic, who could blame her? Listed out like that, Alexis was reminded of all the reasons she wanted to be here. Deserved to be here.

With her best friend, Jenny, busy with law school, Jaz working full-time with crazy-ass hours, and Calli busy at A&M in College Station, girl time was at a premium. Something she rarely got anymore. Time away from her house was the only reprieve she had.

"Where has camping been all my life?" Alexis sighed and kicked the foot still in the water, not caring if she splashed them both. "This is lovely. I may never go back to the city."

"What about your dad? You mentioned him and I interrupted. Sorry."

"He had a triple bypass and valve replacement. He's doing a ton better now, but in the months following surgery had several complications including trouble with some medication, so it's been a long road." Her voice wasn't the least bit defensive. Simply stating more facts. "So no, I may not have a typical job, but you can bet your tush I've been working. Trying to keep my family intact and myself sane. And I'm not after sympathy—"

He shook her ankle to stop her. "None given, so don't worry about it. Just admiration. A lot of that."

That warm feeling flooded through her again. Notched higher with a strong dose of bad-boy lust. Who knew the real Nico would be so easy to talk to? So...kind?

"Okay, let's check out the damage on this one." He tackled the second set of double knots.

"Thank you," Alexis murmured, her lashes quivering until she opened her eyes for the first time since her body had touched the rock.

He shot her a quick glance, making her wonder how many times he'd done that. During all that soul baring, how much had he watched her? She started to tingle all over.

"For what?"

"Hmm?"

"What're you thanking me for?" he asked, shooting her another, longer look.

A look that intrigued as much as it disarmed. Charmed.

Crap, she was starting to fall for him and she knew it.

"For taking care of my feet." *For taking care of me.* "For listening."

"Sure thing. They—you—did a good job today. You kept up, didn't wh—" The knot jerked free and he bit off what he'd almost said.

"Didn't whine. Is that it?" She playfully kicked his stomach then stilled so he could unlace. "Is that what you were thinking?"

Laces *thwoomped* through eyelets. Leaves rustled. And Nico's face reddened above the goatee. "Yeah."

A little slower now, he continued to draw the shoelace free. That tingly awareness set up camp inside Alexis.

Inside her panty region to be precise.

She refused to acknowledge it. Certainly would never act on it. She wasn't here to get all hot and bothered by a former hooligan, no matter how considerate.

Yes, Sticks had shown up that first weekend, had been eager to tell her all about the counselors and volunteers, and their reputations: the good, the bad, and the not-so legal.

The half brother to her two "little sisters" had welcomed her with open arms and his instant acceptance had quickly paved the way for "Lexi" to become part of the group.

Though she refused to let Nico catch her observing him, she'd been entirely aware of his surprise, if not downright amazement, as she blended in and claimed her place. *Take that*, she'd wanted to shout while flipping him the bird.

Something she might think, but would never, ever do. Etiquette lessons and Mother's strict strictures had stuck. No matter what was burning in her mind, Alexis knew how to present a perfectly proper façade. So she kept that middle finger firmly entrenched with its mates, hadn't let her prideful pleasure show.

But now, the secret gloating she'd indulged in seemed childish.

Even more when Nico paused before removing the boot and rested his hands, one on her ankle, the other higher on her denim-clad knee, and said, "About that. I should never have assumed you'd be a whiner. I should never have assumed anything about you. Truth is, I owe you a big apology for how I treated you last month."

"Yep. You do." She might not plan on gloating, but she wasn't about to pretend his hostile introduction hadn't hurt.

It had. A lot.

"It won't do me any good if you don't accept it." The fingers on her knee tightened a fraction, sending another zing of awareness straight up her thigh.

"Your apology?" Alexis clenched the muscles between her legs. "Convince me you mean it this time."

SEVEN

Something Captivating

LEXI LEFT HIM NO CHOICE. Whatever it took, he had to convince her.

A gust of wind buffeted them as Nico rushed to his car, carrying the squirming handful of woman. Overhead, clouds gathered, blocking out the sky visible between the tall buildings.

A grim smile curved his lips. Wouldn't it be appropriate if her wedding was rained out? Too bad the nuptials were taking place inside.

Ineffectual slaps landed on his thigh. "This is crazy! Nico!"

"Woman, I didn't drive all the way here for you not to listen." He dumped her on the convertible's front bench seat.

She glared at him, her plump lips pressed flat, but she issued no protest. Surprisingly, didn't try to scramble from the car, just crossed her arms and scowled.

Judging by the look in her sparking green eyes, she

was dying to know what all he might say, but equally strong was her desire to tell him to take a hike.

In case her defiant submission was an act, he jumped over her and into the driver's seat, fished his keys from his pocket, and shot her a glance. She hadn't moved. "Good girl."

"Go to hell."

Nico couldn't suppress a laugh as he started the engine. He'd missed her fire. She was so sexy when she was angry. Happy. Hell, just breathing.

Granted, he hadn't thought this through. Not like he should have. Ever since learning of her engagement, a slew of sleepless nights had given him plenty of time to review what went wrong in their relationship (mostly him, he was shamed to admit). And everything that had gone right.

Countless times, he'd told himself to leave her alone. Let her live the life she was meant to. One that didn't include a rangy, tattooed former juvenile delinquent.

But the nightly mental pep talks hadn't done a thing to mend his lonely heart or stifle his longing. He loved the woman. Never mind that he'd never *told* her. Never mind that he hadn't talked to her since last fall.

After breaking things off, Nico had worried that he'd made the ultimate mistake.

Pride, and yes, the fear that she might really be better off without him, kept him from admitting it. To her, or himself.

But once Brett and Coon stated their piece, he couldn't hide from the truth any longer. He had to talk some sense into her.

Had to touch her...

"What are you looking at?" Her testy question made him realize he hadn't stopped gazing at her.

"Have you lost weight?" She still had killer curves, far as he was concerned, but her face looked leaner. Troubled.

What would you expect? You just kidnapped her the day before her wedding.

"Yeah." Her voice practically gave him the finger. "Heartache'll do that to you."

So she'd lost weight because of him? Not her mother's harping? He didn't know how he felt about that.

"Heartache?" He tried to pin her down. Make her face reality. "You keep saying you're getting married tomorrow. Shouldn't you be blissful? Ecstatic?"

"Ah, shit." Said as though she realized she'd just admitted how *not* into her pending marriage she was. "Take me to the restaurant. It's—"

To drown out her words, he revved the engine, debating his approach. Did he whip her into his arms, make her submit with kisses that would devastate them both? Or try to calm her down? Reach her rationally?

You're in it for the long haul this time, go for rational.

Okaaaay...

Angling his body, he reached over the seat and into the back, grabbed a small cooler and hauled it into the front. He plunked it in her lap. "Here."

Maybe that'd keep her busy. Long enough for him to formulate some sort of plan. How to get her to listen? A horn blared nearby, jarring his thoughts.

Five o'clock traffic might've been long gone by now, but they were still in the heart of downtown, surrounded by people and cars. Houston never slept it seemed.

Neither would he. Not until he'd won her back.

Decision made, he exited the parking lot in the opposite direction the jerks in the sports car had taken, which suited him just fine. He was heading toward more neutral territory. Getting as far away from the church as fast as he possibly could, taking I-69 out of the city, toward Cleveland, TX, and beyond.

If that just happened to be the same direction that he took every month toward Buccaneer? If it just happened to be one of the areas where he'd lived as a kid, before his dad went to jail—the second time—and he happened to know it like the back of his hand? Well bully for him.

He'd get Lexi among the tall pines and majestic oaks, remind her how things were between them. Bet she'd listen—

"This isn't the way," she said stiffly.

"I know."

"I told you to take me to the restaurant."

He knocked on the cooler. "Open now, complain later."

Or never, if he could help it.

"What is it?" she asked suspiciously instead of simply pushing in the latch and sliding the lid off.

"You think I'd put a basket of rattlesnakes in your lap? Dammit, Lex. Show a little trust."

"Trust?" Did her voice crack? "You want me to trust the man who broke my heart?"

He had to turn this around somehow. Fast. "Call it a peace offering." He thumped the side of the cooler. "A romantic gesture. I don't care. Just didn't think it'd go over very well melted. Or wilted."

He'd already hit the interstate, brought the car up to cruising speed.

And now he prayed.

HOW IN HEAVEN could Nico do this to her? Show up *now*?

And in the car of his dreams, such a beautifully restored 1957 Chevrolet Bel Air Convertible that it took her breath away?

She'd seen the beat-up hunk of metal and rusted parts when he'd bought it, given him a hard time about not doing things the easy way. Though the exterior was rusted in a couple places, dinged up in many more, he told her the engine was still running and that he could fix the rest. And he couldn't wait to get started.

Started and finished. He'd made more headway on this in the few months they'd been apart than he had the two years while they'd been together. The silver metallic exterior gleamed, gold accents highlighted the uniqueness of this special vehicle. The front bench seat was upholstered in a deep plum. She struggled not to cry at that. He'd been thinking brick red, and she'd talked him into the beautiful, not-quite purple color instead, claiming that it'd look gorgeous with the body colors he'd chosen.

She'd been right. And he'd done a marvelous job.

"Nico"—she stroked one hand along the metal dash—"this is spectacular. Impressive beyond what I ever imagined."

He smiled at her and she could tell the praise pleased him.

Just the sight of his strong, dark hand commanding the gorgeous steering wheel, which he'd painted a deep plum to match the vinyl seats, nearly brought tears to her eyes. He'd even added extra touches to the wheel including a pair of little racing flags at the center, something she'd mentioned liking once at a classic car show he'd taken her to.

Everything about the car showed the love he'd put into it. Reminded her how he'd always made her feel so cherished too.

"Open it." He pointed to the unknown surprise sitting in her lap.

Not sure whether she was more afraid of what was actually inside the cooler or how she might react, Lexi pushed in the button and angled the top off. Her heart skipped several beats.

"Damn you." Lexi sniffed, hating that her eyes watered, that the sight of his unexpected gifts had turned her insides to mush. Her will to nothing. "Damn you to hell."

"Lex?" He jerked the wheel when he turned to her, shock on his face.

She righted it without thinking. "Eyes on the road, buster."

With fingers that trembled, she liberated the clear clamshell case from the chilled interior, staring in awe at the orchid corsage it held. Totally extravagant. Totally ridiculous, made up of one white and one blue orchid, white and teal ribbons, and the remaining pieces of her broken heart.

Beneath it lay three King Size Hershey's Bars with almonds.

She tore into one. "You asshole," she said around the first bite, gazing at him through narrowed, watery eyes. "Making me stress eat like this. And the day before my wedding."

His jaw flexed. "Not if I can help it."

Lexi let that slide. "I'm too tired to fight with you anymore. I just need to call—" Where was her phone? Her purse? Shit. "Shit!"

"Lex? Babe?" She could tell she'd surprised him. "I'm not used to you cussing this much."

She stuck out her chocolate-coated tongue. "Yeah, well, you obviously bring out the best in me."

The sexy bastard had the audacity to grin.

His left arm, resting on the car door where he'd lowered the window, casually steered. His right hand was fisted on the seat between them.

So he wasn't as relaxed as he seemed? Good.

He looked phenomenal. Even better than she remembered.

How was that possible?

And the chocolate? Heaven on her tongue. Her eyes nearly rolled back in her head at another bite and the smooth glide of chocolate goodness going past her tongue and throat.

After he'd broken up with her, she'd done more than her share of binge eating. Sugar *was* its own food group, after all. One she'd nearly OD'd on more than once, drowning her sorrows with snickerdoodles and sundaes.

Shortly before she and Bradley started dating and

then swiftly got engaged—easier to go along with the tide that was Mother than stand up for herself when she really didn't care—she'd embraced healthy eating again as one of the few things she could control. Compared to resisting Mother's wishes, placing the right things on her plate was a piece of cake.

"Less than one hour in your company and you turn me into a sugar slave." She finished the first bar, debated the second, and let common sense rule.

But she couldn't stop herself from opening the plastic container housing the corsage. "This is totally frivolous," she accused, running her finger over one delicate purply-blue petal. "It's beautiful."

She brought the flowers up to her nose and inhaled. Refused to acknowledge how this orchid smelled better than ambrosia when her bouquet earlier just made her gag. She didn't care that the blue was fake, the poor orchid dyed for aesthetic reasons only, didn't care that she'd forgotten her purse and phone back at the church, couldn't call anyone or let them know where she was.

Was actually relieved by it, in fact. The burden of playing the perfect daughter and fiancée lifted for the first time in months. Giving her the freedom to cuss, eat chocolate, inhale orchids. And admit, just for a moment, her utter and complete captivation by the man next to her.

"It's stupid," she told him. "Won't make any differ-ence." It can't! "But thank you. Thank you for thinking of me and for your stupid, thoughtful, lovely gifts."

Strands of his long hair whipped out behind him when he turned to give her a tight smile, its brevity making her wonder...just how much restraint was he exercising?

He hadn't said anything for miles. Had simply let her devour the treat in silence, breathe in the delicate aroma of orchids, let the crazy wind tangle her hair while his presence confused her more than anything had since he'd said *adios* months ago without a single backward glance.

EIGHT

Something Old

"MY APOLOGY?" Nico hoped she could hear his sincerity. "I mean it this time, so believing me should be easy."

"Okay, I'm ready to be impressed," she said. "Go for it."

Nico went back to slipping off her boot while he talked. Easier to stare at slightly scuffed leather than at the dare shining from her luminous gaze. "You're one of the hottest women I've ever seen." Now why in blazes had he led off with that? "I painted you with the same brush as the others because they all showed their true colors—bland. Unreliable. Too uppity for a little dirt, much less teenagers with dirty pasts and some bleak futures. Month after month, I watched the more tender, younger kids get their hopes up only to have them crushed. I got riled. Took it out on you."

The boot had been off for a while. He finally met her gaze. "I didn't give you a chance in hell when you got here. For that, I really am sorry."

Too serious much? Lighten up!

She opened her mouth to comment. Nico swatted at her toes. "I'm not done convincing you."

Those sinful lips smiled sweetly. "By all means, carry on."

He refused to acknowledge that same swooping motion his stomach had made when he'd first spied her. Nudging down the second sock, he told her, "I also thought it expedient to push you away."

"Expedient, huh?"

"What?" Was it his fault if he sounded belligerent? "Surprised I know it?"

Her toes gouged his stomach again, harder this time. "You're doing it again. Lumping me in with other people instead of viewing me as an individual. Making assumptions about me."

Damn, she was right. Isn't that what most of the dainty debutantes had done with these kids? With him and Brett? "You're right. I won't do it again."

She rolled to her back and then pushed up to sitting so she could tackle the sock herself. "I was simply curious why you'd use *expedient* in reference to me. Why the need to push me away? Could it possibly be because you considered maybe...eventually...actually *liking* me?"

This foot couldn't have been bothering her nearly as much as the other. She stripped the sock off in half a second and slipped her bare toes in the pool.

"Here." She lifted the opposite leg out and plopped her sopping sock and dripping foot across his lap. "Make yourself useful," she taunted. "And be expedient about it."

Nico couldn't help it. He laughed. Ignored the cold

water soaking clear through his jeans and laughed. "Smart ass," he finally accused.

Did she hear the affection in his voice?

She was actually fun. Easy to talk to. He *did* like her. Not eventually, but *now*. Who knew?

"So why not *let* yourself like me?" She wiggled her foot and it climbed a couple inches up his quad. "Where's the problem in that?"

Nico fought against the urge to pull the sole of her foot against the vee of his jeans. And grind himself against it. That'd sure stop wherever this crazy interlude was heading. "Isn't it obvious? Having or wanting anything to do with you would be complicated. If not impossible. Especially for someone like me."

Way to go, idiot. You just admitted to wanting her.

Worse than that, dickhead. You brought up your background. The gulf between you both.

She didn't get defensive. Didn't back away. If anything, she shifted closer, dug her foot a little more firmly into his thigh. "Who says it's impossible? A girl and a guy can't enjoy some harmless flirting, maybe a bit more, without it getting complicated?"

How much more?

Desire flared. Urges rampaged. Caveman urges goading him to slam her back against the rock and shove up her shirt so he could see, touch, and taste her breasts, suck on her nipples, fondle between her legs.

Kiss those too-wide lips into silence while he let his mouth, his hands speak for them both.

Are you nuts?

No. Just lusting hard.

How much more?

Nico clenched his teeth against the need to demand an answer.

Since he'd been stunned into stillness, she leaned forward and started gingerly tugging the sock down. "If that's what you think, Nico, then it's on you, bucko, not me. Too bad, really, since it's something I'd be willing to explore."

For real?

A slight sound of distress left her throat as she eased the sock past the knob of her ankle; another small grunt when it passed by her toes. Then she whipped it completely off. "Ta-da! Finally. Ew. Would you look at this mess?"

She angled her foot a couple different directions, exposing ragged-looking blisters along her big and little toes, and one humdinger on the inside of her ankle. A smaller one on her heel had already ruptured. Before he could comment, she splashed the foot back in the pool and snared his gaze. "Because that's all I'm after—a little fun and relaxation away from the daily grind of my normal life. See? Nothing complicated. Nothing impossible."

Man, she was so real. So candid. Wasn't making coy or playing games. Despite her bank account, she hadn't had an easy time of it, not at all based on the little she'd shared.

Respect, something he rarely gave much thought to when it came to females, as well as the concept of her proposed fun and flirting, all took root and grew fast.

Nearly as fast as the desire he'd been trying to mask. Was about ready to unleash, whatever the outcome.

A sharp *no*. A yell and slap. A complaint to the paid

counselors. Maybe a reprimand. That'd be the worst to come of it, right?

He was beginning to think the reward of trying something with her might be worth the risk, worth any possible repercussions...

"Nico?" The way she said his name and tilted her head caused him to realize he'd been staring at her. For a while now.

"Lexi," the name he'd heard the kids use slipped out. Because it fit. She wasn't hoity-toity Alexis Templeton. She was cool, casual Lexi. Sexy Lexi. "You're incredible."

Heat flared across those dynamite cheekbones. "And I think you're F.O.C."

"Definition? I know better than to assume anything with you anymore."

"Full. Of. Crap."

"Not true. I already knew that I was attracted to you. I never expected to *like* you. A lot."

"So you admit it, huh? Woohoo." She twirled one finger in the air between them and let the sarcasm fly. "Score one for the useless society chick."

"Don't call yourself that. You're *not* useless." His emphatic statement startled them both.

"Well now," she mused. "If we haven't both flipped the switch on our assumptions today. You sound all defensive on my behalf. Pretty cool." She gave him a pleased smile.

He couldn't help it. He had to know. "How much more?"

She straightened both arms behind her, kicked her feet in the water, and gave him a perplexed look. "How much more what?"

Nico cleared the raw desire from his throat. "You said, 'Flirting and a little more'." But it rumbled out anyway, his voice low and hoarse. "I'm asking how much more."

Then he waited for the slap.

UH…

Say something, Alexis! Answer him.

Tough to do when a newly revitalized part of her just wanted to jump him.

Let saner heads prevail! Your family—

Blast her family. Alexis was thinking about herself for once. Was ready to answer for *herself*.

"Lexi?"

She liked how he said it, how she felt like just another normal-incomed, red-blooded woman around him. How she could, without much effort, practically become another person altogether.

Why not?

"Flirting is fine," she said, forcing herself to hold his intense gaze. "Better than fine." *Kissing too.* "But I'm not about to have sex with you the first time we talk."

"Of course not." He didn't look convinced.

"Really, I mean it." She gave him a light shove. "I'm not planning to sleep with you at all." *Liar!* "If that's what you think, you might as well get lost."

"Bummer," he said with all seriousness despite the sudden spark glinting in his coal black eyes. "Because when I decided to lure you to my lair and convinced you to follow me, I *assumed* you knew my penis expected to come out and play."

A second of pure silence.

One of stillness.

Two more.

Then Lexi laughed. Laughed hard, till her stomach hurt and her eyes watered more than the spring. She laughed till she cried. All the tension of the past few months, all the pain from the stupid hike evaporated. Left her feeling fresh and free.

Renewed, like a bud emerging from the soil.

Lexi wanted to reach out and stretch toward the sun.

And its rays appeared to be emanating from the rough-looking man beside her. While she'd cackled like a banshee, she'd seen the slow smile spread across his mouth.

It didn't make him look younger; she doubted anything could erase the years of experience. But the grin, the flash of teeth, the slightly crooked tilt to his lips, all combined to soften the air of danger that cloaked him like a shield. Made him seem more human. Definitely more approachable.

Infinitely more interesting.

His sense of humor surprised her, delighted her.

Darn near seduced her.

Lexi wiped the lingering moisture from beneath her eyes. "Thank you. I needed that. The laugh."

"Not my playful penis?" He snapped his fingers and shook his head. "And here I thought when you started limping, I was getting luck-*eee* today."

She sobered and hiked one leg out of the water and back onto the rock, angling so she could face him.

"No, you didn't." Her words weren't much louder than the whispering leaves.

"Nah," he agreed just as quietly, taking on the serious tone she'd adopted. "I didn't. But I was worried about your feet. They doing okay?"

She drew her second foot from the water and scooted back, closer to him. "They're great. I'm great. Thanks to you." She had trouble holding his gaze. Now that he'd stopped grinning and stared at her with mysteries blazing from his eyes, she suddenly felt both self-conscious and aware. Both flattered and awkward.

Sex with her high school boyfriend and the two guys she'd dated seriously in college hadn't prepared her for the fierce array of emotions, the unfamiliar drive to hurl herself against him, strip off his clothes, and burrow into his chest. Tangle bare legs together.

To explore him physically. Emotionally...

Explore herself in the process.

Whoa! Weird! Too much, too soon.

As though he sensed her inner conflict, he broke eye contact and shrugged out of his flannel shirt. Leaving only the black t-shirt between her vision and his naked chest, darn it. Scrunching the fabric in his big hand, he bent forward and started drying her feet and lower legs.

Lexi devoured the sight of his strong back and tattoo-laden arms.

Her toes curled. *Thank God you painted them.* Cherry red. Bright and happy. Just like the rest of her right now.

Don't you mean bright and horny?

Lexi muffled a snort.

Once her soles and toes, and the small spaces in between, once her ankles and shins and calves were dry, he leaned back, propped up on one arm, and shifted toward her. "So, sexy Lexi, tell me what you're thinking."

Sexy Lexi?!

That I'm glad I'm here.

That I want you too.

That I can't wait to tell Jenny and the girls all about you.

That my feet never felt so good.

That never in a million-trillion years would I have thought you'd be nice. And funny. And—

"Cat got your tongue?" The words may have been teasing, but the tone was a rumble. "Just stop thinking and kiss me."

Though the command came out a whisper, it blasted straight through her. How his "sexy" Lexi wanted to comply. Regular, sedate Alexis saw flashing *Danger* signs bouncing around like strobe lights on steroids.

Holding her gaze hostage, he slowly brought one strong hand up to her face where he traced a finger from temple to chin before cupping the side of her neck and jaw.

He was so close she could count the individual hairs that made up his goatee. See the three nicks on his skin —old scars dotting cheek, nose, and forehead. Smell the faint spice of his breath when he said, "I dare you, Sweet Lex. Kiss me. Or I'll do it for you."

"You're intoxicating." His fingers tightened on her scalp. *Out of my league.*

But so addicting. Like coconut cream and carob lattes.

"Determined," he said, closing the gap between them to take what she hadn't yet decided to give.

Her stomach swooped, heart fluttered, and lips tingled. Instinct told her this would be like no other kiss she'd had before. She lifted her chin. Braced herself.

Just before their mouths connected, he swore. "Tell me to back off."

She remained silent, curious, apprehensive. Thrilled to her core. This was living. The excitement, the uncertainty.

So much better than managing Mother's stupid afternoon tea parties, subjecting herself to meaningless small talk, or going shopping just to get out of the house. So much better than worrying herself sick over her dad or brother, or pandering to the one parent who refused to handle life like a grown-up.

Her heart pounded and the throbbing in her lips became unbearable. She mashed them together, staring into his dark, sinful gaze. Awaiting heaven.

"Say it, Lexi. Last chance. 'Get back, you bumfucker.'"

She snickered. "I wouldn't call you a bum."

The palm cupping her cheek moved and he threaded his fingers through her wilted ponytail, pulling the band off and coiling her hair around his wrist until he anchored his hand at her nape. "You'd call me a helluva lot worse if you knew how boxer-dropping, cock-hardening, dirty-dream-inspiring I find you."

Wowzers.

"So boxers, huh? Not going commando?"

"Lexi." The growl reached right down to her toes, made her feel all liquid and hot inside.

If he could touch, so could she. She reached between them to test the texture of his goatee. Softer than she'd expected. Especially considering how hard the rest of him was. How easily her other hand fisted in his t-shirt. Rejoiced in the heat and hard muscles beneath.

She'd never wanted a kiss so bad.

Never looked forward to one more.

She tried to lighten the moment. To make it last. "Hey, quit worrying. It's not like my dad will come after you with a shotgun if we make out."

"No, he's likely to bash my brains in with his polo bat."

She laughed. "It's a mallet. And he doesn't even play."

"Then stop thinking of him."

"Done."

"Think of me."

"Can't seem to stop."

The fingers on her scalp tightening was her only warning. He closed the gap between them and pressed his lips to hers. Then again, with more pressure, lingering longer.

But not long enough.

Her mouth came after his, sealed them together, lip to lip. He surprised her yet again. No fierce tongue thrusts, no bold, groping palm to her breast—or one zeroing in between her legs. No fast moves beyond the kiss. Just a sensual settling in against her mouth, a sigh as their lips melded and then lifted, melded again.

A sigh. Then a deep inhale. A twitch of those fingers in her hair. A murmur in his throat.

When he finally shifted, abandoned her mouth to graze his lips across her cheekbone, Lexi didn't know whether to be delighted by the nuanced, near-innocent kiss or offended he hadn't gone for more. Because she was feeling anything but innocent.

With nothing beyond the tender assault of his lips, he had her melting inside, her veins turning molten. Had her heart rate speeding, the muscles clanging in her chest; her whole body going all tingly and squirmy as achy need grew hot and fast, rising like a tidal wave that sped through every limb.

You've never wanted someone this quickly before. Slow down. Get away. Before he takes advantage.

Self-preservation instincts warred with lusty ones.

Ignoring the niggling voice screaming *CAUTION: Trouble Ahead*, Lexi scraped her nails over his shoulders and up his neck until she could grab hold of his ponytail. She pulled it just enough to turn his head. Guided his mouth back to hers.

Taking the lead, she swept her tongue over his lips. Didn't try to delve inside, just tasted. Satisfied in some small—very small—way, the craving he'd roused.

"Okay..." Defying the grip she had on his hair, he pulled back.

Heavy eyelids blinked open and she saw him gulp air. He was breathing like a racehorse, way harder and faster than their simple kiss warranted.

So he wasn't unaffected. Just impressively controlled.

Even that was a turn-on.

"It's time, Sweet Lex," he breathed hotly. "Tell the loser to get away from you. To get lost. *Now.*"

"I'd never say that," she whispered, trying to subdue a whimper when he released his hold on her nape. Failing, because she missed his touch already.

But then he started stroking his fingers through the length of her hair and she moaned. But wait. Was he giving her yet another chance to escape? To cool things between them before they went too far?

His actions were so the opposite of "taking advantage" that Lexi fell further under his spell. Who could have guessed? The hardened, scary-sexy exterior hid a thoughtful man. One she really, really wanted to spend time with. "The loser part," she finished. "It's too rude, and that's not me."

His fingers drifted to her bottom lip. "What about the 'get lost' part? Planning to say that?"

"Nah. Then I couldn't do this—" Lexi released his hair and shoved his shoulder, pushing him down and onto his back.

She leaned over his chest and held his chin while she climbed over him. Boom! That was it. Didn't matter that he was beneath her; he took total control.

One strong hand palmed the back of her head and held her in place as he lunged upward, capturing her lips.

This kiss was totally different than the exploring ones before.

His tongue thrust in her mouth and slid against hers, arousing, rolling motions that caused everything in her to clench. His taste held just a hint of spice, from the pack of cinnamon gum she'd brought that'd been passed around during sunrise. And a deep smoky flavor that was all Nico.

All-encompassing.

His tongue retreated and hers came after it, chasing inside his mouth. He gave a low groan and shifted her until she straddled his prone body, her legs over his. His hardened length undeniable between them.

Part of her wanted nothing more than to strip. To lose herself in the next few moments. To play with his penis—she would've chuckled at the thought if she wasn't so turned on—and ride his cock to completion.

But she knew better. Fun and flirting, *that*'s what they agreed to. And kisses. A whole lot of them, she hoped.

"My clothes stay on," she gasped between voracious kisses that swept over his face and jaw. "But other than that, you can touch me. Anywhere."

Nico didn't need to be told twice.

Before she could blink, strong hands covered her butt and hauled her against his groin. Fingers delved, gripped. His tongue tantalized, satisfied. Rubbed along hers and fanned a deep hunger sharper than any she'd felt before.

More than just frivolous exploring or teenage groping, this was core-deep yearning. Adult cravings.

This was living.

And Lexi couldn't wait to experience it all.

NINE

Something Arousing

IN HIS REARVIEW mirror and overhead, dark gray clouds billowed, obliterating blue sky. So far, they'd outrun the brewing storm.

Nico had driven for over an hour. Night approached and traffic grew sparse the farther they got from the city, the route he'd taken not yet as congested as I-45; one of the reasons he'd chosen it.

Lexi had devoured the first chocolate bar, waited a while and then savored half the second before wrapping it back up and placing the cooler down by her feet. He'd seen her delicate finger stroke the orchids' petals, seen her inhale their fragrance. Then close the corsage up tight and tuck it away.

Like she hoped to do with her emotions?

Not gonna happen.

Once he reached his old familiar stomping grounds, crisscrossed with country roads and blessed with copious trees, he left the highway.

A sideways glance showed Lexi contemplating the

view out the passenger side, but at least she wasn't complaining or demanding he take her back anymore.

She'd changed her belligerent tune after seeing his gifts. He owed Brett for helping spark that idea. Well, Brett *and* his friendly neighborhood florist who was over the moon to hear from Nico again, all too ready to whip something up on short notice. *I lost my best customer when you guys broke up,* the owner had joked. *It'd make my year to see you two back together.*

He seconded that.

As soon as he could, he turned down a remote road, and then another, hoping for any semblance of privacy. The tree-lined drive blocked out what little light was left and he flicked on the headlights.

"This area's beautiful," Nico commented, attempting to ease the tension. She might've been quiet, but he could feel her brooding. "I'm surprised you didn't want to get married someplace like this instead of your fancy church. Beats the hell out of the city."

"Bite me."

"Ah, Lexi. Feisty girl is back. Good. I love it when you talk dirty." Her presence captivated him. The wind whipped her hair, blowing the long cocoa strands around her head, making her look wild. The way a woman should look. Lexi was built for sex and sin—she had no business trying to look innocent. She couldn't anyway, no matter how much she wanted to.

He reached out to run his fingers through the long strands.

She cast him a defiant stare. "Keep your hands to yourself. Eyes on the road."

How he wished it was his teeth on that lush mouth.

"Sweet Lex, you look gorgeous. I've missed you like crazy."

She arched one brow. "Yet you let me go. You miss me but not enough to hold on to me. Not enough to *be* with me. To continue our life together."

A streak of lightning bolted across the gray sky, punctuating her statement. It was growing darker. Silently, he considered her words. Was that really the way she saw it? He had a different opinion, one that made him think he was driving straight into two storms—one inside his car, one outside.

"A life? Like your family would've stood for that. I can just imagine Christmas dinner, slummin' with the mechanic." He thought back to the one and only formal, sit-down meal he'd attempted with her parents. Her mom had apparently *loved* him. As though it was yesterday, he heard the snidely voiced comments he'd overheard the woman make. *Alexis, dear, go find your grease monkey. He should be here by now. Make sure he washes his dirty hands. Supper is almost ready. I do hope he knows which fork to use.*

The offhand remarks, so casually uttered, confirmed what he'd secretly feared—he wasn't family material, especially for someone of Lexi's caliber.

Working on cars was a decent job, he'd told himself. It sure topped stealing them. But *mechanic* didn't come close to what the Templetons had groomed their only daughter for.

Lexi had protested, threatening that if her mother didn't show him some respect, Lexi would ask him to leave *and* go with him.

The damage had been done, though. While her

defense had warmed him, it wasn't enough. Mrs. Templeton had only voiced Nico's suspicions: Lexi was better off without him.

None of that meant she should be with loose-loined Langston. Not even close.

Much to Nico's dismay, the asswipe was a customer at Seven Seas Automotive, the shop Nico had recently bought into with several years' saved earnings and now co-owned with Coondog.

No, it wasn't enough ol' Cooney had shown him Lexi's engagement announcement, tapping the screen and shaking his head, *tsking* over the "mistake of a lifetime" Nico had made, letting "that sweetheart" get away. Hell, no.

Then Langston had to go and show up one afternoon, running late on his way to some "lame" flower shop he complained, to pick up a "tester" bouquet of orchids for his "troublesome" fiancée—all while hovering over Nico, who'd quickly identified the problem and repaired the neglected belt, doing his dead-level best not to belt the fucker breathing down his neck and talking smack about Lexi.

Then the polished-to-perfection ass in Armani just *had* to go and mouth off about his sexless engagement— and brag about his dick-squeezing tart on the side.

Nico did himself proud that day, not committing murder.

"Hey!" Lexi slugged his shoulder, tired of his trip down Nightmare Lane. "What's this you have against my family?"

"It's more like what they have against me."

Lexi released a frustrated sigh and looked away.

Did he even bother to tell her about the time her mother handed him an envelope of cash? She'd blindsided him just as he was leaving work late one evening, after everyone else had cut out. "There's five grand in there, *Mr.* Tonetti," Mrs. Templeton said as though he should've bowed down at her feet. "That's a fine sum."

As if time with Lexi could be bought off so cheaply?

"Squander it. Invest it. Buy yourself something useful or absolutely frivolous, I care not. Guarantee me that you'll leave my daughter alone, and I might be convinced to scrounge up more."

He'd taken her envelope of cash. Walked off with his head held high. Used his key to get into Coon's office later that night where he shredded the whole batch. The next day, he'd mailed the chopped-to-pieces useless money back to Lexi's address, anonymously. Let Marla Templeton stew over that.

The memory sickened him. Made him feel nauseous, downright dirty.

"Tell you what..." He tried again, shaking off the past. "Let's talk about something positive. Tell me what you've been doing with yourself." He was about to ask if she'd finished her Cognitive Science degree, something she'd started working on that last year they'd dated, but she cut him off.

"Planning a wedding." Bitterness coated her words. "One you seem determined to ruin."

"That's it?"

"Nothing as mundane as working, if that's what you're getting at."

He ignored the dig, knowing she didn't mean it. Lexi had never been one to judge him. Never.

Then why didn't you give her a chance? Not lump her in with her mother? Fess up to your insecurities and talk to her instead of keeping everything to yourself?

I'm trying!

"You know, you really ought to turn around." She said the words as though she thought she *should*, no real feeling behind them. "Take me back. I'm expected. I have commitments. Bradley's got to be beside himself, wondering where I am."

Nico sped up. "Let him wonder."

"Sure, until he calls the police to report me missing." She twisted in her seat, facing him with narrowed eyes that spit fire. "Come on, Nico. Whatever this is about, it's pointless."

"Pointless?" Wind gusted against the vehicle. He tightened his grip on the wheel, along with his resolve. "Baby, after that kiss back there"—he gestured behind them, toward Houston—"after how you haven't uttered a word of protest in miles, I'm not buying it."

Silent, Lexi fell back against her seat. Apparently the truth left her speechless. She wanted him. He knew it; she knew it. The question was, what to do about it?

He could think of a hundred things. Only a handful centered around her body. But with the walls she'd put up, he wasn't sure he could reach her any other way. Use sex to weaken her defenses?

Works for me!

He shouldn't let the area below his belt have a say —*but you know you want to.*

No, he should take her someplace public, really talk to her. Maybe even admit the real reason he broke things off. His own damn doubts.

What? Did you drive all the way out here because you're ready to be with her the rest of your life? Stand up to her parents and get married? Have babies and be a father?

Be a father? Nico shuddered, and it had nothing to do with the lowering temps and increasing winds. Given how his own father had died in prison, he hadn't exactly lived with a stellar example of fatherhood growing up.

There's Cooney.

Right. A man who could teach classes on Confirmed Bachelorhood.

Who goes off-grid one weekend a month. Right... He and Brett had been speculating on Coondog's closed-mouth destination for years, figuring maybe Coon had a lady on the side. One who lived out of town.

Huh. Maybe he did have a decent example after all. Maybe—

Lexi made a grab for the steering wheel. "I said take me back!" She sounded a bit frantic. "Please."

"Nuh-uh, woman. I'm not taking orders from you." Nico easily overpowered her with one arm and shoved her back into her seat. "The wind's strong enough to buffet this barge. Do you want to get us both killed? Stay put." He growled the last, suffering anew in silent agony.

The damage had been done. Having her that close, the sweet scent of her perfume, light yet heady, had gone straight to his brain. And below the belt.

Reigniting the desire he'd been trying to bank since that explosive kiss earlier.

Nico licked his lips, remembering the flavor—her flavor—that the golden ball had left in his mouth. One taste wasn't enough. "You got any more of those balls up there?"

He risked a sideways glance.

"Nico..." She closed her eyes as though she could hide from him. From them.

They both wanted more than just a kiss. A lot more.

Maybe, before he worried about convincing Lexi that Langston was a Grade A asshole, he should prove her own feelings to her. She was marrying one man but she wanted another. Maybe even still loved another—him.

Nico wasn't such a gentleman that he wouldn't take advantage of that.

Left hand firm on the steering wheel, he stretched his right to her knee. "Perhaps I should check for myself."

"DON'T YOU DARE." Lexi tried to cross her legs but Nico wouldn't have it. He dug beneath her dress and wrenched her legs apart. His fingers dove past her panties. The big car swerved, one side of tires running onto the shoulder.

"Watch out!" she cried but even she couldn't keep her eyes on the road. Instead, she focused on the juncture between her legs, where his dark, muscular forearm disappeared beneath the white dress.

Nico straightened the wheel. "Everything is under control, sweetheart. You know I can drive—you're just a handful of distraction." Several of his fingers plunged deep. Her traitorous muscles clamped around them and she gasped. "And you know what I can do to you."

Did she ever. She dreamed about what he could do

to her, had spent the last hour trying to obliterate the thoughts, the memories. The yearnings...

Fighting emotions she didn't want to name, she savored the missed sensation of his touch, of his calloused fingers snagging on her lacy underwear, the way he commanded her body's response as only he could.

She'd never stopped loving him. Never. Never stopped wishing, hoping, he'd realize he made a mistake and come back to her.

From the moment they'd met, thoughts of him had consumed her. Had made her joyful. When they decided to date, to become a couple, they'd joked about how he was going to complicate her life.

She was starting to wonder if she'd ever be happy any other way.

Complicated love is better than no love. Isn't it?

Lexi fought back a moan at the sensations rioting through her. She ground her teeth, to keep from crying out, coiled her fists to—

And felt her engagement ring. The heavy weight of it a harsh reminder.

What was she doing, letting him invade her like this? It was one thing to give him time to state his case—part of her still held out hope he was there to profess his undying devotion and sweep her off her feet. It was another thing to cheat on the man she was marrying. *Tomorrow.*

Steering with one hand, Nico leaned over and rolled his fingers deep inside her. Defenseless against him, she lifted her hips, welcoming his touch. How long had it been since she'd felt such ecstasy? Two months? Three? Eight? As long as they'd been apart...

Too long.

Her stomach clenched. Her heart pounded. Sweat beaded on her forehead and her nose. No, wait—it was raining. Cool, wet drops washing away her tears.

Lexi leaned her head back and accepted the moment for what it was. She wouldn't stop him. Didn't want to. Nobody could make her feel this way. Especially not Bradley.

Nico teased her clit and she gasped back a satisfied sigh, thrilled to her core. Her world became a whirl, the trees whizzing by, the raindrops on her face, his hand driving her wild. Lexi rode his fingers, loving the way he varied his touch, circling her clit, stroking ever so lightly over her folds and then pushing deep, always one step ahead of her.

Nico honked the horn. Short, happy blares.

She lifted her head and stared between her legs. The faded switchblade tattoo on his forearm was moving up and down, up and down as he pleasured her. How she loved his arm, the flexing muscles, the dark hair.

She couldn't stand the sight and tore her gaze away, focusing on his other hand. Blindly seeing how his clean yet always stained fingers guided the wheel, so in control yet so out of control as he swerved and fingered her. Thank God the road was deserted.

Thunder crashed closer, echoing in her crotch. Was she really going to come, just from his touch? She gripped his wrist with both hands, holding him to her, when what she really wanted was to rip off his jeans and climb over his cock. Ride it to completion.

She was weak. She'd always been weak when it came to Nico. Vulnerable. It was the main reason why she'd accepted his decision when he broke up with her. Why she hadn't fought harder, beyond a few phone calls. She'd never thought she was edgy enough, experienced enough to satisfy him. Not indefinitely.

Had figured he'd lose interest at some point and she should just suck it up and move on. But her heart hadn't listened, common sense unable to override emotion.

Emptiness gaped in her lower abdomen, the need to be filled overcoming all else. His hands weren't enough. *More.* She had to have more. She had to have all of him, now, deep inside her.

"You've got to stop," she cried. It was raining harder now, making her feel elemental, raw. "Nico! Stop!"

His hand stilled and started to withdraw. Lexi clawed at his wrist and forced him to resume pumping his fingers into her. "No. The car. Stop the car! I need you."

Nico lifted his foot off the accelerator, passed a thick copse of trees, and then maneuvered onto the shoulder. They came to a rumbling halt. He set the parking brake but never paused in his attentions, pushing high in her vagina. "Ah, felt it!"

Her muscles contracted around him. She was so wet, so ready...

The pitch of raindrops increased, coming down harder, hitting the metal dashboard and bouncing off, landing on her clothes, on her hair and sinking in. Sinking in...like his touch.

She humped his fingers, scrambling to get her hands beneath her long dress, trying to reach her clit. She couldn't think anymore, had to come...

Nico's motions slowed. "I've got to roll up the windows and put up the top, Sweet Lex."

An unwilling moan issued from her lips as her lady bits twitched in protest. Nico shut off the engine and turned to face her. Flexing his middle finger in her one more time, he eased his hand from between her legs.

Nooooo. Don't stop!

But he had. Taking that decadent touch away. Leaving her empty. Aching.

"Finally! Got it," he said. "A souvenir, for later."

Still perched on the edge, it took a second to recognize the shiny gold ball he held between slick thumb and finger.

He grinned.

The bastard actually grinned.

A souvenir.

That's what all the fingering and pumping was about? Not pleasuring her or needing her but an effing souvenir?

Because after tonight, there'd be no them. No future. This was just a last-ditch fling to him. She was ruining her life for nothing more than an orgasm?

What was she thinking?

She wasn't.

Pressure stung her eyes. Brought unwanted moisture.

Lightning flashed around them, illuminating the sky. When had it gotten so dark? Directly overhead, thunder cracked, striking Lexi like a whip. She flinched.

What time was it? Nine? Ten? She couldn't imagine what her family, what Bradley, must be thinking.

Nico pocketed the ball and nudged her jaw until she looked at him. His lashes narrowed against the rain. "This wasn't my intention, Lexi. To get so physical with you so fast. I just wanted to talk to you. But it's obvious there's unfinished business between us."

Rain plastered his long, black hair to his face and shoulders. Lexi wiped the wetness from her eyes and saw the drops glistening on his tanned skin, catching on his goatee. He looked phenomenal.

She shook her head, blurring his image. "This doesn't change anything. It can't."

Nico moved his hand, running the fingers he'd had inside her over her lips, allowing her a taste of what she felt for him. She jerked away, avoiding his gaze. She saw the ridge in his jeans. "Stop, just stop. You have to. Take me back to the church. I…"

Her heart thudded. The ache in her pelvis grew stronger, her desire seeping through her panties. It was all she could do not to throw caution to the wind and jump him right then.

I'm so confused!

He leaned over and kissed her forehead. "Stay put. I'll be right back."

Run, Alexis! her inner—boring—good girl begged. *Steal his car and run. Before it's too late.*

Instead, she found herself mesmerized, unable to move, unable to resist his magnetic pull as lightning flashed twice more and she watched him in the pouring rain, struggling to get the top up.

Nico was ten times more man than Bradley could

ever be. In her eyes, at least. So why was she about to shackle herself to the wrong man?

Because Bradley was right for her. What she wanted —a traditional man, a traditional marriage.

Nico was sexy. Fun in the sack and out. But he'd never settle down or consider her worth forever.

If she wanted forever, then *she* had to settle.

Which is what she'd decided not long after hooking back up with her high school sweetheart. When Bradley proposed sooner than she'd ever expected, catching her completely off-guard, she'd settled.

Succumbed to the pressure from her mother to do the right, expected thing—marry someone in their social strata. Succumbed to the lingering grief in her heart.

In the months since Nico broke up with her, the anguish, heartache, and loneliness over her brother's ongoing absence had only grown. The renewed *joie de vivre* she'd felt since meeting Nico had all but evaporated when he was no longer in her life. That special someone to share life's joys and troubles with; someone who could soften the latter while making the former even better.

Depressed? She'd wondered about that. After the breakup, she'd booked a few sessions with Mother's shrink only to be told a broken heart didn't automatically equal depression.

Yippee. Too bad there wasn't a pill that would meld together the shattered pieces. Just the prescription of time.

Time? *Pfft.*

Lexi didn't want to grow old, skipping out on traditional marriage and a family of her own, all because she'd fallen for a bad boy with no domestic tendencies.

But the bad boy is hot.

Maybe so, but hot wouldn't warm her future. Just her bed.

Get out now! Before you do something unforgivable! She wavered. *Don't throw the rest of your life away for a booty call!*

That's all she was to Nico, when it came down to it. A good time.

His stupid souvenir comment proved it.

He'd left the door ajar. Dual lights from the bottom of the dash lit up his empty seat and her lap. Her knees were squeezed tight together, her fingers a mangled mess. Lexi blinked, focusing on the keys dangling next to the steering column on the metal dash.

In a daze, she wrenched the keys free and threw them with all her might. They skidded across the street.

"Lexi! What're you doing?" Nico yelled, just as he was fastening the top in place.

Blocking out his cry, she levered the heavy door open and hurled herself from the car. Pounding her flimsy sandals into the damp earth, she headed for the shoulder. She had to get away. She had to outrun Nico. Outrun herself. What he made her feel.

If she stayed, she'd succumb. She'd settle. Again. She'd settle for being his plaything. His meaningless piece of ass.

Anything to feel that life-lifting, heart-pounding excitement his presence always brought forth.

Escape. The only option.

Common sense fled faster than her feet. She turned into the trees.

Dodging pines and oaks, jumping over debris, Lexi forced herself to keep moving. Almost pitching head-first to the ground, she slowed her pace. Her girly bits were swollen and aroused. Every step reminded her just how much. Rain beat against her back. If only it could wash away her longing.

She traded safety for the hope of oblivion and moved faster.

Her lungs burned. Vision blurred beneath the shadows. Rain drenched her clothes, weighing her down. She ignored Nico's calls and ran. Fallen pine needles and mud sucked at her soles. One sandal slipped off. Her next step kicked up water.

Lexi stumbled but kept going. Turned away from the road, aimed for the thicker growth beyond. Her body had never needed him this much, to the point that she was ready to forfeit her future. And for what? A quick hump that wouldn't mean shit to him.

How could she even consider it?

With harsh motions, she brushed away tears that wouldn't stop. She hurt, ached inside. Why did he do this to her?

Why do you let him?

Nico complicated the hell out of her life. Always had.

And she was starting to wonder if she'd ever be happy any other way.

TEN

Something Old - The Girls

"YOU GUYS FUCKED YET?"

"Jazmin!" Calli shrieked on a laugh and shoulder-butted the woman next to her. "Don't be crude, girl."

Enjoying the rare time out for herself, Lexi had met her three closest girlfriends midweek for a late lunch at a pool hall/entertainment venue. The place would be hopping in a couple hours when the denizens of downtown Houston started getting off work.

For now, Lexi was basking in the joy of friendships missed. She sat across from Calli, who was attending Texas A&M for graduate school but had come into town for the day, and next to Jenny, in her last year of law school, planning to join the DA's office as a prosecutor —an occupation Lexi found comical given how her petite friend looked more like a kindergarten teacher than a vicious attorney hell-bent on justice.

Mouthy Jazmin, a current social worker and former Big Sister Lexi had met when she went through orientation a while back, only grinned, totally unapologetic.

Lexi loved being around Jaz's outrageous energy. Full of piercings and attitude, at five-eleven she towered over the rest of them.

"Well? Have you, *chiquita*?" she asked Lexi, pointing her fork full of some fruit-based concoction like an accusation. She'd been running late and was the only one of them still eating. "Done the dirty yet?"

Jaz blinked newly purchased purple contacts, spearing Lexi with a narrowed gaze from beneath her super short midnight hair that made those flashing amethyst eyes stand out. The unnatural pale color would've given Lexi the creeps if Jaz hadn't pulled it off so well. "I mean, *all* we've heard the last few times we could pry you away from Momzilla was Nico-this, Nico-that. I, for one..." She paused dramatically, returning the fork to her lips, sliding the bright red fruit off and speaking around it. "I wanna hear how good he is in the sack."

Lexi felt her cheeks heat and turned to Jenny. "Save me!"

"Don't look at me." In deference to the recent rains and over-the-top humidity, Jenny's lively dark curls were knotted up tight. After learning what true roughing it was these last few months, Lexi wasn't about to let a little crummy weather screw with her just trimmed-and-styled look. Her neck could just sweat.

"I might not've asked you outright if Nico's a good lover," Jenny added with a whimsical smile, "but I'm as curious as the next lovelorn girl."

"Lovelorn? I'm totally lost, you guys," Calli said, bewilderment showing on her classically pretty face. Lexi had met the small-town transplant sophomore year at college. Calli had saved her bacon when it came to biology lab and they both loved the same hairstylist, where they'd gone today before meeting the others. Gorgeous blonde hair, thick and long, usually braided but down at the moment, and funky earrings kept the country gal from being a total tomboy. "Aren't you and Carter hot an' heavy?" she asked Jenny. "Livin' together?"

"I'm cooling things off that direction."

The strain in Jenny's voice caused Lexi to look at her long-time friend with a more discerning eye. "What'd he do now? I thought you said he was getting—"

Help. Counseling Lexi was about to finish but stopped when Jenny gave a slight shake of her head, panic flaring in her eyes. She knew Jenny's boyfriend could have jealous tendencies and a righteous temper that vied for dominance with his practical jokester, always-up-for-a-laugh personality.

Given how Lexi was the flypaper who brought their girl group together and Jenny didn't know the others as well, it made sense she might not want to advertise her business. Especially if it wasn't pleasant.

"Your parents still away?" Jenny asked, in a bid to change the topic.

Lexi was game. "Yep. And I am *loving* having the house all to myself." With her parents on a ten-day Caribbean cruise, the first vacation they'd taken since learning their son was missing, Lexi had encouraged their housekeeper/cook to take off too.

Having the freedom to dance naked down the hall-way, eat coffee ice cream for dinner, and binge watch *Justified* and her favorite season of *Friends*—twice—had been a pure delight. "They get back Monday. Unless I can talk Dad into marooning her on an island."

That led to a round of chuckles. But really, convincing her folks to go radio silent, taking a true breather from tech and life stress was doing *Lexi* a world of good.

"Wishing you'd joined 'em?" Calli inquired.

"Not at all." Lexi reached toward the ceiling, getting in a good stretch before picking up her tea glass and draining it. Late lunch had been terrific. The camaraderie exactly what she needed.

"Any word on Phil yet?" Calli asked.

"Still the same. Just missing." *Missing.* Such a simple-sounding word for the deep void left by her brother's MIA status. "Anything new with you guys? Calli? Are you seeing anyone this semester? I thought I heard you mention someone when we were at Mane Street, but then the hair dryer came on and that was all she wrote."

The blonde who Jaz had once dubbed Tomboy Barbie, gave a self-deprecating laugh. "Just professors and lab assistants these days. After Marc asked me out that third time, and I was worried he was going to be gropey...you know *expecting something*, at the end of the night, you know—"

"We *know*," Jaz said on an impatient sigh. "I keep telling you, South, there's no need to get squeamish every time you talk about S-E-X. That third-date rule is ancient. Archive it. Forgettaboutit. Do what feels right for you and stop over-stressing. *Puh-lease.*"

"Well." Calli was hardcore blushing. "Turns out the last thing I had to worry about was him sleeping with me just to dump me after. Nope. That turd just wanted to butter me up so he could *cheat* off my midterm in Quantitative Phylogenetics. What a jerk."

"Yeah. An absolute dickwipe," Jenny commiserated sympathetically. Then looked toward Lexi and Jaz, mouthing *No idea what she just said.*

Covering a snicker, Lexi too made an appropriate response, feeling a tad envious of Calli's schoolwork, even knowing the classes had gotten harder.

Jazmin slapped one hand on the table, jarring Lexi back to her expectant gaze. "What?"

"You're not getting off that easy. Did you think *we*'d forget? Nuh-uh. Calli shared about her Midterm Cheater wannabe. Now it's your turn. Spill, Lexi," Jazmin insisted, wiping her lips after the last bite of fruit disappeared and pushing her plate to the side. She glanced at her phone. "I'm due back at work in fifteen, gotta leave in three. Give me something juicy to get me through this next appointment."

Jazmin assisted clients as a caseworker. Her past and somewhat rough exterior camouflaged a gentle soul who loved nothing more than helping others. Well, that and gossip. "It's a rough one, abused mom and her two kiddos. Please, I *need* to be reminded all men aren't savage a-holes. To hear how good your mechanic is with his *tool*."

Calli stifled a snort. "Jaz, you bad."

Beneath her spiky black bangs, Jazmin winked. "Can I help it if being bad makes me feel so good?"

Jenny nudged Lexi's shoulder. "When do you see him next? Isn't Buccaneer this weekend?"

"What about it, Lex?" Jaz said. "Have you been

feeling *good* lately? Thanks to your Mr. Mechanic Camper Man?"

Any more and you wouldn't believe me. Lexi knew Jazmin wasn't asking how Nico made her feel emotionally, just sexually. But did she really want to admit it? Out loud?

What all they *weren't* doing?

For five months now—make that four, if she didn't count the one she'd had to miss when her dad reacted to some meds and ended up in the hospital—they'd met every second weekend. Flirted, made out, even indulged in some seriously heavy petting when they could get away with it. He'd gotten under her shirt, even under her pants—with his hands.

But that was just the physical stuff. It was the emotional that had *really* gotten to Lexi. The time they spent together, just the two of them, either hanging back from the other kids or counselors, or when they stayed up late after Lanterns Out, just being near the embers of the banked campfire. Talking back and forth, really getting to know each other. She made him laugh. He made her forget the stress of her life. Sometimes it seemed as though she lived for those times more than anything else.

Lexi didn't care that it wasn't a real relationship, that he hadn't asked to see her beyond their weekends, had never asked her out. Requested her phone number.

At least she told herself that she didn't care.

What they had was enough.

Enough to give her the push she'd needed. Knowing Nico had improved her life in ways he couldn't imagine.

1) She'd convinced her dad that Mother needed

counseling. Medication, maybe. The woman was at a total, miserable standstill with Phil still missing, needed to find a way to either grieve and move on, or accept the not knowing and stop letting his absence affect every second of every day.

2) Even though Lexi's handicap was outrageous, she'd started golfing with her dad twice a week. Just the two of them. Father-daughter time she cherished.

3) She'd finally stopped pandering to her mother, not only accepted her friends' invitations to lunch and movies, but started instigating her own, such as today's. Things she'd stopped doing while trying to make Mother happy.

And best of all?

4) Lexi had made an appointment with her former college advisor to talk about getting back in school to finish her degree; never mind that she was changing it, again. She couldn't wait to tell Nico about this one.

It was time to celebrate. A toast to all the recent improvements in her life. And she wanted to do it by being intimate with Nico.

Definitely not all stuff she wanted to blab to her girlfriends, especially before "it" happened. But everyone was staring at her expectantly, including Jenny.

Jenny, whose eyes had widened, suspecting the talk would turn her direction if Lexi didn't give up something tantalizing soon. So she said, "I go up early Saturday morning."

"And?" Jaz pressed.

Taking one for the team—or in this case, for Jenny—Lexi admitted, "I don't know how good he is with his toolbox. I haven't exactly opened it."

"Meanin'?" Calli asked on a squeak.

"We haven't slept together yet."

"Why the hell not?" Jazmin demanded, as though it was completely unacceptable. "As much time as you spend *talking* about him, I figured for damn certain you must be *doing* him."

"Not everybody jumps in the sack so dang quick," Calli defended, her small-town values shining through.

"These days they do," Jazmin insisted.

"Uh-hello?" Jenny said. "She only sees him once a month, *camping*. With kids all around."

"True dat," Lexi said, deadpan.

"Shit," Jazmin snorted, getting up, her demure blouse and nice jeans at total odds with her heavy biker boots, studded leather jewelry and multiple piercings. "Now I gotta head off to work without anything smokin' to give me a kick of adrenaline."

"What about your own sexual escapades?" Calli asked in her breathy drawl. "Don't you—"

"Escapades?" Jazmin laughed loud and long, slinging her backpack over one shoulder. "Truly, South, you crack me up." Slapping a bill on the table to cover her tab and tip, Jazmin leaned down as if to impart a confidence but her rough voice still carried. "All my best 'escapades' these days take place with my happy dildo collection. That or my hand. Not much worth getting kicked up over. Adios, chicas, until we meet again. And, Lexi?" She pinned her with a look that meant *business*. "Next time, I want dirt, capeesh?"

"I'll bring you some dirt," Calli said with bravado, as though standing up for Lexi. "Dirt filled with maggots and slugs and—"

Already five feet away, Jazmin spun on her booted heels and marched back, aiming her finger right at Calli's nose. "Don't be spewing that bug bullshit my way," Jazmin told the entomology major. "Not if you want to graduate with your master's *and* all ten fingers."

"Yikes," Calli said watching Jazmin stomp off. "Sure wish I had her confidence."

Lexi thought she heard Jenny whisper *You and me both.*

"And guts," Calli continued. "Dildo *collection*? Dang. I barely got up the gumption to buy my first vibrator on Amazon. I mean—" Calli slapped palms to reddened cheeks. "Just think what the box-packing people must be imaginin'!"

Lexi smiled, more than a little excited to think instead about the condoms she'd bought, and already packed in her weekend duffel.

Oh yeah, she thought, idly watching Jenny and Calli connect over a slight fear of Jazmin coupled with extreme admiration, wondering if her cheeks had gone as pink as Calli's. While she might not've been able to satisfy Jaz's demands for dirt and details today, that certainly didn't mean Lexi didn't have plans of her own. Sexual plans she intended to carry out, and soon. This weekend in fact.

After spending increasingly more time with Nico, after dreaming and kissing and longing...

She didn't care if he considered her nothing more than an occasional weekend fling. The positive changes she'd made in her life since meeting him made it worthwhile. Sure, she'd love to date, to see him away from the campground, but there wasn't any reason why she couldn't have her very own sexual tent buddy, was there?

As long as they kept any amorous activities away from the other counselors and kids, Lexi was beyond ready to make her move. To satisfy her craving for the Texas bad boy.

ELEVEN

Something Old - The Guys

"THURSSSS-DAY, DA-DA, DUM-DE-DOO," Nico hummed under his breath as he parked over the lift and climbed out to elevate his next diagnostic, his stomach already growling for lunch—an hour early. "Thursday, Thursday."

Best damn day of the week.

Get through today and only one more workday till the weekend.

Around him, the familiar hiss of air hoses, tools clanging against metal, and masculine voices interspersed with frustrated grunts and colorful curses made him feel right at home. The smells of sweat and oil, grease and gasoline fumes comforted his nose. He loved it. Every second.

Being here, working here. Every moment brought him closer to seeing Lexi this weekend. He couldn't wait to tell her about the beat-up Bel Air he'd bought and his plans to restore—

"Nic!" Coondog hollered, coming out into the garage

from the reception area that fronted the customer entrance.

Grateful for the reprieve—some jobs were a bitch—Nico lowered his arms from the underside of the Mercedes-AMG he was checking out. Shrugging the kinks out of his shoulders, he turned to his fifty-something boss, all faded tattoos and weathered skin on his craggy, bearded face. "Yessir?"

"You boys know what time you're takin' off tomorrow?"

Boys, as if he and Brett were prepubescent. Hardly.

They'd talked about going up a day early, tomorrow after work, to get in some fishing and quiet before the masses arrived Saturday morning.

"Hang on." He held up one finger, asking his boss to give him a minute. Then he turned toward the private office opposite reception where his buddy had taken to clearing out Coon's twenty-plus years of mess. "Yo! Brett!" he called across the noisy garage. "You get ahold of Ranger Dick yet?"

The camp caretaker's name was Richard and as teens, they'd saddled the old geezer with the nickname. It'd stuck, poor guy.

"Talking to him now!" Brett hollered back, the ancient office chair squeaking beneath his weight.

In time for fall semester, Brett had pried himself away from the gym long enough to enroll in some business courses. Between his school schedule, training for some powerlifting competition he'd signed up for, and now working part-time at Seven Seas, Nico didn't know how his busy friend kept his ass afloat.

One thing was for sure. Seemed every week Brett's

gym-honed muscles grew bigger even as his buzzed hair grew shorter.

The chair squeaked again and Brett appeared in the doorway. "That was him just now. You were right—last week's storms did a number on the place. Flash flooding down the creek bed tore up the roads."

"Can we still get in?" Ranger Dick lived on-site year-round, in one of the few actual buildings on the property. After taking a little-used exit off the interstate, one still had to navigate a handful of low-water crossings on a couple county roads to reach the Buccaneer's entrance and then another four miles of dirt before coming upon the designated campground. "Tell me they haven't canceled this weekend."

Nico ignored Coondog's grumbled retreat—"Just asked a simple question. Didn't want a blame play-by-play."—and checked the clock over the office door. 11:22 a.m.

If things were still a go, in a little over forty-five hours, he'd get to see Lexi. Not that he was counting or anything.

Nico knew Sweet Lex was only slumming with him. Getting her summer kicks.

So she found him hot and liked fooling around with him. Big honking deal. There wasn't any more to it than that. Not on her part.

His? After their first big conversation by the waterfall, after that first make-out session, it'd been pretty easy to cool things off with the couple of women he'd been sporadically seeing. Neither occupied a fraction of his thoughts like Lexi did. Easy enough to jack off in the shower to memories of her; hell of a lot easier than faking it or calling someone else her name in the heat of the moment.

Yeah, he'd fallen pretty hard, had taken more than one ribbing, first from Brett and then from Coondog too, but he didn't care.

Lexi had come through. The kids had taken to her, she wasn't squeamish about baiting hooks or cleaning fish, wasn't above pissing in the woods or digging a hole to shit in.

Nico was impressed.

Near captivated too.

It'd been too long since he'd seen her smile. Caught her fragrance on the breeze.

Heard her laugh.

He couldn't wait to see her again, to touch—

"Yeah. We're good," Brett called across the garage, approaching as he spoke and shaking Nico out of his lust-inspired reverie. "Ranger Dick said they've been clearing the roads since it dried out enough, should finish up this afternoon. With the heat and sun this week, the ground isn't too soggy for tents, so we're fine there. They haven't gotten to all the hiking trails yet but we should be good to go."

"Yo, Coon! Got a report!" Nico yelled toward reception, heading to a side counter to chug some of the Dr Pepper he'd opened just before starting on the AMG.

Coondog blasted in through the door. "When are you boys gonna start using that intercom thingy Brett installed?"

While Brett just grinned, Nico swallowed the last bit of sugary goodness. Then he wiped his forearm across his lips before spouting back, "When I fuckin' remember we've got it."

"Touché," Coondog said around the chew of tobacco he'd just pocketed along his gumline, knowing he'd forgotten more than all of them put together.

In addition to the gal helping Coondog out front, five other employees were busy in the garage with Nico. There were four bays designated for major repairs. Another two for diagnostics and easy fixes—where Nico was currently stationed.

"Ya got that figured out?" Coondog gestured toward the vehicle beyond Nico's shoulder.

That. The Mercedes-AMG GT giving him such a headache this morning.

When he'd brought it in, Mr. Kruger had bragged and bragged about the "steal deal", how he'd paid only forty Gs for the used three-year-old model. What an asshole. He'd totally been had. In good working condition, the car was easily worth twice that—and more. After his last stupid purchase, Nico had counseled Mr. Kruger to always bring them in prior to finalizing anything, let him or Coondog give things a once-over before the deal was done.

Drink finished, Nico tossed the can in the recycle bin. "Part of the problem is I'm running up against some non-standard parts in there. The guts are a mess. It'll take until after lunch to straighten out, prep an estimate, and get the correct shit ordered *if* Kruger okays it."

What a hassle. That was one phone call Nico was sure glad he didn't have to make. Coondog liked handling the money calls, and he was welcome to them.

Nico went on to give a report on the other vehicles in process, wrapping up with, "So, after we complete Ms. Dryden's Hummer, if we get the Trailblazer, Tundra, and that little Escort finished by close of business, any chance you'd let me and Brett head out early? Like after work today instead of tomorrow? Storms destroyed the trails. It'd be great if we could help—"

"Like how you lumped me in there," Brett said with a bit of attitude. "I might not want to leave early. Might have a big date tonight."

He didn't. Or Nico would've heard about it.

Coondog was already waving them off. "Yeah, yeah," he said walking backward and connecting his gaze to Nico's. "You get those four finished *and* call Kruger about his Benz, an' you boys can take off. Where's Sid?" Nico heard Coon bark at the girl he'd hired last week as soon as he left the garage. Sid was their tow truck driver. "Ain't he back yet?"

The thought of getting to Buccaneer early, where he'd soon see Lexi, gave Nico renewed determination. Was even worth having to do the Dreaded Call.

Twenty minutes later, he was elbows deep under the hood, after having lowered the vehicle to try another angle. "Stubborn, sonofa—"

"Miss! You can't be in here."

"—bitch!" As if it had a mind of its own, the wrench slipped and tore a chunk off his palm. "Goddammit."

Shit, that hurt. He grabbed a bandanna from his pocket and wrapped his hand so blood wouldn't screw with his grip and got right back under the hood. "Okay, you motherfucker, this time—"

"*Miss!* I said you can't—"

"N-Nico?"

The feminine voice jetted his head up so fast he nearly gave himself whiplash. He angled toward the muffled sound. Lexi? Here?

Here!

She'd actually sought him out? Away from camp? Approached him on *his* turf. On his side of town. Wow. Maybe there was more to this thing between them on her part too. Maybe she wasn't just slumming—

"Nico, I n-need..." The breathy sound quavered forth across the expanse of the suddenly quiet garage. "I tried not t-to come but..."

Before his surprise could fully turn to satisfaction, he realized something didn't seem quite right. She definitely didn't sound quite right. He straightened, releasing his hold on the wrench which clanged to the concrete floor.

The guy who'd been telling her to leave backed off when Nico's throat gave a low, involuntarily growl.

Keep it cool, he reminded himself.

Trying to look casual in front of the guys, he started a slow amble toward her. She waited about forty feet away, backlit by the late-morning sun that cast her face in shadows.

Was she trembling?

The closer he came, the more he saw. The more he worried. Because this Lexi was unlike anything he would've imagined.

Her eyes were puffy and red, lips swollen. She looked downright awful. "Ph-Ph-*Phil!*" she sobbed from five yards away.

Nervous energy thrummed through him. His heart

picked up its battering pace. His feet followed suit, advancing toward her despite his attempt to act like this —like she—wasn't a big deal. "Lexi, what—"

"Oh, Nico!" She fairly flew to him, hurled herself into his chest and curved her arms around his waist.

She felt so good. Smelled wonderful. To hold her again after twenty-nine days of yearning. But still—

"Lexi, sweetheart..." His palms smoothed over her head, down her hair and across her shoulders as he tried to pry her away from his chest so he could see her face. She resisted, stayed firmly snuggled in, attempting to catch her breath. "Renegade Girl, what's wrong? Tell me."

A snicker behind him made Nico aware of their audience. That he hadn't lowered his voice.

Screw 'em. He didn't care.

She was here! And, by God, she *needed* him.

"Phil. My br-brother." A big, snotty sniff followed the frantic cry. "I just got word that they've recovered his body."

His body? "Recovered? You mean rescued?"

Please, no.

No. Don't let her brother be dead.

He forced her arms down and pushed her away, took a step back so he could see all of her. "You don't mean that," he all but begged, remembering the light in her eyes when she'd first told him about Phil, how close they were, how he'd defied their sometimes tyrannical mother to do his own thing.

How Nico had secretly compared her to the brave brother she so admired when he'd coined her nickname.

He and Lexi had been cleaning fish just last month after a decent haul while Brett and the paid chaperones corralled the kids and started cooking. Fried fish and corn fritters. The meal was as hick Texan as they came and pure dee-licious, especially after the trust exercises and morning hike they'd exhausted the crew out with that weekend.

"Man, that smells good," Lexi said beside him as the aroma of frying fish reached the bench where they worked. He took a moment to admire her efficiency, lopping off fish heads, slicing back scales and getting to the good stuff like a pro. "Almost makes this grody task not so bad."

"Grody?" He'd laughed. "I hear 1980 would like its dictionary back."

"Ha-ha." She wiped the inside of her arm across her forehead, smearing a couple of strands that'd escaped her ponytail across sweat-damp skin. "I'll have you know my gnarly language is totally tubular, dude. Totally."

"Right on, sister." He butted her hip with his, enjoying the moment.

They worked quietly, flying through the remaining fish until she surprised him by saying, "I like being here with you, Nico."

"Back at you, Renegade."

"Renegade?" She'd paused on her last fish. "Where'd you come up with that?"

He grimaced, not really having thought the offhand comment through. Or planned on sharing it.

"Nico?

What the hell. "My boss said that's why a fancy girl

like you would be interested in a guy like me. Dangerous renegade type, blah blah," Nico finished, feeling like a dope. Why had he brought it up in the first place?

That wasn't all Coondog had said, not by a long shot. *Don't sell yourself short, Nic, there's plenty of good in you, reasons for any number of women to fall for you. But a rich, society type?* Coon had guffawed around a fresh chew of tobacco. *I know all about those, son. They're drawn to the danger—don't matter if it's real or perceived. They get a rush from the thrill. Just keep a level head and have fun. Maybe just not too much fun.* Nico's confident "I hear you," had ended the advice giving but hadn't stopped him from thinking about it—or Lexi.

Or stopped him from wanting her with every breath.

"Welllll"—Lexi seemed to ponder—"that's true to a point. Your sexy bad-boy shtick *is* what drew me at first."

"My *shtick*?" Tempted to toss some fish guts her way, he nevertheless chuckled.

"But it was your surprising thoughtfulness that sucked me all in," she continued. "Your so-so kisses that took over from there."

"Funny girl," he muttered. "I'll show you a so-so kiss the next time we're alone."

"See? Your boss is right. *That*'s what I'd expect from a renegade—kiss threats."

"Ha-ha."

Both done, he whistled for one of the kids who jogged over to retrieve the last container of fillets. "Thanks, Mr. Nico, Miss Lexi."

"You're welcome, Sticks."

After the young teen departed with the last of everyone's ready-to-be-cooked dinner, Nico scraped the remaining scales, bits, and bone into the lockable trash bin they hauled out after each trip and led Lexi over to the spigot so they could wash off their equipment.

"I'll have you know that I gave it some thought, Lexi mine." Sounding possessive much? "Decided that between the two of us, I'm not the renegade, the rebel. *You* are." Just like her brother before her, she'd stood up for herself, gone after what she wanted. In this case, independence.

And, dare he hope, him?

She paused and glanced up from her task of cleaning their knives. "Me? How do you figure that?"

"Because I'm not the one rebelling. The one crossing boundaries and taking chances. That's all you, baby."

She stared at him, the growing awareness in her eyes twisting his gut into knots. "Nico." There was a wealth of need in her voice. "I'm craving one of your so-so kisses right about now."

"Counting the seconds, Renegade Girl. Tick-tock."

The seconds till they could be alone.

The seconds he'd have with her.

This weekend. Next month. And beyond.

He'd cherish every single one.

And pray for just one more.

But not like this.

Never like this.

When she wore unmistakable grief like a shroud. There was no denying it any longer. Her brother was dead.

"But why are you *here*?" he asked as the full import of her presence registered. "Not with your parents?"

The racking sobs started again and she launched herself against him.

He staggered back a couple steps before he found his footing, secured his grip around her back and butt, and shook his head when Brett approached, his expression asking if Nico needed any help.

"Keep everyone out of the office," he ordered, holding tight to the emotional woman.

Brett nodded and motioned the guys back to their assigned vehicles as Nico carried Lexi away from multiple sets of curious eyes.

She was sobbing in earnest now, her staggered breaths choppy against his ear as she held on for dear life.

"Wrap your legs around me." She did, that clawing grip along his back and shoulders doing something unfamiliar to his insides. Turning him protective. Into a warrior.

One who was ready to do whatever it took to help his woman.

TWELVE

Something Thrilling

UNMINDFUL OF THE COLD RAIN, Nico secured the car and tore after her. "Lexi! Come back!"

Foolish woman. "You'll hurt yourself. Quit running!"

Her pale dress flickered through the shadowy trees like a ghostly beacon.

It wasn't supposed to be like this.

What'd you expect? That she'd rip off her engagement ring, banish "Bradley" from her vocabulary, and welcome you with open arms?

Yeah. That would've worked.

Been a hell of a lot better than her braving the elements to flee. To literally run from him. He powered forward, his booted feet eating up the distance between them. Before he reached her, she barreled away from the road into thicker brush.

Lexi. Oh, Renegade. She was breaking his heart all over again.

Was the very thought of reuniting with him driving

her? Or was she simply running from herself? From how he made her feel?

There! He caught a flash of her white dress. The sight lent wings to his feet and he caught up with her seconds later, snagging her wrist about fifteen yards from the road.

He whipped her around. Light from a distant strike filtered through the trees, illuminating her face for a second. Tears, mingled with raindrops and mascara, tracked down her cheeks.

"It guts me to see you like this," he told her hoarsely. "Please don't run anymore."

"Why are you doing this? *Why?*" she cried, gripping his upper arms. Her fingertips delved beneath the edge of his t-shirt, holding tight, not pushing him away. "I'm going to marry Bradley. Tomorrow. I am!"

"Who are you trying to convince, Sweet Renegade? Me?" Nico hauled her close and ducked beneath the nearest pine tall enough to shelter them both. "Or yourself?"

She hugged him, nuzzling her face against his neck. Sure wasn't acting like a woman about to be married.

Which only made him more determined than ever to save her from Langston. To win her for himself. "Answer me."

Instead of responding, Lexi kissed her way up his neck and latched on to his lips. Hints of the chocolate she'd consumed couldn't disguise her sweet and sexy flavor.

The rain pounded harder, hitting the ground like staccato drumbeats. Large drops traveled past the branches and slammed over his head. Inside his mouth, Lexi's tongue dove past his, slamming into his soul.

He kissed her back, raising handfuls of her skirts to get at her skin. She rubbed against him and her fingers tangled in his hair, pulling his head back. Rain dripped down his neck.

"Are you still going through with it?" he muttered, sucking on her collarbone. No matter what she said, he wouldn't stop. Not now. Not when he held her against his heart.

"What?" Her breasts heaved against him.

"The wedding. Are you still marrying that bastard?"

"You haven't given me a reason not to."

How could she say that when she was pulling his shirt free from his waistband, scraping her nails over his torso? "You want a reason? Do you ever respond to him like this?" Nico flexed his fingers over her thighs, edging them beneath the crotch of her damp panties. Slick heat met his skin. "Does he make you feel like this?"

She arched against him. "It's not you. The balls. Ben...ah..."

"You can lie to yourself, Lexi, but not to me." He swallowed, hating that he had to ask. "Did you catch anything from him?"

"What?" Lexi had his shirt shoved up to his armpits. She was kissing his chest, biting him.

"Sex. STDs." Nico struggled to get the words out. When he'd taken off after her this afternoon, goaded by Coondog and Brett, he'd been intent on making her *listen*. Hadn't planned on abduction—or seduction. He hadn't planned on wild sex and losing his mind in the process. "Dammit, Lexi, have you caught anything from Langston?"

Her tongue was all over him. She abandoned his pecs and attacked his jaw. "Course not. I've always used protection with him." She grazed her teeth over his skin. "And we haven't... Haven't since I visited my doctor. Was waiting until after...the wedding to, um..."

Her words trailed off as her kisses increased.

"Thank God." Nico pushed her against the tree and knelt, shoving her dress up to her waist. The sharp scent of her passion went straight to his head. With a quick tug, he ripped the crotch of her lacy panties aside.

His mouth watered. "After sucking on your gold ball, I'm dying for a taste of you."

The little ball tucked securely in his pocket, right next to the battered rabbit's foot. Mementos he hoped they could laugh over years from now. Souvenirs, to commemorate the night they got back together.

If he could only win her. Make her believe his devotion. As though his tongue was intent on convincing her any way possible, he lunged forward and latched on to the delicate folds, suctioning them, drinking the arousal dripping from her.

Unable to be gentle, he seized one breast and massaged her flesh, delighted in her whimper, how her nipple pearled in his palm. Through the layers of her filmy dress and bra, her beaded breast heaved against his hand. Between her thighs, his tongue licked over her folds and delved deep, as he gave her breast one more hard squeeze before using his fingers to spread her juicy flesh.

Growling, he teased her clit with slow glides and

deliberate circles, coaxing the bud from behind its hood. Once exposed, he sucked the pearl, flicking the tip of his tongue over it until she thrashed. Then he changed things up, licking her with the flat portion using long, sensuous sweeps as he tried to tell her how he felt.

Lexi pulled on his hair and he loved her harder, with everything inside him.

Breathing heavily, she thrust against his face. "More. I need..."

"I know what you need, baby." He pulled back and licked his lips. Guiding her with a hold on her upper thighs, he turned her around and spread her legs. "Hands on the trunk," he ordered. "And brace yourself."

He opened her buttocks, nosed past her torn panties and licked her from behind.

She gasped. "No..."

He overrode her weak protests and satiated himself on her flesh. His mouth dove deep and he drank her in, imprinting his wondrous Lexi on his tongue, his brain, for all time. Only when he had to, Nico came up for air, rested his head against the plump mound of one butt cheek, inhaled and soaked in her very being.

He fingered the slick flesh that'd bathed his tongue, glided the side of his hand along her cleft and roused her further. She was crying, moaning. But it wasn't enough. He wanted her to scream. To beg.

To never desire another man again.

He slid into her with two fingers, then three, stretching her, making her call *his* name. She rode his hand as she had his mouth, bucking like a wild woman.

"Nico, please." She gasped. "Come inside me."

With his free hand, he kneaded her ass. His fingers dug into her flesh, slowing her movements.

He plunged his fingers inside her sleek channel. His thumb caressed the dark crevice of her bottom. She flinched, tried to move away from the intimate invasion but he held her in place. Her body clenched tightly around him and she shuddered, her legs shaking. "Nico...mmm..."

"Shhh, Lexi-girl." He pressed higher, going faster, harder. "Just feel me. Need me."

Want me...

Love me...

"I do. Can't stop." Her words were strained, sounding as if she were in pain. He kept rubbing, not hard but fast, until she screamed, her shout echoing in the night.

Like angels singing.

His need for her became unbearable. He couldn't play any longer. Time to *take*.

Standing, he grabbed her by the shoulders and whirled her around, trading places with her. He leaned against the tree trunk and fumbled with the button-fly of his jeans.

"Yes. Yes," she all but panted, clutching at his shoulders. "I need this so bad. Need you..."

"Hold on, sweet girl." Nico felt her feet climbing the legs of his jeans and he clasped her butt, lifting her. Her body hugged his tight, her limbs wrapped around him as she humped against his freed erection, sliding along his length.

He shifted her until he was poised at her entrance. She was soaked from his attentions. Hot, humid air enveloped his cock. He trembled and steadied his legs. Then he rubbed the tip of his erection past her opening. Sex juice dripped from her center, coating him. Nico's shaft swelled in his hand.

With a hoarse shout, he lunged inside. Coming home.

LEXI SCREAMED. She bore down against Nico's cock, taking him all the way. Her inner muscles rippled around him, pulling him deeper. He grunted and shifted his legs to a wider stance. The action caused him to surge against her.

Her ass tingled; her loins throbbed. The last of her tears dried as she *finally* got what she'd been craving. Needing. Not just tonight but forever it seemed.

She coiled her arms over his shoulders and straightened her spine, trying to find friction against her clit with his pubic hair. After what he'd just done with his tongue—she could still feel him *there*, licking and biting —she was primed. She concentrated on his every thrust, on how he filled her to perfection.

His strong arms. His demanding, yet gentle ways.

Lexi hadn't felt this full, this close to another human being, in months. This excited, adrenaline pumping through her like a hurricane. This happy, emotions chasing the storm and twisting her into knots.

The tempest raging in her loins had never gusted so hard, blasted from her cleft like a blizzard, blotting out past and future, blowing away thoughts of regret or remorse. Centering her on right now. On—

Nico changed tempo and captured her mouth. She

gasped against his tongue and the hard kiss, flailing in his grasp. It felt so good. So good. But her anus ached, wanting...

At her moan, he moved his fingers, sliding them to the crevice of her butt. Before tonight, she'd never encouraged him to invade that virgin territory but now... Something about his decadent touch excited her beyond her comfort zone. Like a dangerous but thrilling squall that threatened to capsize an innocent ship, she was ready to drown in his arms.

Lexi ground herself against his cock and arched her lower back, inviting his touch, secretly hoping he'd do more with his fingers.

He kissed her mouth with renewed ardor, rolling his tongue against hers so thoroughly her body squeezed hard around his shaft.

Streaks of lightning flashed through her while a stray bolt blazed overhead. Shook the ground beneath. Cracked harshly against her eardrums.

"Good God," Nico exclaimed with a shudder, pulling back. "What in the hell are we doing here? Under a pine! Talk about dangerous."

She licked up to his ear, sucked on the lobe. Then bit it. "Stop and you're a dead man."

If lightning struck them both, she pondered on waves of approaching ecstasy, then she wouldn't have to worry about tomorrow. About the wedding. *Or the marriage.*

At the thought, she humped him with abandon.

With every thrust of his hips, Nico's fingers continued to move inward. They teased her crack. She felt her anus tighten and then bloom. In welcome?

She could give him this, give them this. It might be all they'd ever have.

"You can do it," she whispered against his ear.

"What?"

"I'm giving you permission to..." Her bottom thrashed within his grasp, asking him silently. The storm raging inside her increased at the thought.

"Renegade, we can't," he gasped. "Not here. Not like this."

"But I want you to. I want—" *This to be only yours.*

She couldn't say it, not out loud. But Nico heard her anyway.

His hands dipped past her anus and toyed between her spread thighs. She felt several fingers swirl against them both, where they were joined. Felt him gather moisture as he slid in and out. She flinched, so sensitive it almost hurt. So turned on, she didn't care.

"Ready?" he murmured, slipping his hand free to trail it straight up her crack. She felt him settle one finger at her anus, just before he pushed it slowly inside and pumped within her.

The forbidden touch set her off and Lexi exploded around his shaft. The orgasm flashed through her faster than a bolt of lightning. Every muscle in her body strained against him. Her legs tightened. Her sheath clamped down and she bit his earlobe so hard he grunted.

She writhed in his arms. Loved him with everything in her because this was the last time. It had to be.

Nico groaned and lurched beneath her, driving his cock high. He came with a shout. She felt the hot spurt of semen as he pulled his finger free and scraped his nails over her butt.

Their breathing was loud in the dripping stillness. The fierce rain had passed. The breeze instantly chilled her body. Lexi scrambled from his hold.

Her legs zinged with sensation. Her crotch ached. A good, satisfied, once-in-a-lifetime-fuck kind of ache. Her bottom...well, she refused to think about it.

No longer in the throes of unrelenting desire, her mind cleared. Sharpened. Started brimming with thoughts, consequences, enough guilt to drown a barge.

What have I done?

This wasn't real. It wouldn't lead to anything more. It couldn't.

Without stopping to look back, she ordered her lethargic limbs to move and staggered toward the road.

She didn't care how far it was, she was getting back to the church—and her car—if she had to walk the entire way. Or crawl.

And with every torturous step, if her swollen center protested the hurried pace, if Nico's essence, hot and thick, dripping from between her legs reminded her how reckless she'd just been—no condom? When she didn't think to ask him if *he* was safe? How many women he'd been with? When she was getting married tomorrow, for Christ's sake—then Lexi couldn't hate herself any more than she already did.

THIRTEEN

Something Old - Thursday into Friday

"YOU ALL RIGHT?"

The words Nico spoke from the driver's side of his 1990s Camaro Convertible, over the wind and engine noise, could have come from a million miles away instead of a couple of feet.

At her request, after they left the automotive shop, he was driving fast and far. Just cruising the interstate north of The Woodlands, putting miles between Lexi and home. Between her and heartache.

"Sure this is where you want to be?"

Lexi focused on the husky sound of his voice when he spoke again, grateful for the distraction.

"Don't want me to take you to your aunt's?"

Her spinster aunt Myra. Every bit as stiff, pompous, and proud as Lexi's mother? No, thank you.

Aunt Myra could find out later. And not from Lexi.

She thought about her dad's brother, awesome Uncle Andrew, and his wife, Indygo. They'd always been fun and welcoming. Childless too, perhaps why they'd doted on her and Phil, provided a safe haven any time the maternal smothering or expectations became too much.

Her uncle had died several years ago, though, and Aunt Indy, an energy-loving boho type, had moved to West Texas to mend her broken heart in the mountains. Indy's last text said she'd started tending bar part-time at Bottoms Up, a hopping watering hole near the tiny town of Rustlers Junction.

The thought of Aunt Indy belly dancing on the bar —that was the kind of crazy thing she'd do, and out of the blue—made Lexi smile. Then realize that the next time they talked, she'd be telling her aunt about Phil.

Her heart spasmed as Lexi choked on a sob.

"Lexi? Your aunt—"

"No. Thanks, but I'm sure." She swallowed down the pain. Nodded. Mashed her lips together to tame their trembling.

She'd finally stopped crying. For like the seventeenth time. Wasn't about to start up again.

Seemed like the last thirty-six-plus hours, that had been her primary modus operandi: cry uncontrollably for a while; pull herself together. Feel calmer, cognizant, mindful that she'd really already known this. Known her brother was gone. Learning of Phil's death in an official capacity hadn't been a surprise, only a confirmation.

Wednesday night, the doorbell sounding just after 9:00 p.m. had startled her. She'd been hanging out in the kitchen, debating what goodies she could bake to take to Buccaneer this coming weekend. Chocolate chip cookies? Brownies? Or Nico's favorite—lemon squares? Decisions, decisions.

Heck, why not all three? If she ate too many, oh darn, she'd just have to bake more. For once, Mother wasn't here to poop on Lexi's parade, monitor every single calorie she put in her mouth with a snide remark, a disapproving stare.

Could Lexi help it if her body was, well, naturally *not* skinny?

That was one of the things she'd always adored about Bradley. In public, he could politely put Mother in her place, often shut down the snarky comments before they ever started. And he never once made Lexi feel shamed about her food choices.

In private, he'd compared her to the females painted by William Etty and Gustave Courbet. Though several of their works made her blush, the compliment was clear: she didn't have to wear size six or eight to be beautiful. Bradley's support during those formulative teenage years had gone a long way toward helping her feel good about herself.

She made it a point to eat healthy for the most part, so she could indulge without remorse one weekend a month. She'd just pulled the sugar and cocoa out of the pantry, was digging for the vanilla when the bell sounded, and paused at the unexpected interruption.

Who'd be at the door this time of night? And without calling first?

The second set of chimes, before she'd gone ten feet, hastened her pace.

The loud knocks accompanying the third ring, coupled with the masculine trio standing on the other side of the door, visible through the decorative glass, two of them in dress uniform, cemented what she'd sensed for a while now. Her strong and stalwart older brother, good friend and goofball, was finally coming home. In a box. And only pieces of him, she soon found out.

Just thinking about it now, her breath hitched in her throat, contracted her lungs. She breathed through the pain, congratulated herself when she didn't start wailing. "You can turn around now, though," she told Nico. "Take me to your place, if that offer's still open."

"You bet it is."

Without a speck of judgment, a shred of doubt, Nico zoomed toward the first exit they came to, slowed, did a quick U-turn, and got back up on I-45, heading south this time.

Proving his worth over and above, he'd already offered a host of options: drive her to a neighbor's or friend of her parents', or take her to one of her friends, their church pastor, a relative. Whatever she wanted, whoever she wanted to be with, he'd be happy to see it done. See her cared for.

But there was nowhere else she'd rather be. Not at the moment.

Had to have been a shock, how she'd shown up out of the blue at Seven Seas. How she'd totally lost it in front of everyone at his place of business.

But Nico had handled things—handled her—like a champ. With calm control. Needed affection. He'd tenderly carried her into the private office where she'd told him about the formal death notification she'd experienced last night, how one of Phil's friends from high school—Clay, who'd enlisted at the same time and was currently stationed in northwest Houston working at a recruitment office—had accompanied the upper-level officer and medic who came by to give the grim news.

They'd expected Lexi's parents to be there as well. Had made sure they had a medic in case her father's heart couldn't take the news. In case Lexi or her mother fell apart.

Upon learning her folks were out of town, having their technology-free holiday, and seeing the remarkable composure she'd exhibited, they'd proceeded without demanding she first call in reinforcements and emotional support. Having Clay there helped. Phil's best friend might have been presenting a stoic façade, but the red-rimmed eyes, the occasional quiver to his lips told the same tale—they were both grieving, and would be for a while.

Jaz and Jenny had come over and stayed the night. Jenny had midterms Lexi refused to let her miss and had reluctantly headed out early morning, leaving Jazmin with babysitting duty.

When a crisis call came for Jaz a little after 8:00 a.m., Lexi assured her that she was fine on her own, which she thought was the truth.

Only once alone, everything from the past few hours, all the devastating facts and unavoidable feelings, swirled and circled into a cyclone of sadness. The silence pressed in on her until reaching unbearable proportions.

A frantic call from Calli, who'd just found her cell and listened to messages—she was a pro at misplacing her phone—came at just the right time. Helped bring

Lexi off the edge without ever having to admit she'd been on one.

Calli offered to abandon everything and come over, distraught at the idea of Lexi going through this alone. Lexi declined with convincing reassurance.

Yes, Lexi swore to call if she changed her mind. But she wouldn't, pinky swear.

Yes, she was fine, truly, Lexi promised. Doing so much better now. Feeling more tranquil, perfectly fine waiting until Jenny got off work later. Didn't need any handholding. Yes, she was positive.

Yes, Lexi was a good liar—over the phone.

After hanging up with Calli, the thought of staying solo with her chaotic thoughts and riotous emotions proved impossible. When only one solution presented itself that might help console the inconsolable ache in her heart, Lexi sought out Nico. Ventured into a section of town not horribly far off, but one she'd not frequented previously, taking a chance that she'd found the right place and that he'd be at work. Receptive to her surprise visit.

Not only had he received her with open arms, with chivalry and more consideration than she had a right to expect, after a brief conversation with his boss, he'd left work for the day, escorting her to his vehicle while promising Lexi her car would be locked up tight when the shop closed for the night and that Brett would make their excuses this weekend.

He was taking care of her, and that was that.

For once, she felt weak enough just to let him.

She'd talk to her parents upon their return but decided to make no effort to track them down any sooner. As she'd told Nico to explain why she wasn't with them, given the circumstances, "They're out of town, on a cruise. The first vacation Dad and I could talk Mother into taking since Phil went missing. I couldn't call them and ruin it. I won't. Bad news can wait. Good news can't. That's my motto."

The last thirty minutes had been mostly silent. When Lexi declined listening to the radio, Nico had reached across the console and taken her hand; he'd laced their fingers and tugged until the back of hers rested on his thigh. She'd been content to leave it there. Her hand secured in his. His muscular thigh warming her skin through his jeans.

Nico himself, warming her heart with just his quiet presence.

The fall day was warm, muggy. The convertible's top was down, but he had the windows rolled up and the a/c on, blasting cool air over her face and front; nothing to salvage the sticky sweatiness of her neck and back-side. Just her turbulent thoughts providing more distraction than she wanted. So she studied him.

Let herself absorb and appreciate the man at her side.

Her eyes tracked up his strong profile, dangerous on the surface. Gallant beneath. Sexy facial hair, manly ponytail. Distracting muscles.

Oh yeah. Distraction was good. So she kept looking, enjoying—

That was when she noticed a jagged scrape across his left palm when he changed positions on the steering wheel. "Nico!" She tried to gesture with their joined hands. "What did you do—"

"Oh, that?" He gave his head a derisive shake. "That's nothing. Just banged it up at work earlier this morning."

It didn't look like nothing to her. *Men.* "Do you have hydrogen peroxide? Antiseptic? Bandages—"

"Yes, Nurse Nightingale"—he gave her fingers a squeeze—"and antibiotic ointment too. If it will make you feel better, you can doctor me up when we get home."

A few miles later, he exited the highway. After several minutes and side streets, he pulled into an apartment complex, and she took note of the past few turns. It was an older complex, only a two-story, with traditional brick construction in a dark red-orange color and black shutters at every window. Each unit boasted covered parking. Giant oak trees shaded the ground in front of and in between the buildings so that not much grass grew beneath.

Stepping over a few surface roots, bypassing the buckled sidewalk in favor of a shortcut, Nico led her to a corner unit on the bottom floor. He unlocked the door and stepped back, allowing her to precede him with the caution, "Don't expect much. It's certainly not what you're used to."

Sure, this older section of Houston just inside the Loop was a lot different than the exclusive neighborhood where she'd grown up. Just made it different, not inferior.

Lexi crossed the threshold, not sure what to expect. The inside was clean and bright, obviously updated since the original construction. A quick look took in the main living area and open doorway to a bedroom at the far end. The faint hint of lemon cleaner met her nose and brought a half-smile.

She glanced at him. "It's neater than I would have imagined." He was a guy after all. "You live alone?"

"Yeah, since I was seventeen. Now that place was a dump. This is a castle by comparison."

A weight machine took up the "dining" room. "Guess you eat at the bar?"

It opened from the dining room—er, weight unit—to the narrow kitchen opposite the entry.

"That or in front of the TV." A big beanbag lounger dominated the small living room. A nice collection of books and a couple odd pieces of memorabilia—a six-inch, miniature tire ashtray and a fancy pair of figurines at least fifty years old that reminded her of George and Martha Washington—occupied the top two shelves of a bookcase. The remaining shelves brimmed with video games.

Games that spilled over onto the floor and in front of the television. Long cords to two consoles circled each other in a swirly maze. Lexi flicked her gaze to his. He was calmly watching her assessment. Waiting for judgment? "Wow. I didn't take you for a gamer."

One side of his mouth quirked up. "We all need our secret vices."

"I hear you there." She lowered her voice, confessing, "Mine's a Hershey's bar. With almonds. King Size." None of those piss-ant regular bars for her.

"Gotcha."

"But that's for quick fixes only. My real vice? Nah..." She stopped herself before telling him.

"Come on. What is it?"

"It's stupid. Indulgent." A silly, not-quite expensive habit she'd gotten into once she turned eighteen and her brother had surprised her with a bouquet for her birthday.

"Lexi." Nico pointed to the pile of games on the floor. "I'm good. Really good at most of those. Do you know how much time I've wasted honing these?" He mimed holding a console and using his thumbs to make swift moves and shots. "Chocolate bars and what else?"

"Orchids," she finally said on a sigh. "It's totally extravagant, but I just can't get enough of them. Especially Cattleya varieties and Swan orchids—corsage types. Those are my favorites."

"Considering I don't know an orchid from an orgasm, you'll have to teach me."

Through cry-swollen eyes, she gave him her sultriest glance, her mood considerably lightened. "Teach you about orgasms? You bet."

He coughed into his hand. "Orchids, Renegade. I was talking *orchids*."

"Sure you were."

"YOU WANT TO WATCH A MOVIE? Take a nap? A shower?" Nico asked a while later, after she'd tended his palm with more attention than it warranted and then drifted toward the living room, telling him to go ahead and shower if he wanted, change out of his shop clothes.

Since that was the first thing he did after work every day, he took her up on it, keeping his bandaged hand dry and taking the fastest shower of his life.

When he sought her out less than five minutes later, all Lexi had done was climb on a barstool, toss her purse on the counter, and *nothing.*

She barely acknowledged his return, ignored his question, and only alternated between staring off into space, staring at her phone—without touching it—and scrubbing one hand over her face.

Her red and splotchy face. Just the sight made him hurt. Ripped his guts out to see her this way—so distraught.

So completely the opposite of the capable woman he'd come to admire. To respect. To now want to protect and comfort with everything in him.

He placed one gentle hand on her shoulder. She let out a devastating sigh, big enough to rock an island.

He wasn't sure what to do next. How best to help.

A pang in his stomach guided him. "It's almost four o'clock. I'm pretty hungry. Could go pick up something for us both. Or take you with me. Or anywhere."

She looked up from her blank phone screen, gave a little shrug and he took the single step needed to grab her off the barstool and hug her to him. "Renegade, you look done in."

"Yeah. I look like shit for hours after I cry." She kissed his neck where his shirt collar fell open. "I can go home, sure. I guess." Another little kiss. "Jenny's coming back over tonight. Jaz might too, depends on her schedule. Calli even offered to cut classes. Told her no."

Interspersed with her words were tiny kisses, a nibble or two and a couple of heartfelt sighs.

Nico ordered his hands to remain at her waist, not go gripping her butt. Ordered himself not to take her mouth in a deeper, more fulfilling kiss that might give them both something else to think about. "Or you could stay the weekend," he offered. "Here. If you—"

"Yes, please." Her fingers flexed in his shirt, making him realize she was holding on to him as tightly as he was her. "*Yes.*"

She sounded so relieved as she pulled back to snare his gaze. "If you mean it."

"Hell, yes." He released her waist to thread one hand around her nape. Despite the a/c keeping things cooler in his apartment, beneath her hair, her skin felt clammy, probably from their ride earlier.

If she felt safe with him, and obviously she did else she wouldn't be there, then Nico was going to do the thinking so she didn't have to. "Okay. It's your turn. You go shower. I'll set out something for you to wear and go get us some food. An' I'll lock the door behind me so you'll be all right. Call or text Jenny and Jaz, okay?" he suggested. "After you clean up. Calli too. Let them know where you are so they don't worry."

Her cheeks were flushed, eyes still bright, but he saw the composure that overcame her expression as he listed out specific tasks, told her what to do. "Thank you. Sounds perfect."

As soon as she went into the bathroom, he scrounged a clean pair of boxers, some older loose-fitting sweats, thick socks, and a couple t-shirts for her to choose from. Then he put on the clean set of extra sheets he had and turned down the bed in case she decided to climb in.

When he stepped toward the closed bathroom door, to tell her he was leaving, he could hear her over the running water. Sounded like she was crying. Majorly crying.

Should he stay? Call out? Wait and comfort?

In the end, he figured she could use a few minutes to herself. Didn't need to know he'd overheard her grieving. He'd grab burgers, tacos, maybe a pizza. Definitely a couple Hershey's bars. With almonds. Be back in under an hour.

Next to her phone, he left a sticky note with his cell number. Turned around just before stepping outside and went right back to add a penciled heart and an "N" next to it.

Then he zoomed out of the parking lot, feeling like a dope.

But not caring one bit.

NICO TOOK off work Friday to stay with her, which astonished Lexi and went a long way toward softening the edges of grief.

He'd held her through most of the night, letting her cry or cuddle, sob or snooze, whatever she needed. When she'd finally fallen into a deep sleep, he'd tucked her into his bed and crashed in the living room—which is where she found him.

She'd tiptoed around this morning until he roused on his own, gave her a hug and grabbed a shower.

By noon she felt in sufficient control of herself to call the funeral home that had buried her uncle several years ago. Though she wasn't prepared to make any decisions outright, not without consulting her parents first, she at least wanted to learn *what* decisions needed to be made. And by when.

Brett came over midafternoon to check on her, which she thought was horribly sweet. He and Nico had stayed in contact via a few texts, so she was happy to see another friendly face, feeling leveled off enough to look forward to his visit when Nico asked if she was up for company.

Brett tended to hang back during camping time, run interference with the kids and other counselors, giving her and Nico space. She'd come to value his easy humor and laid-back charm.

Though the one time he'd shaved his head, she did join in with the kids calling him Vin Weasel. It was all in fun, and hey, Brett's muscles were nothing to sneeze at.

She knew he'd had a rough childhood. Probably worse than Nico's, from some of what Brett shared with Sticks and a couple other boys one night, talking about how it was never too late to turn things around if you didn't like the direction you were heading.

Over Fritos, salsa, and chocolate bars, which Nico asked Brett to pick up on his way over, the guys challenged her to one video game after another, applauding when she drove their asses into the ground on one of the car games, laughing uproariously when she sucked at the knock-'em-down, shoot-'em-up varieties. Until she finally left the "men" to do their own thing when Nico graciously offered her the keys to his Camaro when she mentioned going to the grocery store.

"Time for another chocolate fix?" he asked, winking.

"Actually, no. I think I've indulged enough for now."

Between what he'd bought her the night before and had Brett bring today, she was way overdue for a regular meal. Though it'd be easy to smother her sorrows in sugar, Lexi knew doing that long-term, day in and day out would wreck havoc on her self-esteem, not to mention jack with her health. Not something she wanted to deal with.

Nico gave her figure a once-over, his appreciative whistle making her stand up tall in his borrowed clothing. "You're looking mighty fine to me."

She walked over and leaned down to kiss his cheek. "And I want to keep it that way."

"I can go with you if you like." He put down his console and stood. "To the store."

"Thanks, but I'm good on my own. Just want to change first." Out of sight of Brett, Nico squeezed one side of her butt before sitting back down.

The seductive, comforting touch warmed her and Lexi reluctantly headed to the bedroom. It was tough, walking away from him. Part of her just wanted to climb right back in his lap.

Haven't you spent enough time there the last twenty-four hours?

Lexi doubted a lifetime would be enough in those strong, capable, caring arms. What an unexpected balm to her grieving soul Nico had been. What a smart choice she'd made, swallowing pride and gathering courage, to seek him out.

"What about Buccaneer?"

She'd unintentionally left the door ajar and heard Nico quietly ask the question as she changed into a different t-shirt and pulled on the underwear she'd washed out the day before and dried overnight in the bathroom. "You didn't go up yesterday like we'd planned? Help out with the trails?"

"Heck no," came Brett's response. "With you gone, it was all hands on deck at the shop. Cooney even made *me* call Kruger."

"No shit?"

"I know, right? He's just handing over responsibilities right and left. Especially after you *abandoned* us."

She thought Nico may have punched his friend in the shoulder, judging by Brett's playful *Ooomph*. "*That's* what you get for being so good with the numbers," Nico said. "He told me last quarter his bottom line was up almost eight percent over last year."

Nico had lowered his voice even more, causing Lexi to strain to hear.

"No." Brett laughed softly. "*I* told you that. You don't think he's considering retiring early, do you? Trying his hand at something else?"

"No way. That man bleeds motor oil. Coon'll work till he drops."

She started to feel guilty about listening in. But just in case Nico said anything about her overstaying her welcome, she needed to hear it. So she could save face, get out of Dodge before things got awkward.

"Thanks, man," Nico said, "for picking up the slack. I appreciate it."

"No sweat. I know she's not my girl, yours either— until you do something about it—but after how great she's been at Buccaneer? Hell, I think we'd both do anything for her."

A strange, unexpected wave of emotion rolled

through Lexi. She blinked at the sudden pressure behind her eyes even as her lips quavered in a smile.

"Damn straight," Nico said with conviction. "That's changing this weekend, by the way. Her not being my girl."

It was? Heart beating fast, breath held, she waited silently, wondering what else she might glean.

"For real?" Brett asked in a hushed tone. "You're finally going to ask her out?"

"That and more. Just as soon as the timing doesn't suck."

Knowing by then there was no way she was heading back home unless he kicked her out, Lexi slung her purse over her shoulder and sailed out of the bedroom. "Are you boys sure you don't mind me leaving you on your own?"

"Boys?" Nico chuckled as he paused the game and unbent from the floor. He came over to her and handed her his keys. "You still planning on making those lemon squares you mentioned?"

"Sure am. That and meatloaf? Cornbread, green beans? A salad? All that work for you?"

"Aw, Nico, is your woman gonna cook for us?" Brett asked, grinning ear to ear.

Nico sliced him a look before turning back to Lexi. Hands on her shoulders, he tugged her toward the door, a couple more feet away from the living room. "Positive you don't want me to come with you? Will you get lost?"

"I'm pretty good with directions. And you charged my phone, so Google will keep me out of trouble. Are you positive you don't mind me taking your car?"

His thumbs brushed over her collarbone. "Absolutely. You don't have to cook for us, you know."

"I want to." She also wouldn't mind stopping by her house to pick up some clothes. Either that or grab something quick at Target. She definitely wasn't too keen on facing the house, alone, quite yet.

Along with everything else she'd packed for the weekend, she'd left the box of recently purchased condoms at home. Just grabbed her purse, got into her car, and ran to Nico.

Now that she was still with him, thirty hours later, and planned on spending the weekend—not to mention what he'd just said about making her his girl— she absolutely wanted to get those condoms.

The wall of sorrow surrounding her heart had eased. While it wasn't gone—wouldn't ever be entirely gone—Lexi had made her decision days ago. It was nice to hear Nico felt the same.

Though she hadn't put on a speck of makeup today, most of the swelling from her extended cry fest had subsided. At least to the point she no longer cringed when she looked in the mirror. So she didn't feel like a total imbecile giving him a flirty smile. "You sure you want me to come back? Aren't too tired of me yet?"

"Come here." He tugged at his Ramones t-shirt she wore over a pair of his cutoff sweatpants.

Without further ado, he slid his hands over her shoulders and up her neck, until they cradled the sides of her head. Tipping it back, he crashed his mouth over hers, his tongue going deep, stroking hers and lighting a fire down low in her belly. Arousing a tingle that hit between her legs and blossomed like wildfire. Lexi squirmed, pushing her breasts against him as she stood on her toes and kissed him back with everything in her.

Her purse thunked to the floor.

One of Nico's hands left her face to grip her butt. Tug her even closer.

She drank in his hard kiss, the thrusting of his tongue. Tasting him like a woman starved. Inhaling his scent, his flavor—

Something jostled her shoulder.

Nico lifted his lips and swore just as Brett scooted past, eyes averted, muttering, "And that, my friends, is my cue to leave."

"Sorry," Lexi spoke from between kiss-swollen lips, easing her upper body away to take a breath, "didn't mean to rush you out."

Her abdomen was still pressed intimately against Nico's upper thighs, the grip of one splayed palm on her right butt cheek making it very clear that's where she'd be staying.

Brett nudged them out of the way and opened the door. Once through, he turned and gave them two thumbs-up, walking backward toward the sidewalk. "I'm betting you won't be sorry for long," he said with a wink. "Have a great weekend. I'll make your excuses to the kids, mentioning vague family stuff or something, leaving it up to you to decide exactly what you want to tell them next time."

"Thanks, man," Nico called out just before slamming the door on the vision of his retreating friend.

"Brett's a really good guy."

Nico rested his forehead against hers. "He is, the

best. Enough about him. Did you mean what that kiss just promised?"

"Totally," she enthused. Then felt like a ninny. *Overly excited much?*

Lexi lowered her gaze, watched her fingers toy with the topmost buttoned button of his sleeveless shirt. Another custom job she figured, noticing the loose threads where he'd torn out the sleeves. The button, the third one down, was right between his pecs. She itched to slide it free, to touch him all over. "That is, if you want to."

FOURTEEN

Something Different - The Other Guys

"WHAT IN THE WORLD?" The surprised mutter whispered out of his mouth.

Philip Michael Templeton Sr. blinked when his wife, wearing her perfect Mother-of-the-Bride rehearsal-and-dinner ensemble, rushed into the hospital waiting area and beelined straight toward them.

"Diane!" Marla exclaimed, swooping to her knees and taking up the hands of the woman seated next to him. "I'm so very sorry to hear about Ron. Have you had word?" She glanced at him. "Is he out of surgery yet?"

Her concern seemed sincere. But whether it was could be a coin toss. Over the years, Marla had perfected acting how she should—whether it was authentic or not. His sweet Alexis came by her stage talent naturally.

"No, no word yet." Diane sniffed, putting on a brave face as she had all evening. Ever since the panicked call she'd made to him, directly after phoning 9-1-1 when her husband keeled over practically mid-sentence, eyes wide in shock and fear, mouth unable to form anything coherent.

Marla spoke reassuringly for a few moments, still crouched on the hard floor in the sterile environment, heedless of filthying her expensive dress. Ignoring the discomfort the position must be bringing to her knees and back.

Though there was an empty chair right next to Diane, one of the few, Marla remained kneeling, her attention focused on their long-time friend. As the minutes ticked by, the two women talking in hushed voices, he decided her concern was genuine, not an artifice put on for show.

Warmth filled his chest at the realization, reminding him why he'd fallen for her in the first place, before she'd gone all holier-than-thou on eighty percent of the world's unsuspecting population thanks to a combination of midlife crisis, grief, and the wretched influence of her older sister, Myra, a woman who had the personality of a pissed-upon old shoe and enough pleasantness to fill a thimble.

Despite things, his fifty-seven-year-old wife still looked mighty fine to him. Always had, the gray that she swore drove her batty, the wrinkles she bemoaned after rinsing all the gunk off before bed not detracting from her natural allure, one only enhanced, in his mind, when she took care of others.

When she didn't have a righteous stick up her arse; when she wasn't totally self-absorbed, making herself sick with worry, fear, and grief as she had the last several years; when she wasn't nagging their baby girl about her appearance, his wife was capable and compassionate. Faithful in the extreme, dedicated to her family—often to her or their detriment, it seemed lately—but she truly had the best of intentions.

Fortunately for them both, now that he was no longer laid up on his ass with health crap, his low-key approach balanced her high-velocity one pretty well.

"Diane, would you like to stay with us tonight," his wife was offering, "after we talk to the surgeon? Or I can stay with you, here or at your place. If you prefer, I could get us a room at the hotel down the street."

"Company would be nice, if it's not too much trouble." Diane gave a tremulous smile. "I really don't know what I'd do with myself if I was alone."

Though Philip knew his wife had a million-and-one things swarming her to-do list, she didn't bat a single artificial eyelash, only patted Diane's hand. "No trouble at all."

"Oh. No!" Diane gasped, her face turning stricken, taking on the expression it had worn most of the evening. "But no, it's Alexis's special day. I can't go ruining that." Her troubled glance included him too. "Both of you should go home. Be with your daughter tonight. Get some sleep. I'll be fine."

Bullshit. Diane and Ron were childless, and older than Marla and him by close to twenty years. Ron, who he'd become fast friends with before the man retired, had taught him much of what he knew, including a boatload about sailing—his favorite hobby. He wasn't about to abandon Ron's dear Diane in her time of need, nor abandon his friend, even if they were separated by several walls, what smelled like vats of antiseptic, and hordes of people wearing scrubs.

The last few years, he'd had enough of hospitals to last a lifetime. The ER on a Friday night in the middle of summer? Complete chaos. There were two pregnant women, both with youngsters who should have been in bed hours ago practically bouncing off the walls. One gal cradling her arm. Another two on crutches. An elderly lady in a wheelchair, her extended—and extensive—family buzzing around her like bees.

Earlier a loud scene had broken out just inside the ambulance entrance, when three men brought in with fighting wounds tried to finish what they'd started. At the moment, the area was stuffed with four cops and the three combatants, their knives and at least one broken beer bottle having been confiscated. The mayhem had spilled out into the main waiting area when supporters of each had plowed inside, defying cops and hospital security.

"Thank God," he whispered, seeing another two patrol cars pull up. Time to get the circus under control.

It was situations like these when he wished he had his brother's Army training. Might do some good. But no, Philip had taken the boardroom route and for the most part hadn't looked back. Not since meeting Marla after becoming involved with her father's company just out of college.

Marla. Man, she could surprise him sometimes.

He was still coming to grips that she'd shown up. Had pried herself away from Alexis's side on this of all nights—just hours before her wedding. The one Marla had fussed over and planned for months now.

"Nonsense," Marla said, overriding more of Diane's protests. "*Of course* we can be here for you. One of us, certainly. Alexis is a grown woman"—was that a guilty look his wife just aimed his direction?—"perfectly able to manage on her own."

Unease stiffening his spine, Philip opened his mouth to find out what that look meant just as a series of high-pitched beeps went off overhead. A loud announcement followed, blaring over the speakers, paging several hospital personnel. Multiple sirens in the distance heralded approaching ambulances.

Philip stood, gingerly helped Marla up and into his seat before excusing himself to check with reception before they were mobbed by the incoming arrivals, to see whether he could gain a report on Ron's surgery status.

By the time he returned to the women, after sneaking in a quick bathroom break, Marla was nodding decisively at him, Diane was dabbing a tissue beneath her eyes and he was about to realize his long night had just begun.

His wife rose and met him out of earshot of their friend. "It's settled, Philip. I'll be staying with Diane tonight. Either here or at her home. Tell me what you learned." She pointed behind him, toward the reception area.

"He was out of surgery, the doctor washing up to come talk to Diane when Ron crashed." Philip kept his voice from carrying. Not difficult with wailing babies, yelling combatants, the pregnant women and their kids, along with the recent arrivals coming in on gurneys surrounded by multiple personnel.

Gah. The noise was enough to drive anyone over the bend, not to mention the stress of worrying over loved ones. "I'm not clear whether it's his blood pressure or heart, but something took a dangerous dive. They had to call in another physician. They're working to stabilize him before speaking with Diane. By the way, I told them I was her brother, that's the only way I could get anything, and with us having different last names and all—"

"Good. Quick thinking." She stroked one hand down his arm, her eyes darting to the side. "Now do some more. Alexis is missing."

"*Missing?*" he strangled out. "Good Lord, woman, why didn't you lead with that?"

"Because I'm not positive it isn't by choice." Then she met his gaze and firmed her voice, going into Commander Mode. The one he'd always found so appealing when they were younger. "I'll take care of Diane, of things here. See that she eats, sleeps at some point. That she isn't a total basket case once we get word about Ron. You take care of our baby girl. Find her, Philip. She skipped the entire dinner. Where is she? Bradley will be devastated."

He wasn't entirely convinced about that.

Neither did he like the sound of a *missing* daughter. What father would? Tamping down the instinctive alarm, he sought more facts. "When did you last speak to her? See her? How was she acting?"

"At St. Anthony's. She was distracted the whole time. Had me and everyone, even Bradley, leave before her. Said she needed a moment before coming to the restaurant. But she never showed. Isn't answering her phone."

"Have you called the church? Deacon Joe? Checked with Bradley?"

"I've been maintaining a brave façade for the wedding party. It's taken everything I have not to melt down in front of them. And knowing that you were here with Diane? That Ron may not come out of that OR alive? And if he does live through the night, that he'll likely never be the same?" She finally allowed her mask to slip, allowed the strain piling up on her to show. "I'm amazed I'm holding it together this far."

Then Marla grasped his hand and squeezed as she hadn't in years, not since his ticker had given them all such a scare, gripping tight as though she depended upon *him* to make things right. "As to Bradley, I can't have him worrying about his bride the night before their wedding for heaven's sake. He already thought it strange she wanted to stay behind at the sanctuary. Then didn't show for a meal at one of her favorite restaurants? *With all of us waiting for her?* I texted him that she was fine. That I heard from her and it was just car trouble."

"Marla, you really shouldn't lie, you know, not even via text."

"*She didn't come to her own rehearsal dinner,*" said as though Alexis had dared to skip her own birth. "Find her. Make sure she's all right! And get her ass to the wedding tomorrow." The last was hissed. Even through his understandable concern, he was hard-pressed not to smile. His wife rarely swore. He found it sexy as hell.

"Go. Now!" She released his hands and pushed him toward the exit. "Find her. Send word when you do and

I'll keep you apprised of Ron's status. Pray God he makes it through tonight and recovers."

Amen to that.

Sitting in his vehicle in the parking lot a few minutes later, engine running, a/c on, Philip waited for a response to the text he'd just sent George:

> I hear my daughter missed her rehearsal dinner. Any chance you might know something about that?

He sent a second text on the heels of the first.

> Or should I be concerned?

Had the man been able to do anything?

With the wedding tomorrow and Alexis unwilling to talk to him, or even acknowledge her unhappiness when he'd broached things the last couple of months, Philip had felt his hands were tied.

He liked Brad Langston. A lot. At one time thought the man would make a fine son-in-law. He still might, just not for Alexis. Not any longer.

Things change. His daughter certainly had. Ever since—

His phone vibrated. Philip snatched it off the dash.

> Can't promise but thinking the boy went off after her.

He replied:

> No need to worry, then?

There was no denying how nice it'd been, seeing his capable Marla back these last few months. About destroyed her, losing their son. The worry and yes, guilty conscience—deep down, she knew Phil had enlisted because she micromanaged worse than a preschool teacher—had turned her into a raving bitch the last few years.

Alexis playing at being the perfect child during her engagement had pacified his wife. Which meant more peace—and sex—for him.

But he wasn't about to sacrifice his darling Alexis for marital harmony. Hell no, not if—

Wouldn't think so. Wanna meet for a beer?

Philip laughed. That was George for you. Not about to get worked up. His phone vibrated with another text.

If he's with her, she's safe. Beer. At DB?

DB. The Dive Bomber. A military-themed bar where they'd met before. Mostly since Andrew died.

Philip glanced at the backlit clock on his dash. This time of night, highways were pretty clear.

Be there in 20.

Before putting it in Drive, he sent two prayers heavenward. One for Ron and Diane, the other for Alexis.

Then he tacked on a third, for Brad. Whether tomorrow's wedding happened or not, the groom was going to need it.

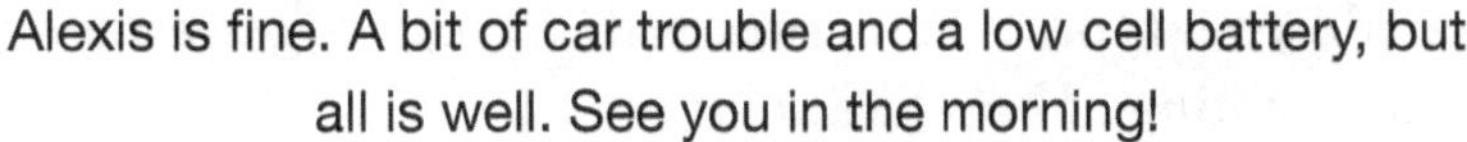

Alexis is fine. A bit of car trouble and a low cell battery, but all is well. See you in the morning!

IN THE *MORNING*?

Too eager, much? The wedding wasn't until 2:00 p.m. Brad planned to get there by one. Plenty of time.

As always, Mrs. Marla Templeton conveyed upbeat positivity, in perfectly grammatical English. No abbreviations for her, even when texting.

"Just wished her daughter shared that same upbeat attitude tonight," Brad murmured. He hadn't been able to do anything right at the church, it seemed, getting caught by Alexis sneaking his first cigarette in months.

"What's that, sweetums?"

More interested in the message he'd missed, Brad had to force his eyes back up to Marionette. Or was it Martinique?

Despite the backdrop of Def Leppard's "Pour Some Sugar On Me" pouring over his ears, a song he'd always liked just fine, the stripper giving him a private lap dance couldn't hold his attention worth shit.

He hadn't wanted the dance, had declined three other girls, but Tom and the guys kept insisting. Finally wore him down if for no other reason than he craved the *private* part.

Being alone for a few minutes the real allure as he followed the perky redhead to a secluded room, catcalls and whistles, shouts of encouragement from his fellow bachelors speeding his retreat. Making him squirm.

The "dance" part? Having Magdalena shimmy and

shake her unfettered boobs in his face? Stroke manicured nails over his scalp and across his nape once he sat down—more like scrunched, trying to get away—shame eating at him like acid?

Not his idea of a good time.

Thanks for letting me know. Need any help with the car?

"Whoya textin', sugar?"

"My mother—" *In Law* didn't make it past his lips; neither did *future*, the wounded huff of pique on her freckled face too priceless to not appreciate.

"Your *mother*?" The nails scraped over his neck a lot harder, not sexy at all. "When I'm doing all I can to entertain you?"

Ow. Might've drawn blood.

"Look." He shifted, ready to explain, or at least try to, his disinterest. But his phone dinged, snaring his attention.

All taken care of. She's fine.

Okay, so Alexis didn't need him. What about...

Philip's friend?

The reason his future father-in-law had been absent tonight. Had Rob or Ron made it through—

At a sharp *zing* of pain, Brad looked up. "Did you just pinch my neck?"

"You're not listening to me," she whined. "Watching me."

Hell. When had his favorite titty bar gone downhill? Granted, he hadn't visited the Twilight Lounge in a while, but still. Inexcusable.

"You must be new," he observed idly, watching for Marla's next text. "Since your—"

He made it through surgery and is in recovery now. We're hopeful. Thank you.

That was good, at least.

The female before him stomped loud enough to rouse an elephant.

He glanced past a nice set of knockers he just didn't have it in him to appreciate, not tonight, and into Maribel's pouting face. "Since your attitude, *sweetums*, determines how deeply I reach into my pockets—"

For a tip, he would've finished. But couldn't.

Because Marigold went straight for his goods.

"I'll see what's in your pockets." Aimed right for his crotch and grabbed herself a winner. "Mmm."

Yeah. He sported a stiffy. Not a big one, but come *on* —he'd been inundated with naked babes the last hour, had a buzz going from the two Coronas and trio of shots his groomsmen had bought. Toasting to Brad's future, his future bride, and to their future happiness.

What about his current happiness? His interest in Millicent so far below zero it broke the thermometer.

The last few weeks and months were getting to him now that time was running out. Were he and Alexis really going to do this? Get hitched forevermore?

Even knowing she'd been ticked at him, he'd missed her presence at dinner. Missed her smiles and friendly demeanor. The way she brightened a room just by walking in and being her vibrant self.

He missed the way they used to be, together. The way they hadn't been this time around.

But after screwing up at work, hiring with his dick and not his brain, dating his seductive Financial Officer for nearly two years and having both pride and heart trampled when he learned she'd only been playing him? Embezzling from his company while working another angle?

It screwed with a man's judgment.

Made him doubt. Everything.

Hooking back up with Alexis had been right. Effortless.

Sweet Alexis would never betray him, play him while working her own agenda.

Not trustworthy Alexis.

Deciding to be with her was one of the best choices he'd ever made. When they'd run into each other one day, surprising them both, they'd instantly fallen back into their old camaraderie. They'd followed that up with a couple of enjoyable, low-key dates. Pleasant, no-stress escapes that worked for them both.

Day trip to Galveston. A museum visit to see an exhibit she liked. She even came with him to a couple Rockets games, well before his favorite team got shut down during the playoffs.

When he casually remarked to his gracious, grand dame of a grandmother that he was seeing Alexis, the joy on her face nearly felled him. He'd known that his poor choices had affected him—and his business—but until that moment, hadn't realized how he'd damaged his grandmother's faith in his abilities. It became very apparent it was time he put his life back on track, started making things right.

Proposing to Alexis, after another few great dates just made sense. If he noticed that some part of her seemed a little subdued, a little less enthusiastic than he remembered, well, who could blame her? He certainly wasn't the same either, not lugging his baggage around.

If kissing her didn't exactly thrill his soul as it used to? He put that down to recently being burned by Lauren, a.k.a. The Swindling Sidewinder, nothing against Alexis.

When they'd slept together the first time, back in high school and early college, their encounters were typically rushed, hurried affairs, whenever they could catch a quickie or their parents were out. He'd never loved her as a man, only a boy. And now? When things should be dynamite in the sack, both of them having gained more experience?

Damn. Was he really ready to admit to himself that he'd been going through the motions, sleeping with her because it's what he figured she'd expect? What engaged couples did.

Sure, a quick orgasm felt great. He'd brought about enough of them with *his* hand lately, ever since seeing his former CFO carted off in cuffs.

Seemed that the excitement, the thrill of sex had nosedived along with his ability to judge character.

Could he help it if he wanted to see whether things would be any better with a partner? With Alexis?

They weren't. Not worse either. Just ho-hum.

Terrific. What every able-bodied man in his prime wanted: blah sex.

Guilt started piling on when he first suspected it wasn't great for her either. Alexis was as beautiful as ever, which just made things worse. She was such a wonderful woman, even prettier now than when she'd been younger, her facial features having matured into the lush body she'd always possessed.

Her generosity of spirit, unselfishness, dedication to her family...none of that had changed. Had only deepened, only showed the maturity and genuineness he valued, given the fickleness of his own parents.

So while it bothered him, nagged at him constantly that sex between them wasn't as compatible as it used to be, as it *should* be, he ignored the disquiet. Unwilling to face it, much less focus on it.

When she'd declared no more sex before the wedding, he'd secretly been relieved.

No more pressure to measure up. To perform.

Once they weren't sleeping together, it was easier to hang out again. A little more relaxed. After the big engagement party her mom threw and once all the wedding details were decided, the frequency of their dates slowed to a pleasurable meal here and there or escorting her to some function he knew her mother wanted to attend, something he wasn't about to put Alexis through without him.

Then they'd wrap up the date with a quick end-of-the-evening peck on the cheek or perfunctory kiss, and *good night*.

No harm, no foul. Just the date of their nuptials, looming ever closer.

So when the woman he'd dated *before* Lauren, a.k.a. The Embezzling Heart Stomper, contacted him out of the blue, he'd been more than willing. Game to give her a whirl. To see whether a one-off with her could rev his engine with a few missing sparks.

It did. At first.

A quick, illicit screw with someone other than his fiancée? With someone he didn't plan on waking up next to every day for the rest of their lives?

Yeah, he got off on it. Secret thrill and all that.

Asininely bragged about it more than once. Trying to bolster his own flagging confidence? Seeking a return to the glory days of his youth? Before heartache and poor judgment took their toll.

Only the one-time thing ended up being a two-time thing. A three-time thing. Before he knew it, he was breaking things off, telling her that it was their last time together because he was getting married and had every intention of being faithful.

"Faithful? You cheating SOB!" she'd screeched, delivering a resounding slap to his cheek. One that wrenched his head sideways. "You could have told me you were engaged. I wouldn't have slept with you. Don't you know anything? A booty call is for *unattached* FWBs!"

Cradling the side of his jaw, Brad had just stared at her.

"Not engaged assholes! It's one thing to call up an old fuck buddy—"

Her tirade continued. While in his head, *Fuck Buddy* kept echoing. That and *FWB*. Friends with benefits. Was that all they'd been?

They'd dated, exclusively he thought, for ten months. Had some good times, a few great ones. Sure, nothing hugely spectacular which is why things had fallen off near the end, but he hadn't cheated on her. Hadn't cheated on Lauren either, not once during the two years they'd gone out.

And here he'd been?

Douchewad of the Year, sleeping around on Alexis just days before their wedding?

"Come on! Get it back *up.*"

The desperate fingers clawing at his slacks finally wrested his attention back to the Twilight Lounge. The secluded room, the muted club noise beyond, the scents of too much perfume—and lust. Just not his.

Brought back Marinara, complaining. "Why'd you go all soft on me?"

Coming alert with sudden clarity, Brad shook off the past, the troublesome memories and his own well-deserved remorse.

He snagged her wrists in a hard grip.

"That's enough," he said in a cold voice, standing and tossing her arms aside so he could do up his pants. She reached for him and he jerked away. "No. Get off me—and stay off."

While his mind had been tripping backward, the tart had unbuttoned his shirt, spread open his fly and liberated a piece of meat that had shriveled beneath her unwanted touch.

Alexis! his wounded heart cried.

She was who he needed. Had to be better for. Make the right choices for, so he could deserve her.

Alexis. In his mind, she appeared before him like a benevolent angel, showing him the way.

He would change for her. Be the man she needed. For her.

Please his grandmother, restore his business. His integrity. And reclaim his self-worth. For Alexis.

Feeling dirty, soiled, and more than a little sick to his stomach—how many shots had he downed?—Brad palmed the fifty Tom had shoved at him before pushing him toward Matilda here. He held the folded bill between them and rasped out, "Take it."

"But we didn't, haven't—" She looked crestfallen, way too young and inexperienced to be here. In this place.

He wanted to tell her to shave off the attitude, get a clue if she had any hope of pleasing customers, of ever gaining repeat ones.

Instead, he intentionally filed the hard edge off his voice. "Stop trying to turn tricks in a back room of a bar. If you want to dance, get one of the other girls to teach you some moves. Or hell, take classes. Better yet"—he thrust the bill her direction and rubbed a hand over his face, feeling razor stubble and exhaustion—"go back home. Find a job you *want* to do. With your clothes on."

Shaking the aura of distaste and regret from his soul, he wrenched the curtain open and headed toward the exit, her shout of "Bastard!" chasing his steps down the hall.

FIFTEEN

Something Old - Friday

"WANT TO?" It took every bit of restraint Nico possessed not to strip her bare, throw her on the floor and take her right there. "Good God, woman, how could you think I might not?"

"You haven't said much since the first time we kissed. Haven't pushed." She glanced at his face before focusing back on his chest. "I wasn't sure…"

"What? That I craved your body?" His fingers flexed on the firm muscles of her ass. "Wasn't sure that I can't wait to get a piece of this and not let go? Is the sky blue? Do the cows come home? Can—"

"Most of the time cows come home. When they're hungry, for sure."

"Can I boost a car in under a minute?" he continued, overriding her flippant interruption. This was serious. She couldn't be under any illusions about him if they were about to move forward. "Did I get arrested for that very thing? More than once? That and vandalism too?"

His impassioned words brought her gaze firmly back to his. "There. It's out. My seedy past."

They'd alluded to it, but he'd never come right out and admitted how he'd made it a habit to break the law for a good number of years. How he'd gotten caught, more than once. He might've had a reputation for being fast on the nab but that only enhanced his rep. Made sure the other guys in his crew bragged about his speed. Let word get out to the wrong people.

Of course, he should have known. This was Lexi.

No recriminations. No surprise or hesitation, feigned or otherwise. She just calmly slipped one of his shirt buttons free to slide her fingers over his chest. "Cool. You'll have to show me. I've always wondered how to hot-wire a car. Might come in handy someday."

"Did you hear me? I've stolen. A lot." He should shake some sense into her. Make her see reason. Tell her stealing cars had gone way beyond hot-wiring decades ago. But she undid another button, stroked her full hand across his chest this time.

"I figured as much. That's actually loads better than some of the things I came up with after first meeting you."

"Lexiiiii." He drew her name out on a long breath.

"Nicooooo," she returned just as deeply, mocking him with a bright smile. "Did *you* think those kids don't talk? You an' Brett, you're practically legends around there. I mean—Ranger *Dick*? Come on."

So she'd known all along? "It doesn't bother you?" He had to be sure it wasn't going to come up later and bite him in the ass. "That I have a record?"

Never mind that it was sealed. A little older on that

last one, or a less forgiving judge and he could've been tried as an adult, had a *public* record instead.

That was after his mom got sick and he'd lashed out at anything and everything over the unfairness of it all. His mom? Wonderful woman, worked herself near to death, with only a few months left according to her doctor. His dad? Hale and hearty, biggest SOB on the planet. That asshole was living it up, free ride on the state, in prison yet again.

That was also when his mom's impassioned plea that he *please* start listening more to Mr. Cooney and distance himself from the gang of friends he'd fallen back with since she got diagnosed finally reached him. His mom had moved in with her sister, his aunt Rosa, who was busy raising Cousin Lila's three kids, Lila having skipped off with a new guy to Oregon after birthing the third.

Aunt Rosa had helped his deteriorating mom get dressed and into the courtroom that day.

Nico had been standing before the judge, who was deciding how he'd be tried, when Nico caught sight of his mother crying silently in the gallery. She hadn't cried when she told him she'd be dying soon. Hadn't cried when his father had hit her. But the sight of her son standing there in cuffs, his future teetering in the balance, had brought tears to her eyes and resolution to his soul.

He'd cleaned up his act for good from that day on. But someone like Lexi—hell, just Lexi—was in a class by herself. So far above anything or anyone he'd ever aspired to. "Isn't it a problem that I have more than a passing acquaintance with a lot of unsavory types?"

"Are you after my money?" Her nails joined the caress this time, lightly scraping over his skin.

"No."

"Stolen anything lately?"

He patted the side of her bottom where—when wearing jeans—he knew she had a habit of stashing gum. "Not besides the occasional piece."

"Of ass?" she asked with a snicker.

"Of gum, you witch."

"Have you any plans to start?"

"Start what?"

"Stealing. The big stuff?"

"None at all."

"Are you on drugs? Planning any heists? Secretly detest puppies?"

"No. Not lately. Never."

With a flourish, she tugged the lower half of his shirt apart, wrenching the fabric pretty hard when the bottom button proved stubborn. "There!"

Pleased with herself, she grinned and nuzzled his chest. "Then we're good. So, bad boy, got any plans to show me that blue sky and those home-heading cows? Make good on your claim?"

"Hell, yes." He gripped her with both hands, angling her hips and rubbing her against him. "I was just trying to keep things uncomplicated, like you mentioned the first time we went to the waterfall."

"With you, I think I can handle some complication. In fact..." Her butt arched into his hands, delighting him down to his toes with the luscious handful she'd proved to be. "I'd welcome it."

"Oh yeah?"

"Mmm-hmm. Complicate me, Nico. Do it hard and deep and don't ever stop."

And here he'd once thought Sweet Lex might be too uptight for him? Too artificial? "It?"

"Take me."

"As in fuck you?"

"Are you trying to shock me? Run me off?"

"Never."

"Promises, promises. I dare you, Nico. Fuck me hard and deep. Pretty please."

He could almost hear *with a cherry on top*. Damn, she made him laugh. "Hard and deep and all night long? You got it, baby."

"What about supper? Thought you guys were starving."

"Sex now. Salad later." With that, he picked her up, curved her legs around his waist and headed toward his bedroom. It didn't matter that it was still bright with late afternoon sun filtering through the plastic blinds; didn't matter that it was a 12' x 12' square and not a suite at some posh place.

Well yeah, it did.

Laying her on his bed, he started tugging down the loose-fitting sweatpants she wore, exposing her gorgeous self beneath. "I'd intended to search out some fancy-ass hotel, get us a reservation, plan a—"

"Not necessary." Her words came out muffled by the t-shirt she pulled over her head, threw toward the corner of the bed. Her bra followed a second later.

Dazed by the sight of her curves bared to his gaze completely for the first time, Nico sat back on his haunches and stared.

"You're so beautiful." He ran one hand down her side and gripped a solid handful of bountiful flesh right at the curve of her hips.

"Not too chunky?" She gave a slight shrug, the first sign of self-consciousness, of doubt, he'd ever noticed from her, not counting the few moments when she'd shown up at Seven Seas. "Mother's always trying to get me to lose weight."

From what she'd shared, her mother sounded like a real piece of work.

"Lex, you're one of the fittest people I know, can keep up with the kids and the rest of us every weekend without complaining." He slid his hand a couple inches down, to grab that spectacular ass. His other, he brought to one breast, traced its fullness from nipple outward and then drew figure eights around the base of them both. "Stunning. Built for sin and sex."

Either his words or touch—perhaps the captivated look in his eyes—reached her because she stretched her arms overhead in a sinuous motion that went straight to his dick. Did a little shimmy on his mattress and plucked at his shirt. "Way too many clothes."

He agreed and climbed off the bed to shuck his jeans, boxers, and shirt. Before returning, he stood there, staring, absorbing the realization that this voluptuous sweetheart was in his bed, reaching for him. Then touching herself when he didn't return quite soon enough.

Nico grinned, happy to watch. For the moment.

He ran one hand down his stomach to grip his erection. "I can't wait to take you. Want to make it last."

She pinched her nipples between the base of her

fingers and cupped the rest of each breast on a moan. Eyes at half-mast, she murmured, "Condoms?"

"Got us covered." Two strides took him to his chest of drawers and the unopened box of condoms he'd purchased a couple months back. Keeping an eye on her—difficult, when all he wanted to do was dispense with preliminaries and jump her yesterday—he opened the box with forced patience, pulling out a couple rubbers before kneeling on the bed.

"Glad you're back." Abandoning her breasts, she rolled to her side and kissed the outside of his thigh, reaching for his cock. Taking hold, she stroked him. "Missed you," she said on a bit of a giggle. "You were gone so very long."

"Silly girl." It'd taken him all of ninety seconds to strip, stare, and get the condoms.

"I'm glad we're not at an impersonal hotel." She released him and propped herself up on one arm, turning serious. "Though I do wish we were at the waterfall. Alone. Had the entire campground to ourselves. Wouldn't that be lovely?"

"Yeah, that'd be romantic," he surprised himself by saying. Romance? When did that enter into sex?

When you met Alexis Temptation, started fantasizing about her.

When you imagined what type of plush hotel you'd take her to. When you thought about the expensive dinner of lobster and steak you'd eat beforehand. Wondered what kind of dessert she'd want.

Yeah, that was before he knew his Lexi was a chocolate slut.

Which only made him grin. She'd devoured the two

chocolate bars he'd gotten her that first night in record time. Called it stress eating and apologized for "oinking" out. He thought it totally understandable. Cute even. But now...

Now he really wanted to make this special. For her.

"I can get us there," he said confidently. "To the waterfall."

Her brows drew into a sharp frown. "Now? You want to stop? *Huh?*"

He feathered the tension away from her forehead, placed the tips of his fingers on her bottom lip and pulled gently downward. "Close your eyes."

"Not my mouth?" Though his actions had eased the frown, her snarky humor was back.

"I'll be keeping that occupied. Eyes. Closed."

"Yes, sir." Smart aleck or not, she closed 'em. "Now what?"

He intentionally lowered his voice, made it mellow and unhurried as he tucked the two rubbers beneath the nearest pillow and stretched alongside her. "Do you hear it? The rain?"

"What? Are you kidding? It's clear—"

"Shhhh." He anchored her legs between his then brought her head up to the crook of his shoulder.

"It's late afternoon and you're on your own." While he spoke, he caressed from her shoulder, down her arm. "You've been on your own for days. You're surrounded by thick growth, dense trees. Leafy, blooming plants everywhere you turn. Their fragrant scent fills your nose as you inhale." Just as her sweet fragrance mixed with heady arousal and slammed into his gut.

He stroked over her head, past her nape—where he

gave a light squeeze—down the length of her spine, over and over. Telling his dick to slow its jets. While he took his time. Creating a picture. A memory.

Writing the scene they both wanted, something he'd learned early and often in his childhood. Though he hadn't done it in years, it all came back to him.

How to bring everything alive.

The story. The sights. The sounds.

"The rain-drenched earth saturates the wilderness surrounding you. Though lovely and peaceful at first, you're starting to become uneasy. Lonely. Ready for rescue, for human companionship."

"For kisses?"

He stopped stroking her flesh to cup her face. Plastered his lips to hers and gave her a deep one. She ate it up and whimpered for more. He licked her lips and pulled back an inch. "You haven't seen or heard another human in weeks, have about given up hope. Your supplies ran out days ago. But you kept going, kept searching. The jungle is thick, animal cries keep you company at night, guide your footsteps the opposite direction during the day."

She touched him back, eased onto his chest and rubbed her breasts against him. Nuzzled her legs against his. Lifted her ass into his palm any time it strayed near, moaned her appreciation whenever he approached the enticing sexy bits.

"Storms thundered in during the night. It's poured long and loud for hours, renewing everything. Your energy, your hope. The last light rainfall has just trickled to nothing. You come upon a hidden grotto. It's completely surrounded by vegetation, tall trees protecting a small pool. A waterfall roars down the rocks, runoff from the storms making it magnificent. Everywhere around you, leaves are soaked, smell green and fresh—"

"Green has a smell? And to think," she said softly, almost as though she were floating, her lips lighting upon his chin, dancing over his jaw. "I never knew green smelled."

"It does tonight. Just breathe it in."

"Can't. Too busy breathing you."

She raked her nails over his chest. The sting felt so good. He wanted to plunge inside her depths. Beyond ready, he took her unresisting lips and tongue in a demanding kiss, one that sent carnal urges rampaging through him.

One thrust in her honeyed sex and Nico knew he'd blow a geyser. Way too soon.

Got to make it last. Slow it down.

He released her lips and flipped her facedown beneath him, on her stomach, and then slid lower to straddle her hips. Ignoring her wiggles of impatience, he took his time mapping her gorgeous figure, sliding his hands from the feminine flare at her waist where her hips curved inward to feather up her torso. Once there, he edged his fingers downward, toward the plump fullness of her breasts. Along her buttocks, his cock jerked as his inner thighs hugged her marvelous bottom.

"You've just taken off your clothing, soaked and cold from the rains, and waded into the pool. Though chilly, your body quickly acclimates to the sensuous glide against your skin. You make your way over to the waterfall." His voice had gone raspy. "Instead of climbing out and standing under the spray, you stay in the chest-high pool, letting the rushing water pour over your hair and skin, wash off the swelter of the last few days, erase every bit of sweat and grime." He lowered his volume and whispered right into her ear. "Let its caress remind you of your needs and longings."

She angled her head to the side, toward him. "For a man? For *you*."

"That's right, baby, for me. But you don't realize it yet, so you start touching yourself. Your wet hands skate over your glistening body."

"Mmm." She squirmed beneath him, pressed her breasts into his palms while lifting her butt toward his groin. Her feet shifted restlessly. Scooting lower—because if her dynamite ass skimmed his cock again, he'd be done for—he brought his hands to her shoulders, massaged his thumbs into the muscles at her nape.

The sight of his dark-skinned, work-roughened hands on her much paler skin should've shamed him. Made him feel inferior. Brought to light the chasm of their differences.

But it didn't. It inflamed him.

Lexi shifted and he rose to his knees, letting her roll over so he could see as he claimed both breasts.

He milked the flesh, felt her nipples burn the center of his palms.

"Mmm," she murmured, first licking, then biting her lips. Her hands fluttered near his, finally settling along his upper arms. "Harder. You can squeeze me— Mmm, *yes*."

As though to encourage him, she tightened her fingers. Nails came out and gripped too.

"After relaxing in the water, you're feeling refreshed." He cleared his throat. Tried again for his best seductive voice. "Aroused. It's—"

"*Definitely* aroused," she said on a groan, skimming her nails over his shoulders up to his nape. She pulled off the band securing his hair and threaded her fingers through the length, tugging. Felt tremendous.

The expression on her face was a pure delight, conveying both hunger and the dreamy quality his tale wrapped around them both.

"You reach down your body to touch yourself." Suiting action to words, he released one breast to glide his hand between them, to her trimmed curls and beyond. His searching fingers met slick, welcoming heat. He parted the silky folds, covered his fingers in her desire and stayed to play.

His heart clanged in his chest, cock strained. How much more could he take? "A bird calls out. The leaves announce a presence just before a man appears. He—"

"Tarzan? Has he joined me?" She yanked on his hair when she asked that, the sharp tug going straight to his groin.

Nico stifled a damn giggle.

The woman wanted Tarzan? He'd give her Tarzan.

His fingers moved faster, went deeper. "He's wild, wearing nothing but a loincloth. His great muscles—" He swallowed a laugh. "Great muscles—"

Nico lost it. Totally lost it. "Lexi, I just can't do it. Can't keep going," he said in his regular voice. "Not with the Lord of the Jungle crashing the party, trying to make it a threesome. Sorry, baby. I thought I could."

Her nails dug in and held his laughing head still. She blinked up at him, looking so well pleasured it was a miracle that neither of them had come. "You don't need to," she said with lust-filled eyes gone hazy. "Don't need to do anything more. Just you. You're all I want."

Her hands released him to scrape behind her under the pillow until she pulled out a packet. Then immediately surged up to kiss him. "I can't wait. And though Tarzan was a nice surprise, it's *you* I can't wait for, Nico Tonetti. Just you."

He made fast work getting the condom in place and lying down to bring Lexi on top of him, guiding one trembling thigh over his waist, getting her positioned to his satisfaction. "I want you to control the speed, the pressure."

At least at first.

"'Kay." A light sheen of sweat covered her flushed face. Hovering over him, her muscles quivering, she took him in hand, squeezed his cock to a murmur of her own appreciation.

Music to his ears. Death to his control.

Not yet. Not yet... Stay strong.

Her fingers roved over him. As if the rubber wasn't there, he felt every nuance of her hungry exploration.

Maintain control.

He tensed, tried to ignore how good she looked, breasts swaying above him, her bent legs hugging his, her fingers—

Distraction. That's what he needed. Especially when

another cock-firming whimper came from that kiss-swollen mouth.

He clenched his eyes shut. Fisted the sheets at his sides. Wasn't it time to replace several of his tools at the shop?

But what?

In alphabetical order! *Had* to keep from blasting off before he entered her.

Impact wrench, 1¾ inch.

Pliers! He needed pliers, right?

Lexi was doing something equally distracting with her fingers, stroking his erection, yes, but also weighing his balls. Like she was comparing them or something.

Which ones? Dammit. Which pliers?

Diagonal! Needle nose!

And a new mill bastard too.

"Who's a bastard?" Lexi asked with a surprised breath. She now cupped his nutsac in one hand and pumped his cock with the other.

Lord, save him. His eyes flared open to find her watching *him*. Not his dick.

More pliers! Didn't he need new ring pliers too? Both snap and retaining?

A pry bar, a lady slipper pry—

"I'm your lady?" That was asked with extreme delight as she rubbed the head of his cock along her cleft.

Vise grip pliers. Ten inch.

Ten inch? He'd like to give her ten inches.

With a slight angle adjustment, she eased down over him. Covered him completely in her wet heat, encased him in her snug passage and clamped down like a vise, no pliers necessary.

Then she lifted off and sank back down, harder than before.

Her hands came up to push at his shoulders, thumping him back on the mattress. "I finally heard *pliers* in there somewhere. What are you doing, buster? Thinking about work?"

"Trying not to come."

"What's the fun in that?" Bracing her arms lower down on his stomach, she started riding him with a motion that sent his brain into orbit. "I've got the sexiest man on earth, full of tats and attitude, telling me I'm his lady? You can bet I'm ready to come. All weekend long."

She leaned over and bit his bottom lip. Not too hard, just enough to let him know he didn't need to treat her like porcelain.

So noted. He started rocking his hips, ready to get the friction on.

When he released the sheet to reach down and grab both sides of her ass, just to hold her close, she went wild, started swinging her hips with abandon.

Oh yeah, her body was incredible, milking him deeper as a fast orgasm shook through her. Every muscle turned rigid, her nails might've pierced the skin on his stomach. She gave a tiny squeak. Flopped forward and bit the skin just below his ear.

Then she turned molten, fairly melted right over him. Took a deep breath, kissed his abused ear. And thanked him, by God.

"Oh." It was the breathiest syllable on record.

Breathiest "Oh, thank you. That was lovely. I needed that" he'd ever heard.

He wasn't finished, not by a long shot. "Ready for more?"

Please, be ready for more.

"OH, Nico, that was so very beautiful, what you did." After the first *man*-made orgasm she'd had in ages, part of Lexi wanted nothing more than to roll over, snuggle in, and sleep for a week.

The rest of her was raring for more. More sex. More orgasms. More Nico.

Though her lady bits felt momentarily replete, it wouldn't last.

Not with the scene he'd created in her mind, his sexy voice drawing vivid images of them, naked, in a jungle setting. Talk about a fantasy come to life.

Not with the discernible scent of her arousal permeating the air, the taste of Nico flavoring her tongue, which thirsted for him again.

"Beautiful?" he asked on a low growl. "The stupendous sex?"

"That too, but I'm talking about what came before. The waterfall. The way you took me there with your words."

"Yeah. My dad was a mean motherfucker. I got used to taking myself where I needed to go when he was on a tear."

His voice was rough, either with his remarkable restraint and self-denial—silly man; didn't he know orgasms were for achieving, not denying?—or because she'd inadvertently reminded him of the childhood he rarely mentioned.

She squeezed his still thick, unspent cock with her inner muscles, slightly embarrassed at how hard she'd just come, at how much dampness she felt between them.

But his hands just clenched her ass, gave a swift jiggle to the flesh and a single swat. "Don't go feeling sorry for me," he said. "Not when I've got a handful of lush Lexi in my arms."

"Good. Because it's your turn." She squeezed him twice more, making her meaning crystal clear. "Do with me what you will."

"Are you sure, Renegade? Because I'm ready to conquer. Can't wait much longer."

"Wonderful." He was so amazingly wonderful. *Lush Lexi?* "After that workout? I'm more than ready to surrender."

As though she'd released a beast from its cage, he eased her off him, ignored her surprised whimper and flattened her on her back. He palmed her breasts and kneaded. Made sure her nipples were erect before scooting lower to take one in his mouth.

He sucked hard and one hand went between her legs. In contrast to the fierce suction of his mouth, his fingers were tender, but fast. Searching through her swollen, sensitive folds until he zeroed in on her clit.

A satisfied grunt came from him as he switched to her other breast, kissing and sucking, until leaving it, too, hard, wet, and achy as he slid down her body and placed his lips at the top of her slit. Tonguing the flesh and turning her to lava.

Restless, eager for everything, she widened her thighs, propped the soles of her feet on his upper back and rubbed. Gripped his hair and pulled, loving the feel of the long, silky strands.

Her breasts were on fire. Loins too. His wet kisses joining her release and arousing her right back to the pinnacle. The muscles in her arms tightened, fingers clamped on his head as her pelvis arched against his mouth. That sexy, decadent facial hair doing all sorts of wicked, wonderful things between her legs.

A short cry escaped. He turned to the side and kissed her inner thigh. "Again, Lexi. Let me hear you, baby."

The sun had started to set, his bedroom growing dim. Voices passed by the window, heralding the arrival of some of his neighbors. But inside their private oasis, Lexi was ready to ease her own self-imposed restraint. She'd never felt this wanton, this decadent before. Couldn't wait to come again.

His lips fastened around her clit, tongue flickered over the bud despite her rocking hips. She released his hair to hold her breasts, massaging, pinching. Her lower body pistoned against his face. "Nico," she breathed. "Come back. Want your kisses. You. Back inside—"

He forged one finger past her tight tissues and hauled upward, plunging his tongue in her mouth the same moment he fit his cock to her entrance. Both tongue and dick thrust deep. Satisfied. Plundered, aroused. Satisfied again.

Sucking on his tongue, her hands once again gripping his scalp, Lexi met every fierce thrust he granted her with and begged for more. All at once everything seized. Tightened. Coiled. Her body felt more alive than ever. She couldn't breathe. Couldn't move. Froze.

Then released.

The orgasm flooded her loins, rippled through her muscles, bathed every inch of her body in such replete relief that she glued her mouth to his shoulder to muffle her squeal. Four seconds later, every muscle sighed in bliss.

"Oh yeah, baby. Good girl." As though freed, Nico's motions lost any semblance of fluidity. He became abrupt, jerky against her, thrust hard and fast. Quick. Twice more. Grunted against her lips. Then relaxed, sank into her, hugged her to him and rolled over, keeping her close and arranging her legs over his, her head tucked partially on his shoulder, the rest on the pillow behind them. "Man, I needed that."

He stuffed the pillow more firmly beneath her head. "All weekend, you said? I can handle that."

Something Old - Saturday and Beyond

ONCE AGAIN NICO SURPRISED HER, this time Saturday midmorning when he offered to follow her to the funeral home after taking her by Seven Seas to retrieve her car.

He'd already waited, patiently, while she'd ducked into the nearest department store and found a couple casual outfits.

"You do *not* have to tagalong and look at caskets with me." She didn't want to do it either but thought having one or two picked out, along with making any other preliminary decisions, might help smooth things in the coming days.

Nico caught her fingers, stopping their nervous fretting over her car keys. The rest of the automotive shop was quiet today, the garage closed for the weekend.

"Hey." He slipped one hand in a back pocket of the capris she'd bought and tugged her close. "We agreed to spend the weekend together. That means whatever you need, so I'm trailing you there." The funeral home was only a few miles away, one of the reasons she'd thought to stop by. "I can go in with you or wait outside, your choice."

He lowered his face to the side of hers, inhaled and kissed right by her ear, sending pleasurable little tingles streaking down her neck. "I figured after we drop your car off at my place, I could take you to catch a movie. Or maybe to the zoo? Any interest in either?"

It could've been the Texas heat that brought a wave of warmth rolling through her, but Lexi knew it was his thoughtfulness. "I'd love to go to the zoo. Haven't been in years."

Not since she was five and Phil wanted to celebrate his ninth birthday among the primates, howling and screeching and swinging his arms, acting like a monkey for two days until Mother finally agreed he could have his party there.

"What's that secret smile about?" Nico nudged the side of her mouth.

Wow. This was the first time she'd thought of Phil in several days with gladness in her heart instead of agony. It was a wonderful realization. One she couldn't wait to share with Nico, along with the Monkey Memory of her goofy brother. "I'll tell you at the zoo. I'd love to go. As long as you take me by the bats if we're there for feeding time. My dad did and I got a kick out of watching them slurp blood."

Nico laughed. "Well, you're just full of surprises."

"Good ones, I hope."

"Only. Never knew you were the bloodthirsty type. It's kind of a turn-on."

With his words and presence lifting her spirits, they

drove to the funeral home, took care of somber business, and then they made a day of it, together.

LATER THAT EVENING, after Nico cherished her with more of his spectacular brand of loving, Lexi explored his body, intent on cataloguing every one of his eighteen tattoos.

When she paused at the faded switchblade on his forearm, he offered, "My dad took me to get that one when I was thirteen, said we would always remember each other whenever we saw it."

"He got one too? The same design?"

"Nah. Already had his. Got it with his old man. I think he saw it as a rite of passage of sorts."

She inspected several others until she reached the close-up of an old guy with shaggy hair and a mustache on Nico's right shoulder blade. A guy who didn't look Hispanic or Italian at all. "Is this your grandfather?"

He chuckled. "Not even close. Try again."

Not close, huh? So not an uncle either. "Mmm, Einstein?"

His whole body shook when Nico laughed. "Nope. But I like that guess better. It's Mark Twain. *Huck Finn* was my favorite book when I was young. Might still be. Just haven't read it in a while."

Which told her a lot about him. More than he probably realized:

1) He liked to dream.

2) Likely used reading to escape a troubled home life.

3) He definitely related to the independent rule breaker.

4) He had great taste in literature.

After a cursory look at them all, she returned to the beautifully rendered cougar face on one upper arm. "This one is phenomenal." Lexi brushed her fingers over such intricate details, the design looked more like a 3-D photograph than a drawing. "The mountain lion."

"Yeah. I found a new artist about the time I decided on that one. They were my mom's favorite animal. Didn't realize until after she died, I'd subconsciously gotten it for that very reason."

She was quiet for a while, just savoring the beauty of his naked, muscular form sprawled out facedown on the bed, arms crossed beneath his turned head, all that gorgeous dark skin decorated with old scars and deliberate marks, waiting for her to touch, to trace, her curiosity to rouse.

"Tell me about these?" She ran her fingers over a few oriental characters down the side of his torso. "What do they mean?"

Nico groaned and rolled over, capturing her wandering fingers and hauling her unresisting form on top of him. "No clue whether it's accurate or not, but supposedly 'Peace. Protection. Laughter.' Three things my mom told me to remember." He sighed, as though debating how much to divulge. "Right before she died, she said, 'Nic, I want peace and protection for you the rest of your days. Listen to Mr. Cooney. Don't ever forget to laugh.'"

"What about love?" Lexi couldn't stop herself from asking.

"She didn't believe in it."

Oh.

Do you?

"Said the others were what mattered. What I could count on. She also told me to stop getting so many damn tats, that my skin was starting to look like a pincushion."

Lexi knew from one of the rare personal conversations she'd had with him at the campground that his mom had died a few years back, living quite a bit longer than originally predicted. Long enough, he'd told her, to see him finally get his shit together, hold down a job and distance himself from the crowd he'd run with as a kid.

Keeping her voice light, she asked, "What about you? Her little boy? Didn't she love you?"

"Oh yeah. To the grave, making sacrifices she probably shouldn't have." His voice told her so much more than the brief words. Of shielding and protecting. What kind of monster had his father been? He never talked about the man, other than to say *in jail* and *what the bastard deserved.*

"It was romantic love she didn't believe in. What she — L-Lex." Nico—*almost*—giggled. "What the hell are you doing?"

Running her tongue over the Laughter symbol. "Hoping it tickles."

He chuckled as she dragged her tongue up toward the sensitive skin below his arm. "It does."

Good. Wonderful. She'd rather him laugh any day than hear the residue of pain in his memories. Leaving the topic of love, believed in or otherwise—who wanted to ruin the magical thing they were just getting started?—Lexi stopped licking to ask, "And have you? Gotten any more?"

"Tats? Not since then. It's been about four years now. Haven't felt the urge." He shifted beneath her, pulling her more snuggly into his embrace. "It'd take something pretty big, I think, to get me back in the chair. I'm pleased enough with what I got."

As Lexi's legs had slid to the side to straddle his thighs, as the solid erection that'd grown between them the last few moments had drawn a significant portion of her interest, she felt confident saying, "Yeah. I'm pretty pleased with what you got too."

❦

ONCE THE SUN finished its descent, Nico shifted against her. "You sleepy?"

She felt the soft words beneath her ear more than heard them. In a weird twist, instead of sex with him knocking her out, she came alive—especially her brain.

Currently on overdrive. Trying to memorize every second.

Pressed against his naked length, enjoying the afterglow and wondering how long they could make it last. She answered at regular volume. "Not really."

"Hungry?"

"Unfortunately, yeah. I'd rather not move"—wasn't sure if she *ever* wanted to move—"but I'm ready for some real food, not junk."

He disengaged and rolled off the bed with a groan. "I'll figure something out. Hang tight."

"I'll meet you in the kitchen," she called after his retreating back as he headed to the bathroom, not expecting him to bring her snacks in bed.

Who wanted to deal with crumbs?

After snuggling back into another well-worn Ramones t-shirt, which hung down long enough she decided to be brazen and skip panties, she made her way to the refrigerator, to see what might be on tap.

She'd just finished transferring sandwich makings to the counter when he came up behind her, pulling her tight against his chest. "Tarzan, Lex? Really?"

She gave a silent chuckle, too warmed by his nearness, too replete by his lovemaking to take offense at the criticism in his tone. "Yep."

"*He*'s your girlhood crush?"

The cool air from the open refrigerator blasted over her flushed face while Nico's presence scorched her backside, made her hungry for him all over again. Who needed food?

"What can I say?" She leaned back to close the refrigerator, then turned in his arms, looping hers over his neck. "The way he runs barefoot through the jungle, wrestles those alligators? So very masculine. Super sexy. Don't you think? And why tease me about it now?" He hadn't said a disparaging word all day.

"Crocs."

"What?"

"They're crocodiles," he explained neutrally, giving her lips a quick, hard kiss before releasing her and reaching into a cabinet for a couple plates. "Crocodiles in Africa; alligators in America."

"How do you know so much?" It wasn't the first time he'd surprised her with some random tidbit.

"Books. Coon's library. He introduced me to the classics and I never looked back." So that's where he'd gotten such a broad vocabulary, vast array of knowledge about odd topics. "And I was cutting you some slack; didn't want to run you off."

As if that could happen.

He picked up the package of lunch meat and flipped it over, checking the date. "Might be okay, but I've got something better." He dipped into the fridge and pulled out a foil-covered plate, one she hadn't noticed hiding behind a six-pack. "Grilled chicken from a couple nights ago. This'll make a much better sandwich."

"Smells great. Just one sandwich for you?" At his nod, she put two pieces of bread on his plate, one on hers, and then she grabbed the mayonnaise and started slathering.

Nico sliced a block of cheese and followed right behind, adding the thin slices on top and picking up the thread. "Hell, the old relic won't use an e-reader no matter how many times I gift him one—"

"Relic? Mr. Coondog? He's not that old." At the auto shop, she'd seen a framed picture of several men wearing camo who looked to be in their early twenties. "What? Forty-five? Fifty?"

"*Gah.* At least."

She gave him a hip butt, reaching for the slices of cucumber as he created them, adding those to the sandwich pile. "I saw the photo yesterday. The one on his desk." Must've been why one of the men looked familiar —Mr. Coondog, younger. "He was in the Army?"

"Yep, that's him and a few of the guys he served with. Tomato?"

"Please." She'd met the shop owner Thursday as they were leaving Seven Seas, when she'd given him her car keys. "Beneath the beard, he's a good-looking guy."

"Coondog? That old coot?"

"My dad's in his mid-fifties. Despite the health trouble, I don't consider him old. Just old*er*." She'd always thought her dad wasn't half bad in the appearance department. He kept himself trim, hadn't gone all soft like a lot of men his age. Plus he still had a full head of hair. Granted, it was completely gray and short, unlike Mr. Coondog's light brown long ponytail, but other than that, she saw some similarities.

"The same with your Mr. Coondog," she added, topping off his mayo-grilled chicken-cheese-cucumber-tomato creation with the second slice of bread and hers with two shakes of salt.

"You can skip the 'mister'. He'd tell you that if he heard you. I met Coon when I was fourteen. He seemed ancient to me then. But yeah, now that you mention it, I figure he was only in his thirties."

"Guess it's all that hard living," she quipped, having not a clue about the man's past.

The sandwich looked terrific. Nico nodded, slicing his on the diagonal, before presenting her with the knife and a fresh fork and gesturing toward the bar. "That or all the tobacco. Used to smoke it. Coon did. Like a steam locomotive."

"That'll give anyone wrinkles." It sure had her uncle, a four-pack-a-day man, right till the end.

"Even though he switched to chewing a few years

back, gave up cigarettes, the books I borrow on occasion still smell like smoke."

Ripping off a paper towel for them each, she joined him, climbing onto the barstool and sneaking a cucumber slice. "Still borrow?" she asked, swallowing. "Even with your e-reader? So he's got a lot?"

Nico whistled. "He's got wall-to-wall, floor-to-ceiling bookshelves in three rooms. The man likes his literary escapes. Used to reward me for good grades. Hell, for just not cutting class, with a loan of Rudyard Kipling or Edgar Rice Burroughs. Ian Fleming when I got a bit older and expressed an interest."

"Kipling. *The Man Who Would Be King*? Do I have that right?"

"You do." He spoke around a big bite, closing his eyes a moment before grinning at her. "Not sure if it's the food or the company, but best sandwich I can remember."

The compliment made her blush. That or the fact she was sitting on his barstool without underwear. "Great movie. I've only seen it once but really liked it. Haven't read the book."

"Haven't seen the film."

She nearly dropped her fork. "Get out of town. Sean Connery and Michael Caine. It's a classic. And you haven't seen it? *Tsk-tsk*." The chicken was grilled to perfection, even straight from the fridge. She couldn't remember another meal she'd enjoyed more. "So back to books. Authors. Tell me your favorites."

"Twain, you know."

"Um-mmm." Given the tat on his back, she certainly did.

"I really like H. Rider Haggard. He's got some great ones." Nico had polished off his sandwich before she'd eaten half of hers. He leaned back, propped one bare foot on her barstool, looking like there was nowhere else he wanted to be. "An early favorite was *King Solomon's Mines*. That—"

"I love that movie!" she burst out, delighted. "It's one of my all-time favorites. The old one, with Stewart Granger and Deborah Kerr, not that newer piece of fluff from the eighties."

"Haven't seen it."

"Which one?"

"Neither."

"You're kidding." It was a little unnerving, still eating while he just sat there, watching. A little arousing too.

"Nope. But I'd be happy to watch it with you tomorrow if we can dial it up from somewhere."

"It's a date, then." Her insides filled with a peculiar warmth, the ease of being with him a balm to her recently overstressed soul.

"Uh-huh. You about finished?"

She'd just placed the silverware next to the last couple of uneaten bites. Wiping her mouth, she hid the food with her paper towel as her mother had taught her and nodded.

"You sure?" His head tilted as though surprised she'd left some.

"Oh. I should've asked first." She whipped the paper towel off. "Did you want the rest?"

"Nuh-uh." Without warning, he lunged for her like a football tackle, scooped her up into his arms and slung her over his shoulder. "I'm after dessert."

———————◖◗———————

"HALLOWEEN," she mused some time before they both drifted off.

"What about it?" Stretched out behind her, his arm slung over her waist, his voice was a low rumble against her ear.

Granted, it had been a couple weeks back, so she'd have to wait nearly a year. Who knew if they'd still be talking, dating? "Oh, just thinking about the holiday. About costumes. About you."

He started to chuckle. "Renegade, sure as shit, I am *not* dressing as Tarzan for Halloween."

She wiggled her ass and settled in, super happy with that response. Because he hadn't said no to spending the future holiday with her. "A girl can dream, can't she?"

He swatted her hip. "Ha-ha," he murmured on a drowsy chuckle, hugging her closer. "Sleep now, funny girl."

———————◖◗———————

SUNDAY MORNING KNOCKED Lexi for a loop.

Nico pulled a box of Blueberry Pop-Tarts out of the pantry. A simple thing, Blueberry Pop-Tarts.

Phil's favorite growing up.

That and— "Brown S-Sugar Cin-Cinna—"

Cinnamon, she tried to tell Nico. But the words blubbered out instead, nonsense syllables that caused him to look at her sharply.

She pointed to the foil wrapper in his hand and

sobbed, "Ph-Phil." She swallowed, tried a watery smile. "He liked Blu-Blueberry and—" And her dear brother would never eat another Pop-Tart. Never grab the box out of her hand. Never snatch half of one off her plate. Ever.

Never taste sugar on his tongue. Have his own family. Or hug her again.

She lost it. Utterly and completely lost it. The sight of that shiny silver wrapper, evil to its core, sent her into instant and uncontrollable weeping.

Without hesitation, Nico dropped the package and lunged toward her. He hugged her tight. Let her heave wracking sobs against him, curse the universe and God, and cry till she could hardly breathe.

Whatever words he murmured in his strong, deep voice didn't reach her but his tranquil presence did. The soothing strokes of his arms and hands across her shoulders and down her back, nothing sexual in the least, just pure, needed comfort.

His smell and strength, seeping slowly into her being with every shaky inhale that shuddered into her lungs.

Though the emotional tempest passed more quickly than the ones before, it still left her feeling totally drained.

"When will it stop?" she asked, breath hitching. "When will some little thing stop setting me off?"

He cradled her head, running his fingers through her thick hair, tugging lightly. "Eventually, and I'm speaking from my experience here, with my mom. Eventually you'll see that shiny Pop-Tart wrapper and smile. Be happy that something reminded you of the wonderful person your brother was when you least expected it. But for a while now, and don't beat yourself up over how long, could be a month, a week or year, for a while..." His voice went rough with either remembered or renewed grief. "It'll hit you hard. From out of nowhere. Take you to your knees."

Lexi in turn hugged him now, comforted him.

Amazing how pain shared truly was halved. How the near silent encouragement his presence gave brought more solace to her than the thought of anything, save her brother's miraculous return.

After a few still, self-aware moments, she murmured, "You've been fabulous. I couldn't ask for any more. But part of me wishes I hadn't burdened you with this."

After crying buckets Thursday and Friday, Saturday's calm had seemed well deserved. So this morning's upheaval felt like a betrayal. A punishment for enjoying herself yesterday when Phil wasn't at the forefront of every thought. "With *me*, while I've been so weepy, so needy. Wished that I'd waited, hadn't ambushed you at work, that—"

Nico shook her once, firmed his arms across her back, kept her close against his chest. "Enough of that. No more worrying about silly stuff that doesn't matter. I'm glad you came. Glad I could help you through this."

"Really?"

"Definitely. Saves me the trouble of tracking you down to ask you out."

"Yeah, right." Even after the sex—the fabulous, tremendous, mind- and body-blowing sex—part of her still doubted. "If you wanted to, really wanted to, you would've done so before now."

"That's not the whole story."

Pulling back, she looked up at him. He wiped his thumbs beneath her eyes, erasing any remaining moisture, and a horrible thought punched into Lexi's heart. "Oh shit. You're taken." Why hadn't she thought of that before? Of course he was. He was too awesome not to be taken. "Seeing someone."

"No. Not at all." A half grin quirked his lips. "Let's rephrase. If I was *brave* enough, I would've asked for your number, several times over by now."

"Brave?"

She got the feeling if he could've hid his expression behind his goatee, he would have. "As in too proud to risk you turning me down. Laughing in my face."

"That's stupid. As if I'd ever."

"Yeah. Forgive me?"

"It depends. Are you over being stupid?"

"Yes, ma'am. I'd like to go out, date you. Away from the campground. Even away from my bed," a wink accompanied that one. "In real life, Alexis Temptation. You, me, *together*. See where it leads. Do you want to do this?"

Alexis *Temptation*? The new nickname nearly made her giddy. "I do. Are you? Absolutely positive?"

"Hell, Lex. You've seen where I work. Where I live." He shrugged, as if that should explain everything.

"And I haven't run yet."

"No, you haven't," he mused. Nico squeezed her shoulder once, then he trailed his hand down to snag hers. He stepped back on one foot to look around at his modest place. "Are you kidding me? I finally have you, in my arms, in my *home*. You think I'm stupid enough to give that up? Give me some credit, woman."

"Hell yes, you want to date me." She'd never been more sure of anything.

"Damn straight. For as long as we can make it last."

Which sounded great to her.

⸺⸺◦⸺⸺

LEXI CAME AWAKE on a sigh and a stretch.

It was Sunday night. Actually Monday morning, a quick glance at the clock showing nearly 3:00 a.m.

She sank into Nico's bed, rolled over and hugged the extra pillow, surrounded by his presence. But not by him.

When she went to bed, he'd been glued to his gaming console. After a thorough kiss and gentle swat on the bottom, he'd bid her good night, promising to join her when he got sleepy.

Baloney. So where was he?

Scenes from the last few days filtered through her sleep-hazed mind. Thursday night, dutifully forcing herself to eat through constant thoughts of Phil's death. Nevertheless, managing to get down some of the tacos and pepperoni pizza, smiling at the combination when Nico explained how *tacoroni* was considered gourmet cuisine, something coined by Brett.

Sitting in his lap on the big lounger, secure against his chest late into the night, alternatively snoozing and trying not to weep. Crying anyway. Wet, wrenching sobs that drenched his shirt and wore her plumb out.

Friday, glorious Friday and the evening hours that changed everything between them.

Saturday, when she'd explored his bookshelf a little closer, noticed that of the few books he had on display, about half were paperbacks from the last few years; the others were vintage hardbacks. She hadn't opened them, to check for dates or editions, but it wouldn't surprise her if he had a couple near original printings. Valued possessions, for sure.

Sunday afternoon, how they'd streamed their very own double feature, *King Solomon's Mines* and one of the early Johnny Weissmuller's Tarzan movies.

"See?" Lexi had poked his leg with her toes when Johnny, a.k.a. Tarzan, let out his patented jungle yodel. "So sexy, isn't it?"

Nico made a grunt of disagreement.

"Calling his mate." Lexi insisted. "What's not to love about that?"

Nico snorted. "Pretty sure he's calling elephants, Lex."

"Oh. Don't go bursting my bubble, bucko." She hit pause and turned to him.

They'd made a pallet on his living room floor, popcorn and brewskis on his side; the remotes and chocolate on hers. "I was young when I watched these old black-and-white movies the first time. I always thought he was calling his love."

He angled toward her. "Did you watch with your dad? Or Phil?"

"With my mom, actually." She saw the exaggerated astonishment on his face and gave him a shove. "See? I am full of surprises. Maybe that's why the memory seems so vivid, because I was doing something really special with her. A bad dream or something woke me one night and I couldn't get back to sleep.

"She tiptoed me downstairs and put in the DVD, said it was what she watched with her dad when she couldn't sleep. After that, *boom*. I heart Tarzan forever."

He'd come closer and nipped her chin, his beer-scented breath wafting over her like ambrosia. Seconds later, his lips nudged hers as he hauled her beneath him...

They never did finish the second movie.

Their entire weekend had been interspersed with sexy interludes; time out of time as she marveled at how well the two of them got on.

So where was he? Why hadn't he joined her tonight? Her last night with him, until who knew how long, given her parents arrival in just a few hours. The memorial and funeral services she'd be planning. The mother she'd no doubt be consoling.

Desperate to eke pleasure out of every remaining moment, Lexi crawled out of bed, brushed her teeth, and went in search of her man.

She found him on the small concrete balcony, made private by the seven-foot fence around it, sitting in a wooden Adirondack chair. More like lounging, beer bottle in one hand, phone facedown on the arm of the chair beneath the other, his long legs stretched out in front.

"Nic?" She crossed out to him, sliding the glass door shut behind her. Why was he out here in the dark? "Missed you when I woke."

He set the beer down off to the side and pulled her

into his lap. "Figured your body needed a rest. Must be sore. I took you pretty hard yesterday."

Several times.

He kept his voice just above a whisper. She followed suit. "I like it."

And she did. Tender in places she rarely noticed, the sensitive tissues, roused and swollen by his thorough lovemaking the last day and a half, made her feel more like a woman, a valued one at that, than she'd ever felt in her life.

She snuggled against him, delighted in the flex of his strong thighs and the renewed awareness that shot through her. "Like how every step I take reminds me that we're lovers now."

He grunted but she could hear the satisfied sound to it.

She angled her head to kiss the underside of his jaw, brought up one hand to feather fingers over his facial hair. "I've been thinking."

"Uh-oh."

She gave the soft hair of his goatee a yank. "None of that now. I want to ask you something, but I need you to know it's okay to say *no*. I mean, I'm expecting you to say no but if I don't at least ask, I'll always wonder if—"

"Ask away."

"Really. It's okay. I'm not expecting a yes. Not even sure..."

NICO TENSED. He hadn't heard Sweet Lex natter on so since the first time they met out by her daddy's tank of a car. What had her so anxious?

She was leaving in a few hours, going home.

It bothered him, how much he didn't want her to. How quickly and seamlessly she'd fit into his life. His ordinary, blue-collar, former-criminal life. Not a fit he would've predicted.

One he now feared losing. What if a return home reminded her—

Screw it.

And that's why he'd been out here. On his pissant, bottom-floor "balcony" drinking by moonlight and parking lights.

Savoring the stillness. The satisfaction of knowing Lexi was in his home. *His bed.*

While his thoughts tumbled over themselves, she prattled on, practically talking herself hoarse. "I mean, I should just forget it but I can't seem—"

"Lexi. Stop." Just like that, she did. "Kiss me. Now."

Whether she responded to the tone or the command itself, he didn't know. But she obeyed. Turned her lips to his and began one of those deep, open-mouthed kisses he so loved.

When she pulled back too soon, he ordered, "Again."

Lips and tongue met, stroked, comforted, and aroused. Just when her lower half started getting squirmy atop his thighs, he figured he'd distracted her enough. For sure he'd distracted his body. But not his mind. Just what had her so nervous?

He wound one hand in her long hair and gently angled her head till he caught the shimmer of her gaze. "What is it, Ren?"

He purposefully kept his voice hard, didn't let any of

the tenderness or affection he felt soften his tone or expression. "What do you want to ask me?"

"Phil. His funeral. Will you come?"

Nico gave a low whistle. Of all the things he might've guessed, *that* wouldn't have been on the list.

"I knew it, you know," she said quietly. "Knew it deep down. He's been gone for a while now, and I sensed it. But that hasn't stopped me from thinking about him or pretending that he would read my letters when he got back. So I kept writing."

Nico nodded for her to continue. At least she was speaking calmly now, not with the panicked edge before the kiss.

"He would've liked you, I think—"

"Me?"

"Yes, *you*. Phil loved video games as a kid, was an avid Scout. Tent camping and all that. He teased me because I wouldn't consider sleeping on the ground. With bugs. And no shower." Her body shuddered at the thought. "I regret that now, not building those memories with him while I had the chance."

Her slight fist knocked twice on his collarbone. "See what all he put up with when I was younger? So yeah, I'm sure of it. You'd pass muster. You're a no-BS kind of guy. What you see is what you get." She stroked one hand over his cheek. "Except for the soft side you keep hidden."

"Sure you're all right?" Nico used his grip on her hair to turn her head and pretend he was looking for an injury.

"I'm serious. You're a likable guy. Phil would've absolutely approved."

Of what? Them?

Lexi pleaded with her glittering eyes if not her voice. "So will you come?"

Damn. She was serious.

His head spun with all the reasons why he should give her a hearty *hell no* and be done with it.

He didn't fit with her kind.

He wouldn't be welcome.

No matter what *she* thought Phil would've thought, Nico knew her parents certainly wouldn't approve.

He'd be leaving Coon shorthanded for the second time in as many weeks.

Double damn—he'd have to buy a suit.

"Won't that cause all sorts of problems for you?" he asked neutrally, giving no hint to the turmoil of his thoughts. "With your parents?"

"Their heads are going to be so wrapped up in Phil, they'll hardly notice which friends I've invited to the funeral. I know it's asking a lot, but I just... Feel..." She shrugged against him. "For some reason, I feel stronger when I'm near you. Does that make any sense? At all?"

Made scary-perfect sense to him. Because she made him feel nearly invincible.

Unwilling to face the uncertainty in her gaze a second more, he gave her a hard kiss. "You got it, Renegade. I'll be there."

And he would, no matter how uncomfortable it might make him, how judged he might feel. She'd crossed over into his world time and again. It was only fair he returned the favor—and crossed into hers.

SEVENTEEN

Something Old - Eight months ago

"ALEXIS, we both know it's nothing more than a phase." The lecturing tone employed by Marla Templeton went from indulgent to derisive. "A raunchy fling. Because you needed to lash out when Phil—"

Lexi stiffened the muscles in her legs, determined to stand strong until this was over. Leaving the kitchen would only earn her a lecture for running away on top of the one she was currently enduring. Their cook had smartly exited with a look of apology to Lexi when her employer had started in on her only daughter.

Lexi had mouthed *Go*; no sense in both their appetites being ruined. Her hands fisted on the granite island—good thing the giant block was between them. It was the only thing keeping her from slugging her mother at the moment.

"When Phil..." Mother leaned over a simmering pot on the stove to sniff. She straightened, her attention back on Lexi, fluttering her fingers. "When Phil— Well, you know."

Mother refused to say it: died. When Lexi's brother died.

"But it's been two years, Alexis. *Two years!* If your father won't put a stop to it, I will."

"A stop?" The topic of conversation was expected to arrive any minute for his first überformal sit-down dinner with her family. Why did Mother want to criticize and complain now? "You're being unreasonable."

"So says the daughter enamored with a fellow not fit to de-weed my flowerpots. Not fit to polish your father's shoes."

"Mother! That's—" *Just shit!* "Completely out of line. Totally unjustified." If only her father hadn't been stuck at the airport in Dallas, his flight delayed due to afternoon thunderstorms. "You wouldn't speak like that if Dad was here. Take it back."

Marla was totally unaffected by Lexi's growing anger. "Now, dear, you'll soon see I'm right. You'll forget about him soon enough." She waved her hand as though brushing off a pesky fly. "It's exactly like you and college. You change men like you do majors."

Foul! "That's not true. I may have had a lot of trouble *deciding* on a major but I've never been fickle when it comes to guys. Never."

An Undecided major only got her so far. When her advisor insisted she choose something, she had. First Business, then Education. She'd considered switching to pre-med after her dad's surgery, but given how Calli had to hold her hand through biology and she'd barely scraped out a C-, it was back to Business.

Dissection was so not her thing. Except when it came to dissecting fish guts.

Yeah. She smiled inwardly. It was easy enough to clean fish when a girl is trying to impress her guy. Not so much a sixty-year-old professor with a toupee and bad teeth.

"Just look at you." Hands now on her hips, Marla prepared for battle. "It's been *years*, Alexis, and you're hardly any closer to that useless degree—"

"It won't be useless." It wouldn't! She'd decided to double major in Psychology and Cognitive Behavior, and had stuck with it. Lexi had finally identified her life's passion working with the kids, first as a Big Sister, then at the campground. She wanted to make a difference. Help others.

But first she had to help herself. "Mother! That's enough. No more negative comments. *None*."

"Once you put a stop to things, tell your grease monkey to go back to the jungle—"

"I won't," Lexi said with fierce determination. "I love him. L-O-V-E! Nico's good for me. He makes me—"

"Pah. Love is a luxury people such as us cannot afford." She huffed so hard, Lexi felt the angry breath halfway across the kitchen. "Now I'll put up with your grease gorilla tonight. I'll *try* to be civil. But afterward, you break things off with him or—"

Or whatever.

Lexi tuned her out. Too angry to respond. *How dare she?*

She'd seen her mother's faults, had lived with them long enough, but this—

Rigid with outrage, Lexi stayed silent, hoping Mommy Dearest would hurry up and finish. Only she didn't. Just kept going, citing all the reasons why Nico was the worst possible influence her daughter could dally with. Why he wasn't up to par. Sufficiently educated. Moneyed enough for their kind. On and on and on, till nausea encompassed Lexi like a suffocating blanket of puke.

She was going to be sick.

Sick at heart for days, to realize that her mother could spout this sort of uncalled-for venom. This absolute prejudiced thinking against another decent, wonderful human being.

She wished she could be sick all over her parent.

"Or what, Mother?" Fed up to the rooftop, Lexi exploded. Slapped her open palms on the granite and leaned in. "You already lost one child! Do you really want to lose another? Because that's what's going to happen if you force us apart. I'll never forgive you. *Never!* I don't know what the future holds. Nico and I might break up tomorrow, or we might marry and have 2.4 children, a cat, and matching motorcycles. Be deliriously happy!"

"Alexis, dear," the socially blind woman said with a dainty snort and artificial smile. "Don't be droll."

"Are you *listening* to yourself?" Lexi rounded the island and got up in her mother's face for the first time in her life, utterly furious with the woman who birthed her. "The unjustified bigotry you're spewing. If I didn't know Phil's death had influenced what you're saying, I'd be tempted to disown you. You have no right! I repeat, absolutely *no* right to dictate my life like this."

Her mother's serene, insincere smile widened. "Alexis, darling. I have every right. Who pays the bills? Keeps your credit cards and bank account flush?"

Sheer red colored Lexi's existence. An absolute haze that she wanted to punch through so she could shake her mother by the neck and make her understand that money wasn't everything to everybody. It nearly destroyed her, seeing how superficial and financially blinded her parent had become. How did Dad put up with this crap?

She never heard the front door open, nor close.

Never heard Nico's quiet entrance or silent exit.

All she knew was that by the time she felt in control enough to spin on her overpriced pair of Versace pumps and walk as calmly as she could from the room, hoping to seek out Nico before he encountered his bitchy hostess, he was gone.

Gone from the house.

And she learned soon after, gone from her life.

"NICO, I'm sorry for anything and everything you might have overheard before dinner last night. Please call me back. Nothing changed how I feel about you. I pr-promise." She took a breath to steady her voice. "I apologize for my mother. She's not in her right mind but that's no excuse. Lately that woman makes me so mad—"

When Lexi heard herself yelling, she lowered the phone and silently disconnected the call.

It was the third message she'd left. Each one longer and more panicked than the last.

Not that she expected him to answer her instantly. Nico had a life away from their near constant dating.

But they'd spent so much time together at his place lately, they'd been joking about her moving in.

Joking aside, Lexi didn't see herself as "living" with a guy. Eventually, she wanted a family—kids, a home of her own.

Her mother's hit about the credit cards had scored. Lexi might've been raised to marry well, take care of a husband—and have him take care of her. But that wasn't who she wanted to be.

Time to move out of the house—on her own. Support herself for a while before jumping in bed full-time with a man, husband or not.

Over the course of the next week, in between apartment hunting and job interviews for something part-time that would fit with her class schedule, she stopped by the auto shop twice, his apartment three times, and left six more messages. He was never available. Never there.

In the end, it might have been easier if he'd ignored her forever.

But he didn't. He faced her. He showed up at the country club one cloudy Friday, shortly before she and her dad were about to tee off. Strode right into the dining room where they were finishing lunch, wearing his sleeveless denim shirt, tattoos blazing in all their glory. Marched right up to her table, apologized to her dad for interrupting and asked her for a word.

Pleasure and nervous anticipation stalled in her chest as she managed to finish chewing and swallow.

Her dad waved off the beefy security guard that shadowed Nico's steps. Told the man to stand down, that he'd handle things.

She didn't care that Nico had made quite the entrance. That he looked more like a maintenance worker than her serious boyfriend. Didn't care that her dad slowly nodded, eyebrows raised, when she indicated she wanted to go with Nico. After her father had been absent and that disaster of a dinner hadn't happened last week, she still hadn't decided exactly how much to tell him. A complete ghost/freeze-out by the man your daughter's been dating for nearly two years, without any explanation, was, well, hard to explain.

Lexi still didn't fully understand it herself.

Blabbing to her dad how unhappy she was would only upset the tenuous balance in the house. Something she was loath to do before finding her own place, especially given how very supportive her dad had been when she expressed the desire to move out on her own, standing up to Mother in that regard. She hadn't wanted to add boyfriend woes on top of it.

Placing her napkin over her unfinished plate, she rose, battling hyped-up butterflies, and grabbed Nico's closest wrist with both hands. "What are—"

"Not here. Not yet." His fingers fisted within her loose grip. A second later he shook free of her grasp. "Follow me."

Dread coiled at his brusque tone, at the way he rejected her touch. But as he prowled through the fancy dining room with its overhead chandeliers, garnering a multitude of curious looks, she couldn't help but appreciate his power. The grace and strength he exuded without even trying.

Couldn't help but be so damn glad to see him.

She followed Nico to an empty ballroom, cavernous and echoing as they were the only occupants, human or otherwise—no furniture, no tables.

When she started to hug him, he stopped her by holding up a sealed envelope and putting his outstretched arm between them.

"I'm going to make this quick, Lex. You know how much I care about you." Sure she did. He might not've said l-o-v-e yet, but he'd shown her a hundred different ways since they'd started dating. "I'm sorry I bailed the other night—"

"I know you overheard." When she started to apologize for her mother's nasty attitude, Nico's words rolled right over her.

"It's nothing, absolutely nothing about you or your parents or anything else. It's me," he said, meeting her gaze, his face without expression. "I just wasn't comfortable in your home. With your people. It's just not my scene. We both know this was never going anywhere. The two of us, we just don't mix. Oil and champagne—you know how it is." He gave a shrug, the move so practiced, so casual, she didn't buy it—or his words—for a second. "They might try to get together, but physics don't lie. Have a good life, Lexi."

He shoved the envelope at her.

She refused to touch it. "Nico. Talk to me. This isn't you—"

"Take it." When she didn't, he tossed it at her. The corner hit her chest and it ricocheted to the floor. She started toward him—

"No. Stay put," he growled so low, she instinctively

obeyed. He pointed to the letter. "Read that. Stop calling. Don't come after me."

By the time she remembered to take a breath, her lungs burned and he'd long since vanished.

She numbly retrieved the envelope, praying the words inside would make more sense than the ones he'd just voiced. Only they didn't. It was more of the same. A bit more hurtful, if that could be endured, given how he'd listed out a litany of reasonable-sounding reasons why the two of them had just been a fluke. A few good times.

Nothing more.

He stressed what a great gal she was, how much fun she was. How she deserved the absolute best in life. How he'd grown bored. Past time they ended it. Blah, blah. *Bam!*

Sucker punch to the solar plexus. He'd just been fooling around.

Another to the gut.

Fun times with the poor little rich girl.

Boom! She took one on the chin.

Was never really into her...

Kerpow!

The last one staggered her heart.

Her father found her, half an hour later, still sitting on the ballroom floor, gasping uneasy breaths, dried tear tracks on her face.

EIGHTEEN

Something Unavoidable

THE POWERFUL ORGASM left Nico light-headed. Seeing stars. Seeing Lexi take off as though the hounds of hell nipped at her heels.

He cursed under his breath.

How could she run after what they'd just experienced together?

Blood pumped through his loins, pounded his heart. Tendrils of desire and longing intertwined and sent sparks to the far reaches of his body.

He wanted to growl his satisfaction, howl at her defection. No time for either. Because Lexi had run.

Thunder roared around him. New waves of rain began to sheet the air.

Flickers of lightning chased her as she dashed through the shadows, stumbling in the mud, escaping as if he were a monster.

Way to fuck her into compliance. She'll really listen to you now.

Shut up.

He hadn't fucked her. Hadn't. No matter how raw or elemental sex between them was, he still thought of it as making love. Always had when it came to his precious renegade.

He drew deep, earth-scented breaths, trying to steady his feelings. To calm his libido. Figure out his next move.

Was she right? Should he let her go? Accept that the two of them would never be compatible?

Hell no.

There was compatible, and then there was *compatible*. Based on how quickly red-hot lust had ignited between them, Nico knew he wasn't the only one still harboring emotions. Couldn't be.

She could deny it all she wanted, but Lexi cared for him. Else there was no way, *no way* on God's rain-drenched earth, she would have abandoned her principles and had sex with him on the eve of her wedding. Without a condom at that.

Bracing himself against the rough bark of the tree, he scrubbed the proof off his flesh, whistling at how sensitive he still was.

Yo! Don't you have a woman to catch?

Did he ever.

Nico shoved his half-hard cock into his jeans. Even spent, his body still wanted her. He held out his hands, let the renewed rain rinse them clean.

What now? How did he prevent her from marrying Langston tomorrow?

Yeah right, you idiot—what's to stop her from marrying him next week?

I am!

Lightning flashed directly in front of him. He leapt back with a gasp, crashing into the tree trunk as the air shimmered for several seconds. *Shit.* That answered it. He needed to get her someplace safe. Somewhere they could talk. He had to convince her. Even if it meant confessing all.

He'd grown up in an environment where no one said the word *love*. It simply wasn't part of his family's vocabulary. Sure, he knew his mom loved him; she'd proved that every day by how hard she worked to make up for the screw-ups his dad committed time and again. He also knew his sorry-ass father never loved anyone but himself.

But to express the sentiment? Out loud? To actually tell someone he loved them?

Not something Nico had any practice at. Or any desire to even try.

Until Lexi.

Days before his own insecurities were brought to light, thanks to her interfering mother, he'd been ready to declare his feelings to Lexi. If not audibly, then in a way that left no doubt exactly how he felt.

The skin on his groin tingled with renewed awareness.

Sure, he could show her. But it was time to *tell* her.

"Lexi! Wait up!" Raking the dripping hair off his face, he took off running, more determined than ever but hampered by the wet ground. "Sweet Lex!" Nothing. He dodged around trees, heading toward the road. But when he reached his car, Lexi wasn't in it.

Maybe she was hiding somewhere, needing a moment of privacy? "Lexi! Sweetheart! Where are you?"

Nothing.

He flinched when another bolt of lightning landed nearby. But it was timely—he saw her form in the staccato flash, her uneven gait blindly tearing down the road.

"Lexi." Nico glanced at his car, then back at the shadowy apparition growing smaller every second. "Lexi!"

He reached into his pocket, came up with a gold ball and a rabbit's foot but no keys.

Nico fisted his hand around both. The marble-sized sex toy was totally different from when her body had relinquished it to his questing fingers. From warm and slick to cold and hard. Unflinching and unforgiving.

She had to forgive him. *Had to.* His stupidity in not holding on to her. For not pursuing her sooner. He stuffed the items back in his pocket and reached into his other. Nada. Nothing.

"Crazy woman," he muttered, having forgotten until then that she'd tossed his keys.

He searched the road for a glint of metal, started sweeping his booted feet first one way and then the other, moving across the road. No luck. So back again, faster, as urgency built.

An SUV cruised past, the tires picking up and spraying water from the soaked pavement, headlights giving the boost he needed if only for a second. Over there, just edging the grass...

He searched with his boots. Hearing a slight clink, he bent down, rifling through weeds and sludge. Desperate. Praying—

Got 'em!

Keys in hand, he jumped in his Chevy. After the fastest U-turn on record, he raced after her, covering the distance in a heartbeat. He slowed as he approached, his headlights casting her bedraggled form into stark relief.

With jerky movements, he wound down his window. "Hey, good lookin', goin' my way?"

Lexi marched forward, ignoring him. But now he saw why she clomped like the bride of Frankenstein—one of her sandals was gone. Dirt and grit splattered along the bottom half of her once-white dress.

The woman who possessed his heart looked downright pathetic. More than anything, Nico just wanted to hold her. Would she let him?

"Get in the car," he coaxed. "Please. That bare foot has got to be bothering you."

"You're bothering me."

The rain started coming down faster, plastering her hair to her head. Her dress clung to her sweet curves and she shook, body quaking. From the cold, from heartache...or from passion?

Poor woman. What had he done—what was he *doing*—to her? His chest burned as though he'd eaten three double-jalapeño burgers.

"Lexi. Woman. *Please.*"

She continued to stomp through the rain as if he didn't exist.

"Lexi, dammit, enough already!" His tone rose with every word. Why wouldn't she acknowledge him? "If you want to go back to the church, fine, get in. I'll drive you."

It was a lie. The church was the last place he

intended to take her. He *couldn't*. Couldn't lose her. Couldn't let her marry Langston. Not now. Not ever.

But how to keep her?

When, deep down, he'd never figured he was good enough to keep her for the long haul. Always expected she'd leave him when someone better came along. When she got tired of slummin' in his neck of the woods.

What the hell?

Where had that come from? Sure, he'd had those thoughts a couple months in, but after all this time? After the two years of exclusive dating? He still harbored doubts about how she saw him?

The thought was staggering.

Was that why he'd never admitted—out loud—how much he cared? How much he loved her?

Because he feared she'd break up with him? So he said adios before she could—at the first outward test?

Damn him. How chicken-hearted could he be?

"Leave me alone." Her voice echoed with pain. The uneven pace increased. He watched her trip over some loose gravel.

His tires crept along as he idled forward, the speedometer registering zero. Rain streamed in through his open window. As lightheartedly as possible, he started humming the old B.J. Thomas tune about raindrops falling on heads. "Come on, Sweet Lex. Get in."

Nothing.

"My heart's still pounding from what we did beneath the tree." His cock was still pulsing too, but Nico figured some things were best left unsaid. "Don't you want to get in the car where it's warm? And dry?"

Nothing.

"Don't you want your little gold ball back?"

Nada, but a slight hesitation in her step. Aha, a reaction.

"Hey now." So Nico decided to really piss her off. Maybe then he'd finally get a real response. "You can't cheat me like this, baby. I still get to take you in the ass, remember?"

That did it. She shot him a look to singe the hair off his chest.

Ah, progress. "Don't you want to try it?"

"You had your chance. You blew it."

Wasn't that the story of his life?

He was probably blowing it all over again. But at least she was talking.

He gently applied the brake, slowing to a complete stop. "Lexi, this is ridiculous. It's storming."

She rounded on him. "Yeah? Well, it's a lot less dangerous out here than in your car. Go away. You've already caused enough trouble."

There was something in her voice—dread? Fear? Healthy adrenaline?

"What do you mean?" he questioned, feeling cold drops hit his skin. "Come on, girl, you've got to be freezing. Talk to me."

No response. Again.

"I could do that thing you're always begging for, that yell." The one he always swore was too asinine to ever come out of *his* mouth.

She hiccuped.

Great. She was crying. How he wished this night

were over. Both of them snug in his bed. "What's wrong, Lex? Sweet Renegade?"

"Don't call me that."

He softened his tone. "What are you afraid of? Me? *Us?*"

Nothing but a loud sniff.

A horrible thought struck him. "Are you afraid of what Langston will do if he finds out about us? About what just happened?"

Jesus, why hadn't he thought of that before? The guy was axle grease, nothing but an over-groomed playboy with no respect for women. Sure, he didn't seem to have any guilt about cheating on Lexi, but how would Langston feel about Lexi cheating on him?

"If? He's *going* to find out because I have to tell him, now don't I?" Lexi took off again. "And there is no *us!* Scram!"

Was she crazy? Who knew how the bastard would react? His gut told him Langston wouldn't take it well. "He won't hurt you, will he?"

Her silence spiked terror in his gut and he gripped the wheel, unintentionally revving the engine as he jerked closer. "Lexi!"

"Hurt me?" she tossed over her shoulder. "You asked *me* about being safe, if I'd caught anything from Bradley. What about you? You're not exactly an angel in the bedroom, now are you?"

"I haven't been with anyone else," he told her honestly, hitting the brakes. "Not since you."

Her feet slowed to a halt. For a few seconds she looked straight ahead, remaining silent. More wind blasted past, lifting her long hair and creating a stringy, riotous halo about her head. He saw her shiver again.

Finally, she turned and stared. "I guess you *are* an angel."

"Pl-please don't marry him, Lexi." His voice broke.

She squeezed her hands into fists, clamped her eyes shut and just stood there. Fat raindrops sprinkled down as she silently sobbed. "You just don't get it, do you?" she cried. Her sandaled foot stomped once on the gravel lining the road. "I *want* to marry Badley. I mean *Bradley*." She shook a fist at him. "You're not doing me any favors."

"Lexi, please just get in. Talk to me."

She hiccupped. "I can't."

She sure looked as though she wanted to.

Nico grabbed his leather jacket from the backseat and stuck his arm out the window. "Here. If you insist on standing in the rain, put this on before you get sick. If it's not too late."

Why couldn't his chivalrous instincts have kicked in sooner? His fingers drummed on the wheel. What to do? Did he confess his love now—when the timing sucked? Or be brutally honest? See if he could coax her inside? "I believe you want to get married, Lexi. Maybe even *badly*. But not to him. Not to Langston."

Lexi sniffled as she slid the coat on, crossing her arms in front of her. She looked toward the starless sky and allowed rain to wash over her face. "He's a good man. Perfect husband material."

Perfect my ass. "You don't love him."

Lexi didn't deny it.

The truth was, Langston *could* be the perfect guy

and Nico still wouldn't approve of him marrying Lexi. The only man he approved of was himself. And if he didn't act on that, he was going to lose her forever. Even if he wasn't sure he could be all that Lexi needed, he wanted to try. Needed the chance—

"I don't have to love him," she answered, whispering as if sharing a secret. He leaned his head out the window to hear better. "Don't you see? Don't you get it?" She started clomp-walking again. "I've grown up, Nico. I'm ready to move on, to make more out of myself."

"Lex, what are you saying? You're fine. You don't need to be any more."

She increased her pace and muttered, "If I can't be with who I want, at least I can please my parents."

"You can be anything you want," he said decisively. "Be *with* anyone you want."

Even you? When you ran off at the first sign of trouble?

For a moment, he let her go, just as he'd done before. He couldn't reason with her, couldn't make her happy. Maybe he should just let her live the life she wanted, the life she'd planned.

Maybe she didn't love *him* either, not after all this time. Certainly not based on her words—but she'd certainly loved him with her body. Was that enough? One thought of the wild way she'd ridden him beneath the tree and he was hard for her all over again.

He watched her walking out of his life, the rain sparkling in the headlights. Nico felt himself losing her, could see this scene replaying in his mind until the day he died. Him—giving up. Taking the easy way out.

Fearing he wasn't good enough for her, so not even trying.

Do you hear yourself? Hear those pitiful thoughts circling? Instead of silencing the voice, he listened. *Flush 'em, Nico. Have you learned nothing from Coondog? From your time with Lexi?*

Prove that you're man enough for her. The *man for her. Fight for her!*

He knew what he had to do. More importantly, he knew that he wanted it with all his heart. Nico gunned the engine and lunged alongside her. "Marry *me*," he blurted.

"What?" Stopping, Lexi whirled to face him, hugging herself within the confines of his jacket. "What did you say?"

He stomped on the brake. "Marry me, Lexi. Marry me!" he shouted for all the world to hear. "*Marry me!*"

She gawked at him. "That's ridiculous. You can't just swoop in from nowhere, *the night before my wedding,* and pop out a random proposal. Especially one you don't mean."

"I mean it, baby. With everything in me."

She leaned down. The rain had slowed again but her long hair hung over the window's edge, dripping water from its soaked tips. "You're serious?"

"Very."

"You expect an answer—a yes—just like that, don't you?"

"After what we did back—"

"That was just sex."

"Then you need a new grasp on the English language because *that* was lovemaking at its finest. Passionate. Elemental. Unstoppable."

Just like he felt, now that he was certain this was the

right course of action. "Unstoppable. For us both. We're unavoidable, Lex, you and I. Just like the tides. I'll always come back to you, I swear. More than that. I'll never leave again. Never. As long as there's breath in my body."

NINETEEN

Something Different - The Other Girls

"THAT MRS. T AGAIN?" Calli asked in her soft country twang as Jenny hit IGNORE on yet another call.

She'd pacified the woman the best she could throughout their rushed rehearsal dinner. But now that the younger gals had relocated for the bachelorette events Jenny had planned, which hadn't gone as expected given the late start, she didn't need Alexis's overbearing mother putting any more of a damper on things.

"Sure is." Jenny's teeth plucked at her bottom lip. As maid of honor, shouldn't she be chained to the hip with her BFF the night before the wedding? "What is up with Alexis? How worried should we be?"

Strobe lights bounced through the air, creating a neon kaleidoscope over the patrons crowding the tables, bar, and dance floor a ways off. The din of boisterous partygoers, overlaid by flashing lights and laughs, invited Jenny to relax. To enjoy a rare night on the town.

But she struggled, the dull ache in her wrist and

arm reminding her how her last evening out, a few short months ago, had ended up—with her in the hospital, her boyfriend arrested for abuse, and Jenny no longer in denial that things would *ever* improve. Would ever go back to how they were when she and Carter had first dated.

"Yeah, I'm tryin' not to be overly anxious about 'Lexis," Calli said. "Keep tellin' myself that she's fine."

Good, dutiful Alexis. Who, since no longer dating Nico, pretty much did *everything* her mom wanted.

Until this evening.

The yummy rehearsal dinner had come and gone. Brad and his groomsmen taking off as soon as they could shove the raspberry-topped New York cheesecake down their throats. Parents, grandparents, and other sundry relatives either going home or to hotel rooms, eyebrows raised and concerned murmurs about the missing bride but nothing overtly stated.

"I'm sure she'll show up any minute now," Jenny bluffed with a confident air. Time in the courtroom and in front of opposing counsel had honed her bluffing skills at least.

Work lately had been as stressful and satisfying as ever. The further away she got from Carter in time and distance, combined with the hours of counseling and self-defense classes she'd undertaken, all added up to a stronger, surer Jenny. Or it should have, she acknowledged with less self-assurance than she'd like.

Alexis was the outgoing one who could talk with anybody in any situation, the people person who would know exactly what to do.

The introvert of the two, planning party-type events

and heading them up wasn't exactly in Jenny's wheel-house—especially when the guest of honor had vanished. "I miss Alexis. Really wish she was here."

"Any word on our absent bride yet?" Jazmin asked as she arrived back from her trip to the bar ordering another round of a different shot she'd promised would add a full cup to their bra sizes—definitely *not* something Jenny needed—and inches to their short statures —which she definitely did.

Of the bridesmaids, only the three of them remained. The private pole dance lesson had been a riot, all but one of the six bridesmaids getting their sexy groove on—or trying to. They'd been minus Mica, who'd confided to Jenny just before she went home after the rehearsal dinner that she'd just learned she was pregnant. And while hanging upside down on a pole likely wouldn't hurt anything, her newly discom-bobulated stomach took exception to the idea of pole spins.

"Gotcha, girlfriend. Your secret is safe with me," Jenny had told her sincerely. "Now get on home to your man. I'll cover for you."

Hugs and a couple fortifying breaths later, Jenny was climbing up that stripper pole as if her future depended on it.

And maybe it did.

Hadn't her counselor been telling her it was time to stop hiding and put herself out there? Move past her controlling, abusive ex to having fun again?

"I'm starting to think maybe she finally wised up," Jaz observed. "Decided to bolt and jilt."

"Jazmin," Jenny chided over the stupid lurching of

her heart. "You shouldn't say things like that. You'll jinx the wedding."

"Would that be a bad thing, *chiquita*?" The woman who towered over Jenny's petite frame a good eight inches plopped in the next chair, her leather-and-metal cuff bracelet making a thunking sound when she slapped the scarred wood table beside Jenny's phone. "Lexi's better off alone than with someone she doesn't really love. I never thought she got as excited over Brad as she did with Nico."

Jenny refused to acknowledge the weird combination of grief-relief that statement brought. Yes, Alexis deserved happiness, more than most after what happened to her brother, and after living with Mother "superior" all these years. But could Jenny help it if secretly—way down so deep she'd barely admitted it to herself these days and certainly never *told* a soul—she wanted Brad for herself? Had crushed on him before he'd ever asked Alexis out back in high school?

"Here you are, ladies. Goldschläger times four." The waitress announced their drinks, startling Jenny when she plunked not one but two of the weird shots directly in front of her.

"Ew." She wrinkled her nose and pointed. "There's floaty things in there." Gold flakes levitated in the clear liquid. "I'm not drinking that. And why did I get two?"

"Because you're the only one who didn't drink a Jell-O shot the first round," said Jazmin, picking up her glass, tapping it to Jenny's two and the one Calli held up, then tossing it back with a flourish.

"Ayyyy-eeeee!" Jazmin smacked her lips and stuck

out her tongue. "Fire, I tell you. That drink breathes *fire*."

Jenny laughed and slid both of hers in front of the Latina firecracker. "Here. Have another."

"Nuh-uh," Jazmin protested. "You—"

"Already had a smidgen at the stripper lesson. Since I'm driving," she reminded them, "that's more than enough for me."

"No problemo, guess that just means more for me." She ran her finger over the rim of her drained shot glass. "As to Brad, I like the guy. Really hit it off with him at the engagement shindig Mombie threw." Jenny had noticed. Had fought off unreasonable envy toward Jaz at how quickly she and Brad bonded over basketball and who knew what else.

It was one thing to silently suffer her best friend marrying the guy of Jenny's dreams; quite another to watch someone new talk to him as though they were lifelong buds when Jenny still battled the urge to get tongue-tied just saying the occasional "hi".

"Mombie," Calli snickered. "Zombie Mom? Good one."

"Then after the wedding dress thing," Jaz continued, meeting Calli's high-five, "I mean, I could have practically fallen for him myself but—"

"What wedding dress thing?" That got Jenny's full attention.

"Oh shit. Forgot." Jaz looked down into her empty shot glass. "I was keeping that to myself. Oh well." With a renewed grin, she knocked back another before meeting their curious gazes. "Calli, you were off doing one of your bug shows—"

"They're *museum exhibits*."

"Whatever. You were gone the day we"—she gestured to Jenny—"met Lexi and Momosaurus rex. Jenny, you'd gone back to the office, remember? After Lexi found that perfect dress?"

Jenny nodded, easily recalling how excited Alexis had been during the trying-on phase, delighted that her favorite both flattered *and* met with her mother's approval.

Jenny had been with her in the dressing room, undoing what seemed like a zillion buttons along her spine, whispering and giggling, both of them reminiscing over the times they'd dreamed of this day when they were younger: shopping for their wedding dress. Also reveling at how well the exclusive boutique pampered and handled Alexis's parent, with comped mimosas and tiny little apricot-flavored teacakes. Poor Jaz had been stuck out in the waiting area with her.

"What no one knew was that I overheard Momenstein tell the shopkeeper they'd be buying the dress a size down, *smaller* than the one we all thought looked fabulous. Then later, I heard her whisper to Lex 'to encourage your diet, dear'."

"That raving bee-*atch*," Calli murmured.

"Amen," Jenny agreed, chest squeezing as she hurt for Alexis, who hadn't said a word.

"Yeah, well." Jazmin sat up tall, looking supremely pleased with herself. She clinked her two empty glasses together. "I texted Brad. He said not to worry. I don't know whether he overrode Mrs. Tyrant or had Lex secretly return it for the right size, but a few days later, he called and left a message thanking me and saying he'd taken care of it. Good man, that Brad."

Jenny agreed. Enough not to be insanely jealous at learning he and Jaz were chummy enough to exchange phone numbers.

"Even so," Jaz said on a sigh, her triumphant, gloatful look dissolving. "I just don't see it, though I *want* to. Not the two of them. Not till death do they part."

"You ladies doing all right?" Their waitress was back, and with a full tray. "I just happen to have another three Goldschlägers here, compliments of that gentleman over there."

Jenny glanced in the direction the woman pointed but had no clue who their generous benefactor was. Too many bodies and not a one of them catching her eye as someone who was noticing *them*.

"We'll take 'em, thanks." Jaz distributed the drinks around the table. Then she reached into her pocket to tip the waitress.

"No need, hon. He more than took care of me."

"Not about to turn down free drinks"—Jaz grinned —"even if we don't know who they're from. After I met Brad," she said, picking up right where she'd left off, "I gave Lexi the thumbs-up, but the few times I saw them together, I wasn't sure I liked him for *her*. They just don't seem to fit. But what do I know? I certainly haven't found anyone who fits me either. *Not* that I'm looking." Jaz reached for her third shot—or was it her fourth?— and placed Calli's in her hand. "A toast, girlfriends, to not fitting."

"How about to not looking?" Jenny said with a rare edge of sarcasm, miming a drink.

"Hear, hear." Calli swallowed hers, amidst a bit of throat hacking and eye blinking.

"Come on." Jaz gave Jenny's empty hand a doleful look. "This is so not fair. We'll hire a ride if we need to. You can't not have fun with the rest—"

Jenny was saved when a tall hunk in a cowboy hat approached and asked Jazmin to dance. "You're not getting off that easy!" was her friend's parting shot before Cowboy Man whirled her onto the floor.

Calli nudged Jenny's shoulder. "Does 'Lexis know where to find us? I thought you said the bachelorette party plans were a surprise. And with us showing up late to the pole thing, then coming over here..."

"Yeah." Jenny glanced at her phone. "I texted her. Twice." Actually five times between texting and calling. "Haven't heard back. I know Mrs. Templeton called the church during dessert, looking for her."

"Weird as a rabbit bot. The whole thing is, if you ask me." While the rest of them had grown up in the city, Calli had lived in the sticks before relocating for college, where she'd met Alexis. And studied entomology.

Roaches and slugs? Jenny shuddered. Gross. Just plain gross. She knew better than to ask what a rabbit bot was. When it came to things with more than four legs, one was better off not knowing.

"I'm actually with Jaz on this." Calli picked at the label on the beer she'd ordered prior to Jaz's shot craze. "Not convinced she really wants to marry Langston. Think she's just been going through the motions, you know, since Nico crushed her heart. To make Momzilla happy and all that."

"Some maid of honor I've been." Had that secret envy made her so blind as to not notice her friend's ambivalence? Or unhappiness? "Guess it's time to face the music."

As punishment, or maybe a confidence booster, Jenny took a tiny, very tiny, sip of the gold-flecked elixir.

Kapow! Eyes watered. Tongue burned. "Blech. I need a Sprite." But she took another sip anyway, just to prove she wasn't the total wimp she'd come to see herself as. "I should've noticed if she wasn't dancing on air. If this, if marrying Brad, wasn't what she wanted."

"*Thbbbbbbb.*" Calli blew a hearty raspberry. "Jenny, girl, you've had enough on your plate, dealing with gettin' over Carter the Creep." Calli fingered Jenny's arm along the scar. "Wasn't that long ago *this* was in a cast and"—she indicated Jenny's jaw—"that was all bruised an' swollen." She leaned over and gave Jenny a hug. "Honey, 'Lexis is a big girl. Maybe tonight's just her takin' some time out to think things through. If you like, we can finish up here and retrace our steps. Go back to the church, see if we can find out where she went."

"That's a good idea." If Jenny didn't have anything else to drink, she'd be good to drive. Unlike the others who had partaken liberally of the luscious alcohol-laced ice cream beverages at the pole dance venue, Jenny had limited herself to less than half of one. She knew *she* wasn't about to hook up with anyone tonight, but she wanted to keep an eye on the others, just in case assistance was needed if some guy came on too strong or started to get grabby.

She might not have stood up for herself as soon as she should have, but if it came to it, recent defense classes had her ready for a smackdown.

"Whew. He was fine. Damn fine." Jaz blew in like a Texas tornado, spun her chair around and straddled it. "But too friggin' bossy."

"That was fast," Jenny commented. "Short song?"

"Nope, abandoned him in the middle of it."

Calli grinned. "Give him your number?"

"Nah." From between her breasts, Jaz plucked out a piece of paper. "He gave me his." She dropped it in an empty shot glass and snorted. "Who writes their number on paper anymore? What a dipshit."

Momentarily shrugging off the uncertainty over Alexis and the melancholy over her own screwed-up past, Jenny got back in the game. Just knowing she and Calli had a plan, however tenuous, helped a ton.

Jenny plucked the paper out of the glass. "So you won't mind if I help myself?"

"I'm not interested in him." Jaz put on a good show. But she looked flushed. Even more than the pole acrobatics—with her prior gymnastics training, she'd put the rest of them to shame—and shots would account for. She gestured toward the paper. "Be my guest."

Jenny did, spreading it open. "Um, Jaz? Your dipshit didn't write down his number."

Curiosity piqued, Jaz angled closer. "He didn't?"

Not interested, huh? Bullcrap. "Nope." Jenny smiled. "He wrote down something else."

From there, it was a mad, laughing scramble to keep the slightly damp curl of paper away from a suddenly curious Jazmin.

TWENTY

Something Spectacular

BARING his soul had never been so hard. Or so right.

"Hell, Lexi. I know I'm crazy for even proposing. Compared to that glamour boy you're still engaged to, life with me pales in comparison." She stared at him in such a way his throat tightened. Nico forced himself to finish. "You deserve everything Langston can give you. You just don't deserve Langston."

"I don't?" she whispered.

Now that he'd asked her to marry him, had spontaneously uttered the words and repeated them several times over, the rightness of it settled over him.

If he could just get her to agree.

"You deserve to be loved," he told her. "I can do that the rest of my life. I'm a better man for knowing you. Being with you. And I think I'm good for you too. Maybe not in the obvious ways but on some gut, soul level, where it really counts. We're both better together than either of us is alone. I believe that with all my heart."

Her hands gripped the edges of his jacket. She started shaking her head and Nico feared the worst.

"No. Don't answer me." He scooched toward the shoulder, set the parking brake, killed the engine, and scrambled out, pulling her into his arms. "Don't say a word, not yet. Just let me hold you, Sweet Renegade." Damn, his voice cracked again. "Hold you near my heart."

What could he do? What could he say or do to convince her?

"I never should have left you. I screwed us both. Forgive me, Lexi, for the pain. The stupid mistakes." A tremor quaked through him, the emotions and storm, the fear of losing her forever, coalescing into near panic as he brushed his hands over her wet hair, secured her against his chest. A sedan approached, and his protective instincts kicked in, so he guided them both just beyond the shoulder as he talked. "I wasn't good enough for you in the past. But I am now. Will be forever. If you'll just..."

He took a deep breath, hugged her as if he'd never let go. "I love you. *Love you*. Sorry I didn't tell you sooner."

"NICO," Lexi breathed past the awe clogging her throat. "What do you mean not good enough? You were *always* good enough. Still are."

"Strong enough, then," he conceded, "ready to stand and fight for you."

Wrapped securely in his arms, shaking inside and out from what he was saying, she struggled not to instantly accept everything so they could dance merrily on their way.

He hurt you!

That's why she was being cautious. Knowing she needed to pull away, to see what she could of his expression in the dark, she turned her head and inhaled, fortifying her courage before pushing out of his embrace.

He reached for her, then let his arm fall back. Giving her space.

Time to think. To absorb what he'd just said. Marry him? He loved her!

"Lex..." Nico looked desperate. She'd never seen him like this. Confident, dangerous, bold, yes. Lost? Never.

No matter that she'd put distance between them, his scent, a sexy combination of oil, leather, and hard work —the smell of *her* man—still buffeted the humid air between them. Drew her as nothing else.

"Even if you don't believe me"—he scraped one foot against the muddy gravel—"believe that Langston won't make you happy. Isn't the man for you."

Processing everything, she gave a slow nod. "I've known Bradley's cheated on me toward the end of our engagement. I'd stopped putting out so I made excuses for him but..."

"But you finally realized there's no excuse?"

"No, I finally realized *why* it bothered me so much." Unable to stand not touching him, she caught his fisted hand in hers. At the gesture, he seemed to relax, his fingers unfurling to clasp hers. "Because it *didn't* bother me. I was just relieved he wasn't pressuring me to fill his bed."

Nico gave a low whistle.

"That's unnatural, right?" she pressed. "To simply not care."

She was still coming to grips with his admission that he'd never felt good enough for her. Because she'd struggled with the same thing, only in reverse—always thinking, deep down, that *she* was too inexperienced, too naïve for him long-term.

Sure, to someone on the outside, money divided them. That was so simplistic. So very wrong. Not something that had ever come between them.

Not until her mother made such a vocal stink. One Lexi realized had precipitated Nico's actions.

Would he do the same thing now? Abandon her and walk at the first sign of real trouble?

The man talking to her now had matured beyond the man she'd dated. Nico had always been fun and up-front with her, blunt, honest about things if she asked, just not one to volunteer personal stuff, his past and the emotional baggage she'd always sensed he carried.

She'd known from the beginning there wasn't a veneer about him. What she saw was what she got. And she'd loved him for it.

But she'd also known better than to say it.

To frighten him off. To ask for anything more than what they had—an exclusive dating relationship which included a fabulous friendship and terrific sex.

Had he changed enough to really want more with her? Could she take him at face value again? Trust he wouldn't break her heart a second time?

"I'd say it's unnatural not to *want* to sleep with the

man you're about to marry," he said. "Not to want to fuck his brains out."

"Yeah. There is that." She smiled at the forceful way he said it. Then she turned solemn. "You always had a way with words. In your letter— What all you wrote…"

A car drove past, a welcome distraction from the remembered pain.

"God, Lex." His muscles contracted, fingers gripping hers. "Lies. All of it. It about ripped out my heart, coming up with that garbage. Blasting out anything I could think of to convince you—convince myself—that we didn't belong together. Oil and champagne not mixing—pure bullshit."

A couple of nearby soft thumps tried to snag her attention—car doors?—but Lexi remained enthralled by his words.

"Renegade Girl, I love you with everything in me. Have from nearly the start. It just took me too long to own it. To tell you."

He brought their joined hands to his mouth, kissed the back of hers, and Lexi couldn't keep from smiling.

"How can I prove it to you, baby? How can I make you understand I'm man enough to fight for you, no matter what? Wait!" Excitement infused his tone as he pushed her away, his hands going to his belt. "Let me show you."

"Nico!" she burst out, a little dismayed when he unbuckled and unzipped. "I thought we were beyond—"

• • •

"NO, NO. YOU DON'T UNDERSTAND." Feeling elated, hopeful, not caring that his jeans hung partially undone, Nico took possession of her hands, threaded their fingers and drew her palms against his. "Promise," he struggled to speak past grinning lips. "It's *not* what you're thinking."

Light blasted his eyes. Pain squeezed them shut. "What the—"

"Miss!" Fast steps approached as the beam zigzagged across his face. "Is this man bothering you?"

Startled by the abrupt shift, Nico tried to blink past the blinding light.

"Release her!" Hurried footfalls grew closer. "Let her go," a rough voice ordered. "Now."

Nico tried, but couldn't. Lexi had started laughing. Was holding on to his fingers to keep herself upright.

"I said *release*—"

"Off-Off-i-cer!" she gasped. If he hadn't known her so well, Nico would've thought she was in pain. Sobbing. "No, it's fine, I promise—fine."

"I'll be the judge of that. Dispatch got a call about a man molesting a woman out here—half mile back, or so the report went. No one else here. That leaves you two. Step away from him."

"Off—Officer!" Her giggles finally became apparent and the flashlight swung from Nico's abused irises to Lexi, starting at her muddied feet and hem and sweeping up to her face.

"What happened to your other shoe?" Instead of concerned, the deep voice now sounded accusing. Suspicious. "Ma'am?"

Nico blinked her into focus. "Oh, *hell*."

Lexi didn't cry pretty. Never had.

Thanks to tears and rain, mascara trails tracked down her face. Eyes red and puffy, with a glassy sheen from the emotions of the evening, didn't bode well for their story. No matter that it was the truth.

"What?" she asked him, ignoring the cop. "What's wrong?"

"You look—" *Like you're using. Like you've been attacked.* Double hell. "Done in."

For some reason, that set her off again and she laughed. Loud and long.

The cop shifted closer. "Ma'am! What are you on?"

"He thinks I'm on drugs?" She only laughed harder.

"Did this man accost you?"

"No. Well, yes." She swiped at her running eyes. "But not like you think—"

"No tolerance for a bastard who attacks women." The partner who'd hung back till now jerked Nico around. "Hands on the hood," he barked. "Spread 'em."

No stranger to the scenario, Nico did as told, resting his fingers on the convertible's soft top. He remained unresisting when the man applied heavy pressure to hold him in place while the cop checked for weapons. "Gentlemen, if you'll just give her a minute to calm down—"

"Oh, Lordy!" She was still at it.

"Lexi," Nico growled. By damn, he was starting to get the giggles himself. He couldn't see her since Cop Two had him shoved up against the car door. "Lex! If you don't stop cackling, get serious and explain, they're going to haul us both in."

"Jim!" the guy behind him hollered. "His pants are undone! Here, this knife on his belt is all I found."

Choking on his relief—he was starting to think he'd finally gotten through to Lexi, and in the nick of time—Nico spoke over his shoulder. "Can I do up my jeans?"

"Ma'am?" the first one, Jim, asked carefully. "Did he rape you?"

"No!" That sobered her. "No. Not at all. If anything, I attacked him."

Cop Two grunted.

"My jeans?" Nico prompted.

"Fine." Two finally released the pressure between Nico's shoulder blades. "Go ahead."

He spun around, caught sight of the flashlight. "Wait. The light. Shine it here—no! Not my face. My waist—" Nico reached out and aimed the light toward his groin.

"What the hell?" the cop protested.

Nico spread his fly open, pointed to the colorful skin just left of center. "Sweet Lex—do you see? It's all for you."

"Good God, man," One cursed, approaching with a growl. "That's it, you bastard. I'm hauling you in for indecent exposure."

"Hold up, Jim. Step back." Two shined his light on Nico's abdomen and lower—the manly bits covered, if barely. "Look. It's a tat."

"You got another tattoo?" Lexi said with a note of wonder. "After your mother asked you not to?"

Yeah. Because it'd been as important as anything he'd ever done. A way to show Lexi what she meant to him. A way to commit even if he'd been too chicken to come right out and say it.

"Let me see." Lexi dropped to her knees in the mud and grabbed the flashlight.

Hell. Nico's eyelids slammed down, his head fell back.

His embarrassment should be complete. Talk about baring all. And not just before Lexi, no—in front of strangers. Armed ones.

Her fingers lit upon him, quavered over the skin, traced the healed tattoo. The one he'd gotten just days before the ill-fated dinner that didn't happen.

He might not've been good with the words, but when he'd gone to his favorite tattoo artist, the gal surprised to see him after such a long absence, he'd known exactly what he wanted: a beautifully rendered orchid intertwined with a heart. *Lexi* written on one of the petals in an ornate font; *forever mine* on another.

"Oh, Nico." The delighted words breathed hot over his naked skin, her touch threatening to ease the embarrassment of sharing something so intimate, something meant just for the two of them, *here*—in front of an audience. "Nico, my love."

Her tone is what did it.

What loosed restraint and inhibitions, freed his lungs to inhale down to his toenails. Freed his vocal cords to holler loud and long, to yodel out the best damn Tarzan yell to ever be heard on film, screen, or back country road.

Amazing in both intensity and duration, given how it wasn't something he'd planned or ever—*ever*— thought to attempt.

The melodious notes went on for seconds, eons, conveying the depth of his feelings. It went on till the cows came home, till he turned hoarse and finally ended on a high note.

Stunned stillness surrounded them, the crickets and cops shocked silent. Nico came back to himself to find his fists anchored to his chest where they'd pounded away during his declaration.

"Good God," Jim whispered, almost reverently. "I've heard it all now."

"Incredible," Two complimented in an astounded voice. "Crazy-insane, but it'll make for a great story when—"

"Don't you dare," Lexi hissed, her fervent breath blessing his groin. "Don't either of you *dare* speak a word of this," she ordered from her crouched position as though she expected the men to listen and obey. "This…"

"Promise, Ren," Nico swore, breathing deeply of the cool night air, eyes still closed as he concentrated on his vow. "My promise to you. You're my mate, if you'll have me. The only one I could ever want. The one I *need*."

"Forever," she whispered between them for his ears only. Her fingers feathered over his exposed skin with greater urgency. Making the loss of pride so very worth it, even if it had come at such a cost. And in front of others that had no business being party to—

When he felt not just her fingers tracing his vow, but her tongue, his head snapped upright, eyes wide open.

He placed one shielding hand behind her head, holding her to him. The damp strands of her hair instantly clung to his fingers. "Ahem." He angled his head toward the two hovering cops. "Any chance my dick can stop being on parade?"

Lexi smothered a laugh against his skin.

His fingers tightened on her scalp. "That you gentlemen can—" Scram? Vamoose? Get the hell out of here? "Leave us be?"

Jim shifted, holding on to his menacing posture. But Cop Two asked, "Can you both pass a breath test?"

"Yes, sir."

"Prove it."

Thankfully the storm had moved on. It took another ten minutes to convince Deputy Jim and Deputy Two—he'd been corrected after calling them "cops"—that he and Lexi were both sober, and to wait for confirmation that Nico had a clean driving record and no outstanding warrants.

What got them both cuffed and stuffed in the back of the patrol car, and hauled in was good ol' Deacon Joe.

The man who reluctantly admitted to witnessing her "kidnapping" when Lexi told the deputies to call the church, checking for her purse and to confirm her identity. The same man who said two of her friends had just stopped by the rectory and woken him up, looking for her.

"*Oops.* Guess I really should have called the girls, to let them know I was with you."

Just before she settled against him, shoulder to uncomfortable shoulder, she glanced up and said, "At least we can call my dad from the sheriff's office. He'll straighten this all out."

"Hell no. No way am I seeing your father again for the first time since breaking things off from a *jail cell.*

We'll call Coondog. He can bail our asses out if necessary, hopefully keep it from coming to that." His former boss and current partner *knew* people.

At least they were in the same county as Buccaneer Campground, a place Coondog had been frequenting for decades.

"Whatever you say," she sighed, relaxing as well as cuffs and high emotions—and two eavesdropping deputies—would allow. "You've convinced me. I'm ready to listen, as long as you like. Talk to me."

Deputy Jim, who'd remained a grump even as his partner had thawed toward them, climbed behind the wheel, alerted dispatch they were on their way and took off.

Now or never. "I love you, woman." It was actually getting easier to say. "I am so in love with you that I want to spend the rest of my days showing *and* telling you."

Before he could mention marriage again, she spoke. "I know."

Her happy sigh lifted him up as the patrol car headed toward the nearest town—and away from his abused '57 Bel Air, languishing on the side of the road until their tow truck driver, Sid, could answer Nico's plea to please pick her up and get his beauty to safety.

"Have known for a while," Lexi continued. "You just needed to be reminded of it." The smile in her voice calmed his raging nerves. It wasn't every day he told someone he loved them, not once but several times over.

"I won't marry you, though," she said, conviction in the words, as though mind reading his recent thoughts. "Not yet. Not on the rebound. Or spur of the moment."

She let that sink in, and while disappointed, he agreed. What they shared wasn't a rebound love. He shouldn't treat it as such.

"Slow up, Jim," Deputy Two said from the passenger side.

"Why?" Deputy Grump asked, taking his foot off the gas from the feel of it.

"If you ever decide to ask again," Lexi continued quietly, "after you've given it a lot of thought, and us some more time, *then* I'll say yes."

"Over there, on the shoulder," Deputy Two said. "What's that?"

"My sandal!" Lexi exclaimed, sitting upright. "What a great end to the night. If you'll get it for me, please?"

Nah, a great end to the night would be when he had Langston's ring off her finger. For the first time in months, Nico was pretty certain that's where things were headed.

Yeah, he thought, relaxing back against the seat as the two deputies argued about who was going to get out for shoe duty, all in all, a fantastic evening.

Coondog would never let him hear the end of it, lucky rabbit's foot and all.

TWENTY-ONE

Something Forever

"HOW ABOUT DARTS?" Sitting in a plush leather chair in Philip Templeton's masculine study, with one booted foot crossed over his opposite knee, Nico shook the ice in his drained bourbon glass. "I can throw sharp objects with the best of them." He finished answering Templeton's query of what he'd like to do now.

He'd already gotten the grand tour of the place, inside as well as the inviting, manicured backyard complete with new grilling setup his host had been eager to show off.

Clean-shaven, with short gray hair and a golf tan, wearing boat shoes, sans socks, Bermuda shorts and a knit polo shirt, the elder man looked cool and comfortable playing host to the overdressed, scruffy-faced, long-haired ex-con in his spacious inner sanctum.

Nico still hadn't worked up the courage to ask what he'd come for. But he would, and soon. Wasn't sure how much longer he could portray the calm, casual attitude he was striving for, not with the way his heart kept kicking up into his throat, needed swallowing down.

Lexi and her mom were out—a peacemaking, shopping excursion that Lexi had initiated, groaning when she told him. "It's not like I *want* to spend the entire day with her. But I've got to. It's time we mend this thing between us. And since I have no plans of letting you go"—this was accompanied by some thoroughly appreciative kisses—"then I need to make nice with Mother where I can."

Nico figured he had half an hour or so to locate his balls. Man up.

Ask for Lexi's hand.

"Darts, huh?" Templeton didn't seem ready to jump on the idea.

Pity, the dartboard across the room was one impressive piece of craftsmanship. Definitely a custom job, not some mass-produced piece of crap.

Grasping at straws, Nico hazarded, "I could always teach you how to hot-wire a car." Between his Bel Air and the classic stepside pickup he knew Templeton housed in his garage, he'd have something to work with. "I'm out of practice but might be fun."

If one had a sense of humor.

Nico waited, breath held.

Templeton chuckled and raised the bourbon decanter. "Another?" At Nico's shaky nod, the man refilled his glass with four fingers. "As to practicing your hot-wiring skills on my vehicles, let's consider that a no-go. Lucky for you I know you're joking. Had you investigated, young man." Templeton saluted Nico with his iced tea. "Doctor's orders, so if Alexis asks, you can tell her I followed them." Lowering his arm, he finished with, "I know you aren't up to illegal escapades anymore. Haven't been for some time."

"You had me checked out? Hired a P.I.?" Nico didn't know what to think of that.

"Of course. Alexis is rich, obscenely so. You didn't think I'd let her get involved—get *seriously* involved—with someone unsuitable, did you?"

"Sir, if you don't mind my saying, are you insane?" He spread his arms out to the side, opening himself up. Despite the sport coat he'd worn for the occasion, his tats were easily visible at his wrists and neck. The glass wobbled in his outstretched hand, the ice clinking in the silence. "Hello? In your circles, aren't I the very definition of *unsuitable*?"

Templeton took a slow, deliberate drink, evaluating Nico from over the rim of his tumbler before lowering it and arranging the bottom precisely on the coaster.

Nico refused to fidget or relax his arms. Wasn't easy. Condensation made the glass in his right hand slippery.

"On the surface, yes," Lexi's father began, holding Nico's gaze, "and for some in my 'circle' that'd be sufficient evidence to condemn you. Fortunately for you, and Alexis, that's not how I operate."

Using all his control to appear unaffected, feeling his very future hanging by a hopeful thread, he gripped the slick glass and lowered his hands. "Oh?"

The older man gave a decisive nod. "Regardless of what you did in your youth, I know that you currently don't pop more than the occasional Tylenol, snort more than a laugh, or smoke—at all. I know the only thing you've stolen in the last several years is my daughter's heart.

"I know you work hard and responsibly, and that George thinks of you like a son."

George? Who the hell was—

Just as Nico realized his brows had come together in a confused frown, Mr. Templeton clarified. "Ah, you know him as Coondog, I believe."

"You know Coon?" Nico may have worked on some impressive engines, including some with owners in those so-called elite circles, but he'd never touched one of Mr. Templeton's, had never seen one of his vehicles at the shop.

"I do indeed. Knew when he texted, told me there'd been remnants of cash in his shredder bin that things would likely be getting interesting around here."

What?

"Never expected to find the rest of them in the mail." Templeton laughed. "Gave me heartburn to see that much money destroyed. But the look on Marla's face? Heavens, Nico, now *that* was priceless.

"And when I demanded an explanation?" The man shuddered and Nico could practically feel the imaginary sweat pop out on his brow. "That was a row unlike any we've had before or since. I promise you, now that you and my daughter are back together, my wife will never interfere again, believe you me. Not directly. Or indirectly, not if I have any say about it."

"H-how?" That was all he could manage. A strangled, "*Coon?*" and a garbled "*How?*"

Templeton was smiling now, taking another methodical drink instead of offense. The old man was enjoying this. "Alexis's uncle—my younger brother Andrew—served with him in the Army. Both were engine mad and mechanically gifted. What my investigator couldn't find out about you, George supplied once we made the connection between you and Alexis."

Nico finally took a drink. In fact, he took several. He'd been investigated? Found *suitable*?

Lexi's dad knew Coondog?

Her uncle Andrew was *Drew*, the Army cohort with his arm slung over Coon's shoulders in that old picture on his desk? Incredible. "And here I was having no reason to think you'd ever met." Then he choked, spewed fine bourbon down his new sport coat. "Wait a minute—his name is *George* Cooney?"

All Nico had ever seen on official paperwork or mail at the shop was G. A. Cooney.

"Why do you think he encourages people to call him Coondog?" Templeton gave a self-satisfied smile. "Where do you think he disappears to once a month? Ever since reconnecting at Andrew's funeral, George and I hit the golf course." He brought one hand to his chest. "Except for when I was laid low, we tee off every fourth Saturday like clockwork."

Golf's not so bad, he remembered Coon saying the day of the rehearsal. *You might want to try it sometime.*

Would wonders never cease?

"We follow that up with a bit of sailing whenever the weather cooperates," Templeton continued, further blowing Nico's mind. "George is a fair hand with a fishing rod, and I think we both need the downtime to decompress. Be ready for the grind come Monday.

"Now, back to Alexis..." The man's voice lost all trace

of casual. "I knew when she brought you to Phil's funeral that you were special to her. I wasn't sure things would last. Or, if they did, whether you were man enough. Not for the long haul—"

"I wasn't. Not then." Nico held Templeton's gaze without flinching. "I am now."

They sat there in silence a few moments, taking each other's measure.

Finally, after what seemed an interminable trial of sorts, his host nodded. "I think you are at that. I'd challenge you to prove it, to stand up to Marla," the older man chuckled, "but hell, son, even I have trouble doing that, and we've been married nearly thirty-five years."

"Lexi means the world to me, sir. I'd give my life for her." Here went everything. "I want to ask her to be my wife. Preferably with your blessing. Without it, if I have to."

Templeton gave a deep exhale and leaned forward. He could have easily intimidated Nico with the intense glare directed his way. Hell, the man *did* intimidate Nico for a few seconds. Every shred of friendly vanished, and Nico got a glimpse of the boardroom powerhouse Templeton must've been in his heyday.

"You broke her heart once. If you do it again, I guarantee unrecognizable pieces of your body will be showing up for a week. A year! Coyote-shredded piranha victims would look prettier than what I'll do—"

"Sir! Mr. Templeton—enough with the scare tactics." Chills crawled over his skin beneath the fitted jacket. "I let myself get swayed by reverse discrimination, painting all you rich folks with negative brushes. I didn't stand and fight for Lexi when I should have. I let my own inadequacies override my common sense and my love for her." Nico stood then. Stood and stared Templeton right in the eye. "I won't make that mistake ever again."

"See that you don't." Templeton nodded as if the subject were closed. He gestured for Nico to return to his chair. "Now, son, Alexis tells me you have an interest in learning golf."

Nico couldn't read the man. Was he serious? Still standing, Nico replied, "Then Lexi would be mistaken."

"Good. Good. You're not going anywhere, so sit." Nico complied as Templeton reached for the decanter and spiked his tea, granting Nico's glass a larger splash. Nodding to his tea-and-bourbon, he said, "This stays between us."

"Yes, sir." Man-to-man confidences he could keep.

"Glad to see you aren't afraid to disagree with me. I needed to know you'd correct me when I'm wrong." So that golf question was a test? One he'd passed? "That you're strong enough to speak your mind and risk my displeasure. My mistake, Nico, not hers. What about billiards? Any interest there?"

"Plenty." Truly relaxing for the first time since he'd driven his '57 onto the immaculate grounds, Nico found his gut unclenching, lungs exhaling as he considered the majestic table commanding the other side of the room. "I'm a decent shot with a cue stick, but I know bar pool, the kind that comes complete with a cold Budweiser and a smoky dive. I'm not sure how different billiards might be."

Polishing off his drink, Templeton grinned. "Then are you ready to get off your duff and join me? No

Budweiser, but I do have some imported ale. Haven't had a good game here at the house since the last time Phil was home on leave. It'll be nice to play again."

Nico glanced at the fancy granite-and-wood clock on the desk. He'd already stayed longer than he'd expected. Figured Lexi and her mom might drive up any minute. "But, sir—"

"Enough with the 'sir' nonsense. It's Philip." The man surprised Nico by sticking out his hand, giving Nico's a hearty shake when he automatically met the sign of respect. "Considering how it's about to be official, I might as well welcome you to the family, son."

A bit taken aback, Nico floundered. "Uh, haven't asked her yet." Not formally, with intention and planning. "What if she doesn't say—"

"You're about to, or you wouldn't have called asking to come over, all spiffed up to seek out my approval. She'll say yes. My daughter's head over heels for you. No worries on that score. She might've had a tolerable life with Langston, but we both know you're the one she loves and who lights up her world."

There was that. Nico's eyes were drawn again to the ornate clock. "Won't the ladies be home soon?"

"They will, but as you'll be staying for dinner, what does it matter?"

"Dinner?" Nico choked out on a laugh. "Trust me, that will matter a great deal to Mrs. Templeton."

"Then it's a good thing I'm the one calling the shots around here."

"No." Nico relinquished his remaining bourbon and stood, intent on leaving. "I don't want to come between you and your wife. Already, with me and Lexi—"

"You won't. You aren't. Marla has her faults—plenty of them. But underneath the veneer, she's a good woman. Unfortunately, she's followed in her sister's footsteps, too often lacking in acceptance and compassion." A tremor passed through the older man, his eyes glazing for a second before clearing. "Especially since Phil's disappearance and death. That did a real number on all of us. But never you mind." He gave a slight smile, one that actually reached his eyes. "We've been working through some things in counseling. I have a hunch that *you*, and her daughter's love life and future happiness are about to dominate the next few sessions.

"Take off your jacket, son, get comfortable so I don't hear any excuses when I tan your hide at the table." Templeton got to his feet and motioned for Nico to follow as he retrieved a couple cue sticks from the wall. "It might end up costing me a Caribbean vacation or two, but Nic, you keep making my baby girl shine, and I can manage Marla's moods. What's life, if not full of surprises?"

Surprises indeed.

And, man, was Lexi in for a big one when he got her alone later and took her to his place where a giant orchid-and-rose bouquet awaited. One tied with a bow securing a lovely engagement ring he couldn't wait to see on her finger, certain the modest pearl-and-diamond design would look perfect. *Tiny* diamonds.

Hey, he was in love. Not loaded.

The
End

Thanks for reading *Renegade Kisses*. I hope Nico and Lexi's journey toward lasting love satisfied your inner romantic. If you have a chance to write a review, it's *always* appreciated.

Renegade Kisses originally started out as a super-short story that was published over a decade ago. When I pulled it out and dusted it off, I quickly realized my particular *favorite part* of romance books was missing from this one: seeing the characters first meet, savor that first kiss, and fall in love. That's where the entire camping storyline stemmed from. I wanted to *see* them meet and how things progressed from there. I'm delighted with how the story turned out and hope you are too.

What's next? - TEXAS BAD BOYS

Of course, I also have a super-short story of Brad and Jenny finding true love. But once again, it felt unsatisfying —even though it's always been an absolute favorite of mine. (I mean, who doesn't love a sexy pirate with a very talented tongue?) But still, I want to know what made Jenny crush on Brad in the first place and the big question —can this bad boy be redeemed?

I certainly think so! And hope you'll join me for ***Devastating Kisses***, Jenny and Brad's journey coming out sometime next year.

Turn the page for a preview of the blurb.

He'll claim her heart one kiss at a time—if he doesn't destroy her first…

Filthy rich bad boy Brad Langston, reeling after getting dumped at the altar, spirals into the bottle until a one-vehicle accident lands him in the hospital with a very uncertain future.

Jenny Beckman might've crushed on Brad since they were young but, after how he treated her best friend, she's determined to move on. If she can just get her heart to agree. And stop visiting his bedside, where she shares way more than she should with the unconscious man.

When Brad recovers and runs into Jenny, while attending a costume party as a bearded pirate, he *thinks* he's out for revenge. It only takes a kiss or two to know he wants Jenny for all time. But the soft-hearted woman's been hurt in the past.

Can he stop devastating them both with kisses long enough to win her trust?

Up next, Devastating Kisses is the second novel in the steamy Texas Bad Boys Romance series. It's a stand-alone book with HEA, occasional profanity and sizzling, fun encounters.

Ready for more sexy, fun reading now? Swipe on to learn a bit more about me, for links to a couple free, short stories, and for blurbs about my other, available contemporary romance books.

A lifelong Texan, Larissa writes sexy contemporaries and steamy regencies, blending heartfelt emotion with doses of laugh-out-loud humor. Her heroes are strong men with a weakness for the right woman.

Avoiding housework one word at a time (thanks in part to her super-helpful herd of cats >^..^<), Larissa adores brownies, James Bond, and her husband. She's been a clown, a tax analyst, and a pig castrator (!) but nothing satisfies quite like seeing the entertaining voices in her head come to life on the page.

Writing around some health challenges and computer limitations, it's a while between releases, but stick with her...she's working on the next one.

Learn more by visiting LarissaLynx.com.

—————◦—————

instagram.com/larissa_lyons_author

amazon.com/author/larissa-lynx

bookbub.com/authors/larissa-lynx

goodreads.com/larissalynx

facebook.com/AuthorLarissaLyons

Contemporaries by Larissa Lynx

POWER PLAYERS HOCKEY series

*My Two-Stud Stand**

*Her Three Studs**

The Stud Takes a Stand (2022)

**Her Hockey Studs - print version*

SEXY CONTEMPORARY ROMANCE

Renegade Kisses

Devastating Kisses (TBA)

Starlight Seduction

SHORT 'N' SUPER STEAMY

A Heart for Adam...& Rick!

Braving Donovan's

No Guts, No 'Gasms

Historicals by Larissa Lyons

ROARING ROGUES REGENCY SHIFTERS

Ensnared by Innocence

Deceived by Desire (2022)

Tamed by Temptation (TBA)

MISTRESS IN THE MAKING series (Complete)

Seductive Silence

Lusty Letters

Daring Declarations

FUN & SEXY REGENCY ROMANCE

Lady Scandal

A SWEETLY SPICY REGENCY

Miss Isabella Thaws a Frosty Lord